BF1

BIG TOP OTTO

WITHDRAWN

FOR MY NEPHEW TIM, WHO KEEPS RUNNING AWAY
WITH THE CIRCUS, AND FOR LAURIE, WHO STAYS
HOME WITH THE PUGS.

Text © 2013 Bill Slavin with Esperança Melo
Illustrations © 2013 Bill Slavin

Kids Can Press acknowledges the financial support of the Government of Ontario, through the Ontario
Media Development Corporation's Ontario Book Initiative; the Ontario Arts Council; the Canada Council
for the Arts; and the Government of Canada, through the CBF, for our publishing activity.

Published in Canada by
Kids Can Press Ltd.
25 Dockside Drive
Toronto, ON M5A 0B5

Published in the U.S. by
Kids Can Press Ltd.
2250 Military Road
Tonawanda, NY 14150

www.kidscanpress.com

The artwork in this book was rendered in pen and ink line and colored in Photoshop.
The text is set in Graphite Std Narrow and BadaBoom Pro BB.

Edited by Tara Walker and Karen Li
Designed by Bill Slavin and Marie Bartholomew

The hardcover edition of this book is smyth sewn casebound.
The paperback edition of this book is limp sewn with a drawn-on cover.
Manufactured in Buji, Shenzhen, China, in 3/2013 by WKT Company.

CM 13 0 9 8 7 6 5 4 3 2 1
CM PA 13 0 9 8 7 6 5 4 3 2 1

Library and Archives Canada Cataloguing in Publication

Slavin, Bill
     Big top Otto / written by Bill Slavin with Esperança Melo ;
art by Bill Slavin.

(Elephants never forget ; 2)
ISBN 978-1-55453-806-5 (bound). ISBN 978-1-55453-807-2 (pbk.)

1. Graphic novels. I. Melo, Esperança II. Title. III. Series:
Slavin, Bill. Elephants never forget ; 2

PN6733.S55B53 2013   j741.5'971   C2012-908359-3

Kids Can Press is a Corus™ Entertainment company

BIG TOP OTTO

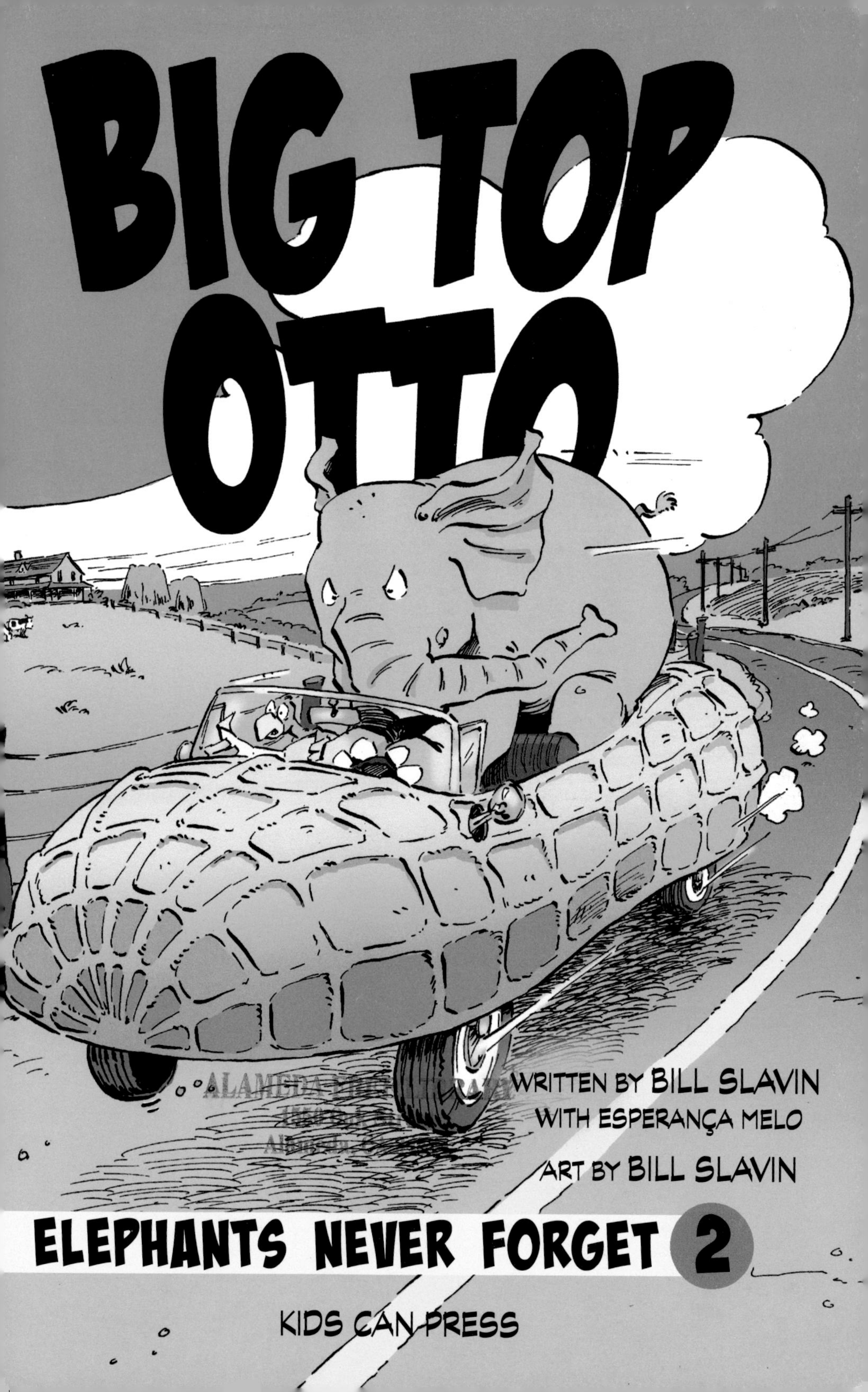

WRITTEN BY BILL SLAVIN
WITH ESPERANÇA MELO

ART BY BILL SLAVIN

ELEPHANTS NEVER FORGET 2

KIDS CAN PRESS

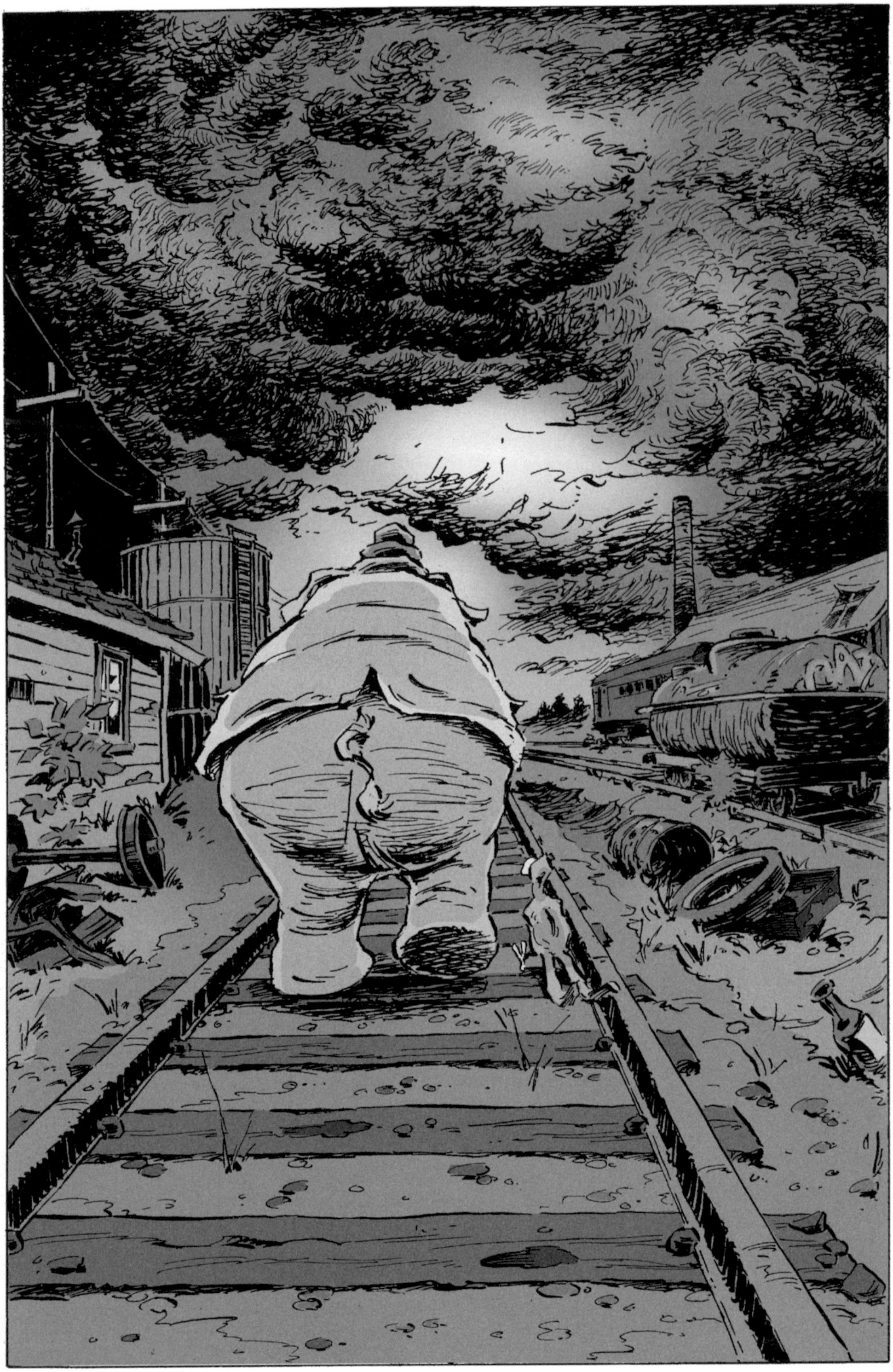

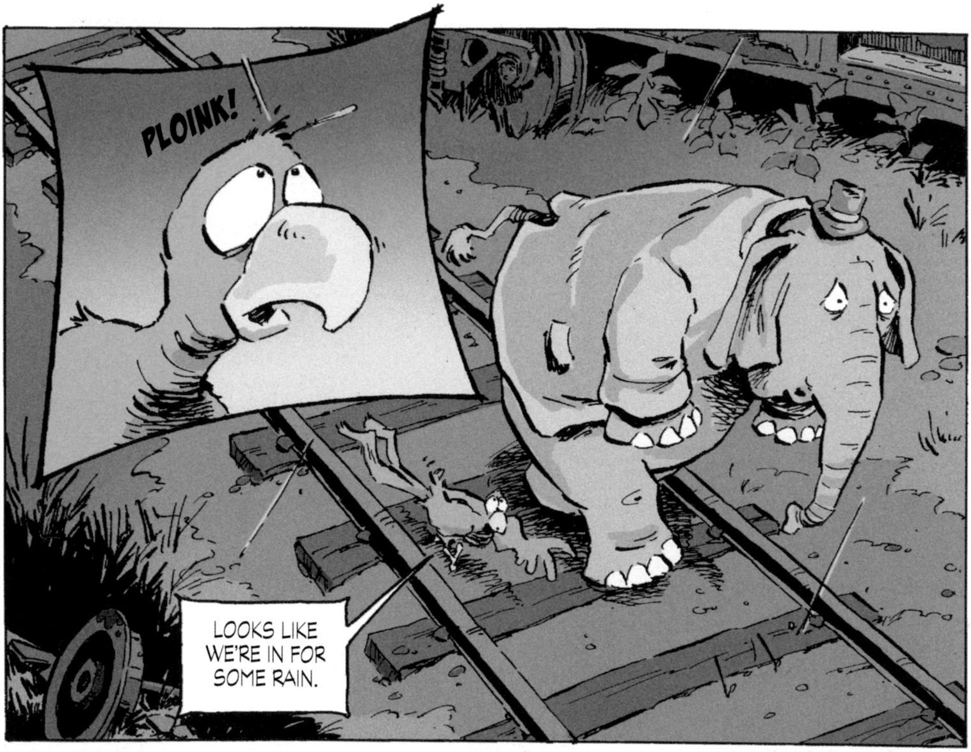
PLOINK!
LOOKS LIKE WE'RE IN FOR SOME RAIN.

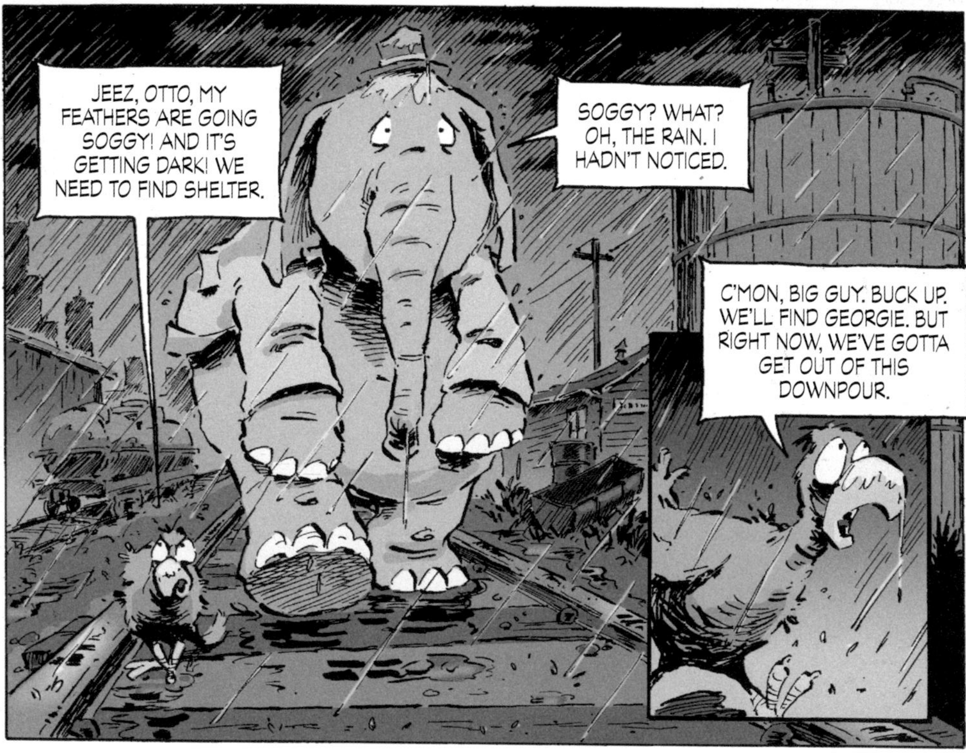
JEEZ, OTTO, MY FEATHERS ARE GOING SOGGY! AND IT'S GETTING DARK! WE NEED TO FIND SHELTER.
SOGGY? WHAT? OH, THE RAIN. I HADN'T NOTICED.
C'MON, BIG GUY. BUCK UP. WE'LL FIND GEORGIE. BUT RIGHT NOW, WE'VE GOTTA GET OUT OF THIS DOWNPOUR.

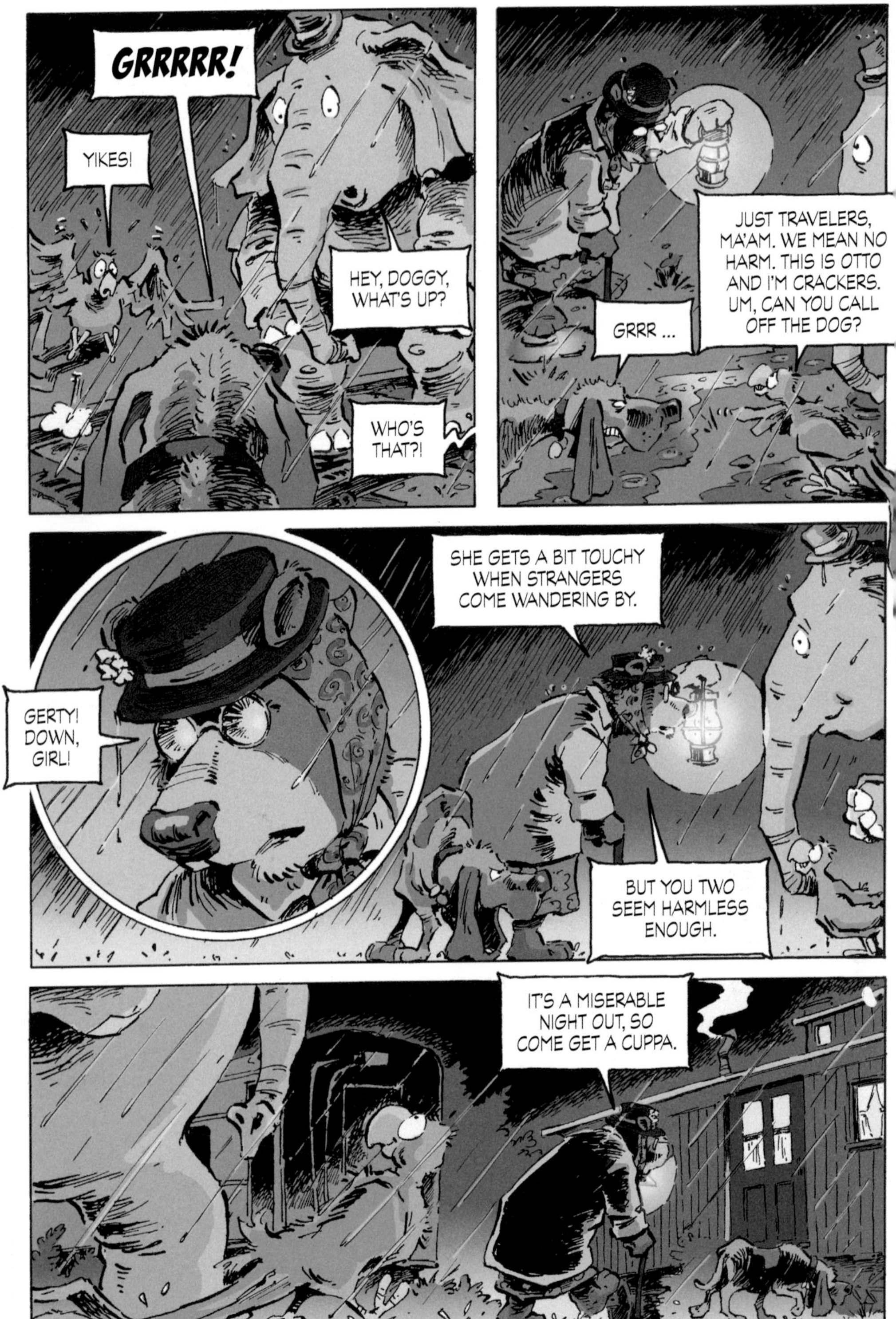
GRRRRR!
YIKES!
HEY, DOGGY, WHAT'S UP?
WHO'S THAT?!
GRRR ...
JUST TRAVELERS, MA'AM. WE MEAN NO HARM. THIS IS OTTO AND I'M CRACKERS. UM, CAN YOU CALL OFF THE DOG?
GERTY! DOWN, GIRL!
SHE GETS A BIT TOUCHY WHEN STRANGERS COME WANDERING BY.
BUT YOU TWO SEEM HARMLESS ENOUGH.
IT'S A MISERABLE NIGHT OUT, SO COME GET A CUPPA.

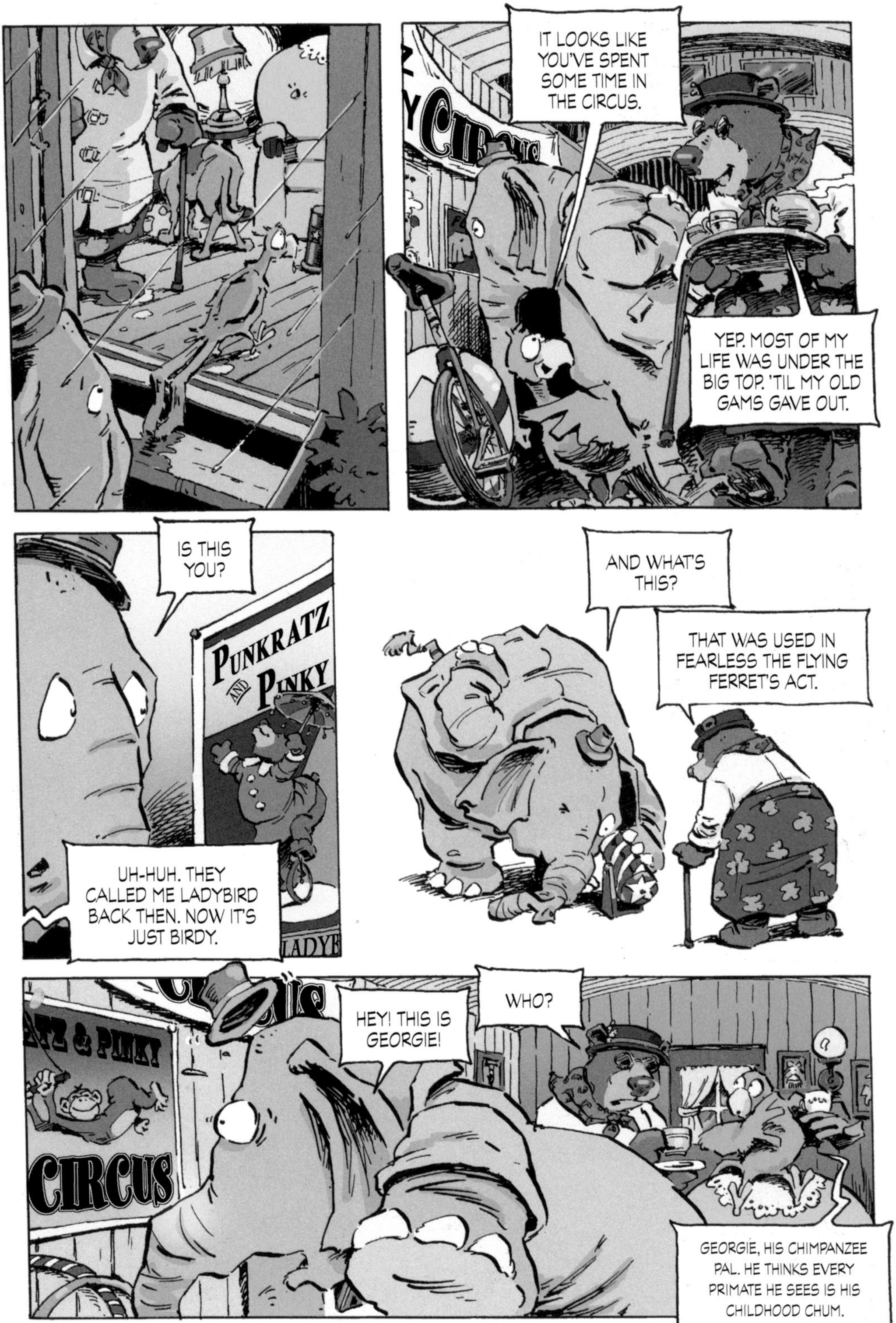
IT LOOKS LIKE YOU'VE SPENT SOME TIME IN THE CIRCUS.
CIRCUS
YEP. MOST OF MY LIFE WAS UNDER THE BIG TOP. 'TIL MY OLD GAMS GAVE OUT.
IS THIS YOU?
PUNKRATZ AND PINKY
UH-HUH. THEY CALLED ME LADYBIRD BACK THEN. NOW IT'S JUST BIRDY.
AND WHAT'S THIS?
THAT WAS USED IN FEARLESS THE FLYING FERRET'S ACT.
HEY! THIS IS GEORGIE!
WHO?
CIRCUS
GEORGIE, HIS CHIMPANZEE PAL. HE THINKS EVERY PRIMATE HE SEES IS HIS CHILDHOOD CHUM.

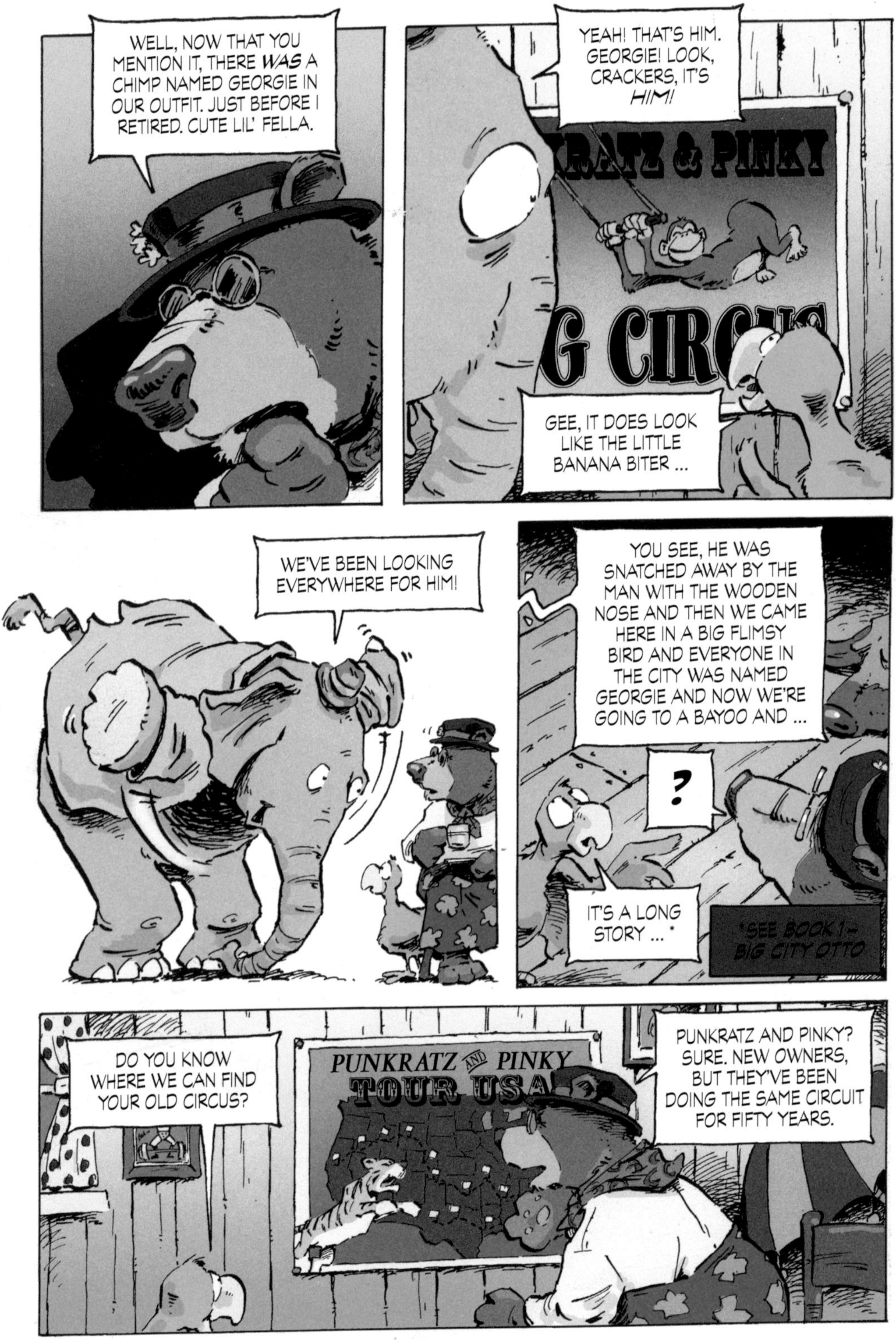
WELL, NOW THAT YOU MENTION IT, THERE *WAS* A CHIMP NAMED GEORGIE IN OUR OUTFIT. JUST BEFORE I RETIRED. CUTE LIL' FELLA.
YEAH! THAT'S HIM. GEORGIE! LOOK, CRACKERS, IT'S *HIM!*
KRATZ & PINKY
G CIRCUS
GEE, IT DOES LOOK LIKE THE LITTLE BANANA BITER ...
WE'VE BEEN LOOKING EVERYWHERE FOR HIM!
YOU SEE, HE WAS SNATCHED AWAY BY THE MAN WITH THE WOODEN NOSE AND THEN WE CAME HERE IN A BIG FLIMSY BIRD AND EVERYONE IN THE CITY WAS NAMED GEORGIE AND NOW WE'RE GOING TO A BAYOO AND ...
?
IT'S A LONG STORY ...*
*SEE BOOK 1– BIG CITY OTTO
DO YOU KNOW WHERE WE CAN FIND YOUR OLD CIRCUS?
PUNKRATZ AND PINKY
TOUR USA
PUNKRATZ AND PINKY? SURE. NEW OWNERS, BUT THEY'VE BEEN DOING THE SAME CIRCUIT FOR FIFTY YEARS.

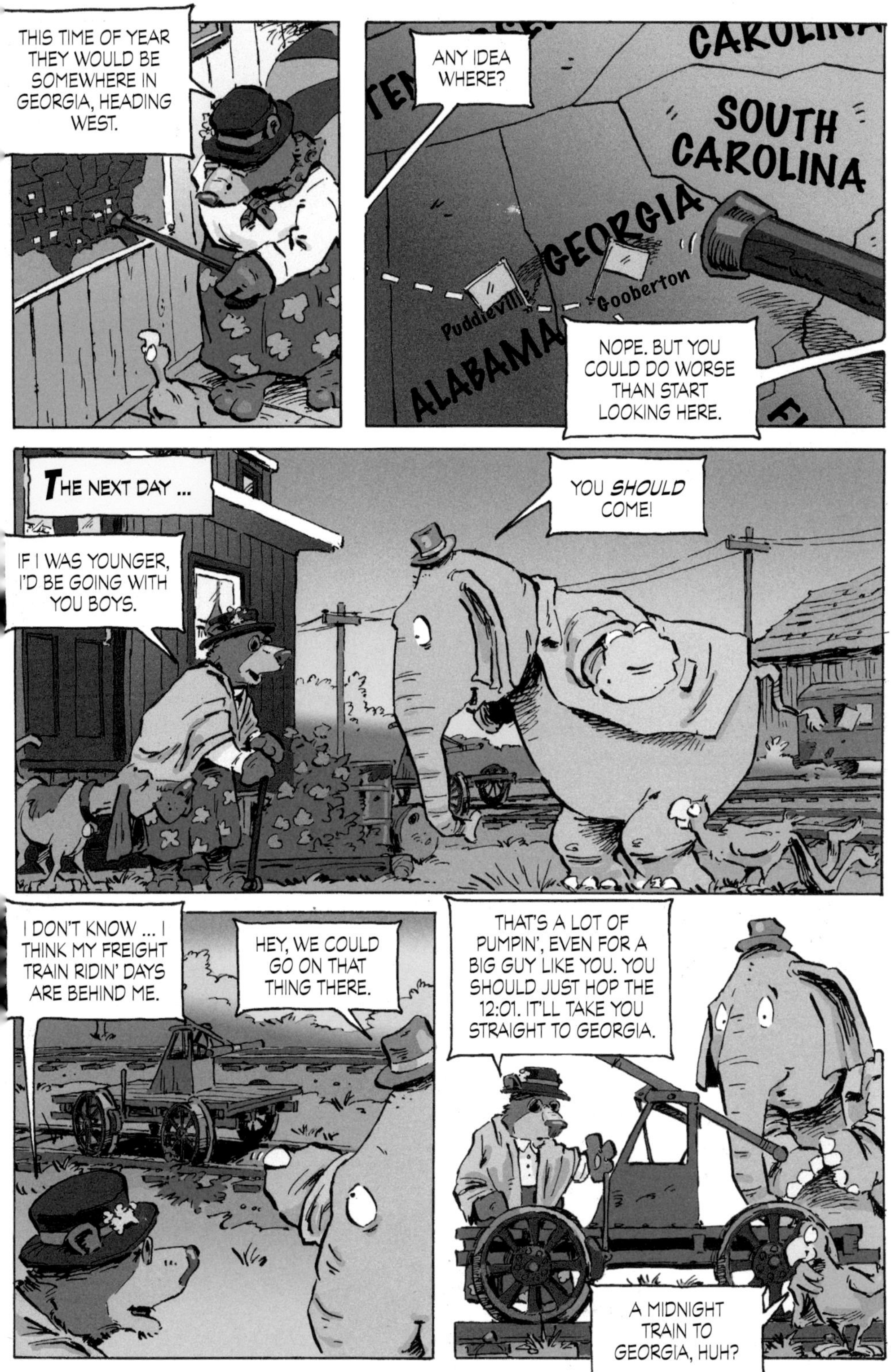
THIS TIME OF YEAR THEY WOULD BE SOMEWHERE IN GEORGIA, HEADING WEST.
ANY IDEA WHERE?
CAROLINA
SOUTH CAROLINA
GEORGIA
ALABAMA
Puddieville
Gooberton
NOPE. BUT YOU COULD DO WORSE THAN START LOOKING HERE.
THE NEXT DAY ...
IF I WAS YOUNGER, I'D BE GOING WITH YOU BOYS.
YOU *SHOULD* COME!
I DON'T KNOW ... I THINK MY FREIGHT TRAIN RIDIN' DAYS ARE BEHIND ME.
HEY, WE COULD GO ON THAT THING THERE.
THAT'S A LOT OF PUMPIN', EVEN FOR A BIG GUY LIKE YOU. YOU SHOULD JUST HOP THE 12:01. IT'LL TAKE YOU STRAIGHT TO GEORGIA.
A MIDNIGHT TRAIN TO GEORGIA, HUH?

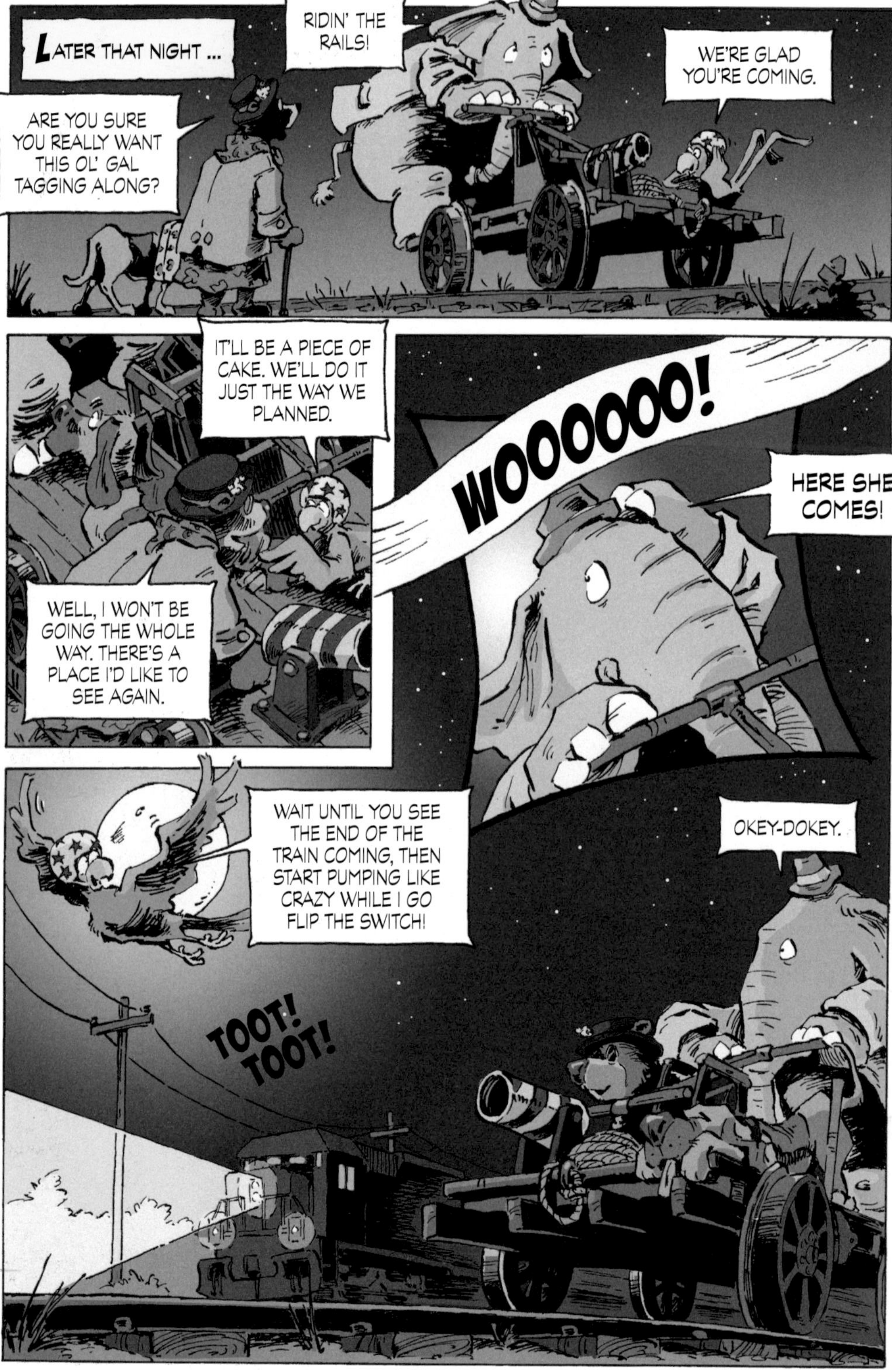
LATER THAT NIGHT ...
ARE YOU SURE YOU REALLY WANT THIS OL' GAL TAGGING ALONG?
RIDIN' THE RAILS!
WE'RE GLAD YOU'RE COMING.
IT'LL BE A PIECE OF CAKE. WE'LL DO IT JUST THE WAY WE PLANNED.
WELL, I WON'T BE GOING THE WHOLE WAY. THERE'S A PLACE I'D LIKE TO SEE AGAIN.
WOOOOOO!
HERE SHE COMES!
WAIT UNTIL YOU SEE THE END OF THE TRAIN COMING, THEN START PUMPING LIKE CRAZY WHILE I GO FLIP THE SWITCH!
OKEY-DOKEY.
TOOT! TOOT!

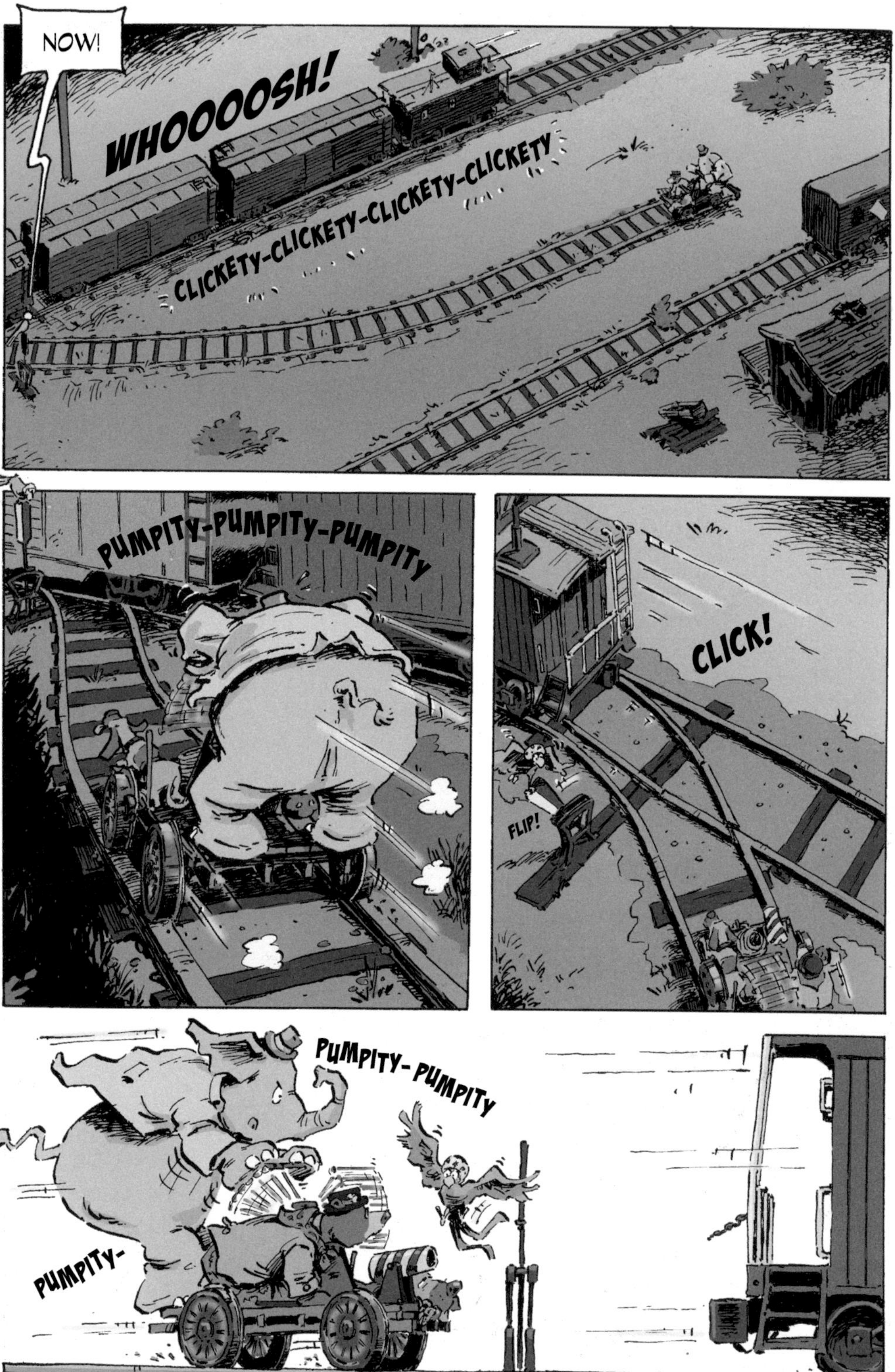

NOW!
WHOOOOSH!
CLICKETY-CLICKETY-CLICKETY-CLICKETY
PUMPITY-PUMPITY-PUMPITY
CLICK!
FLIP!
PUMPITY- PUMPITY
PUMPITY-

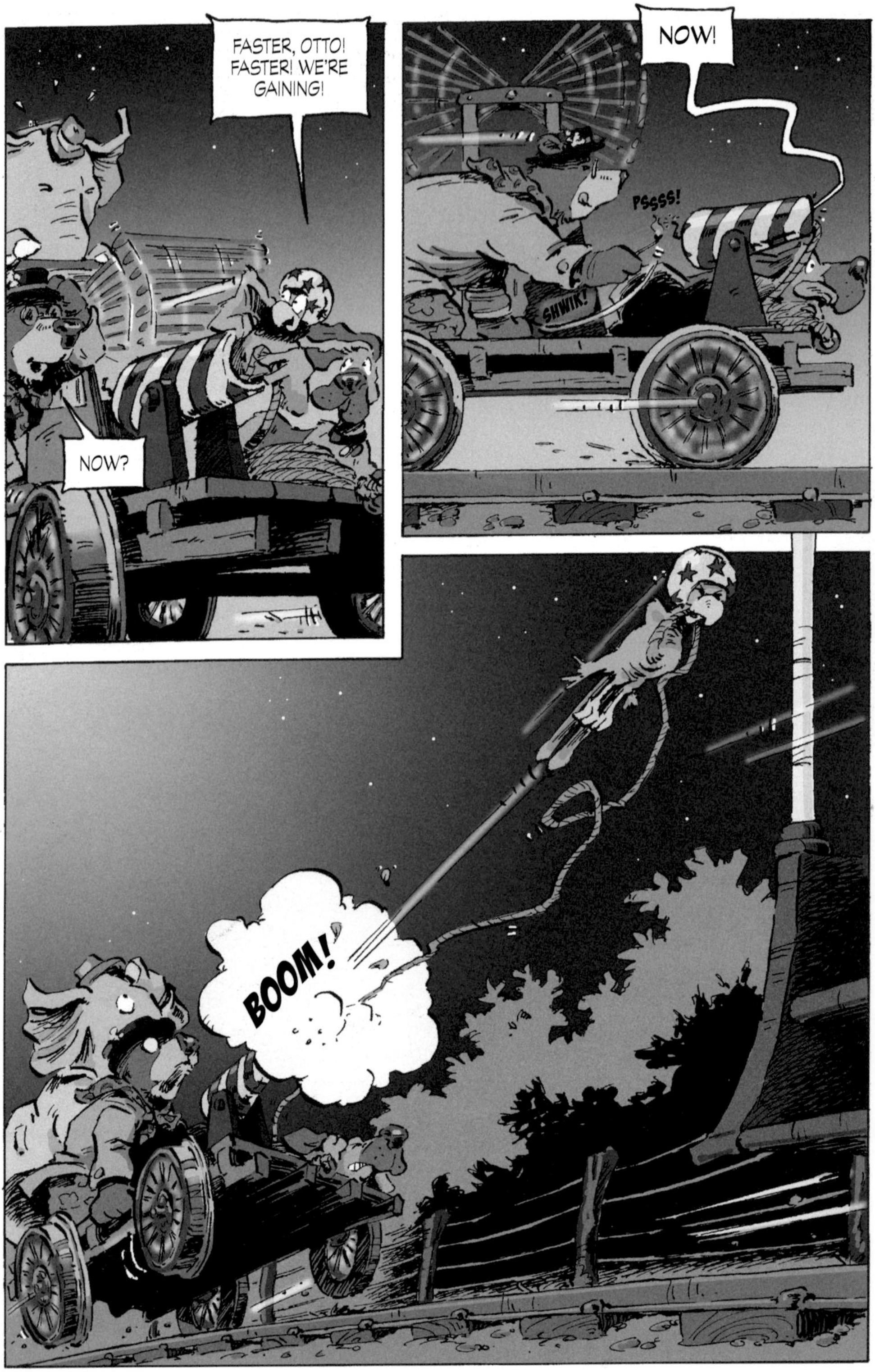
FASTER, OTTO! FASTER! WE'RE GAINING!
NOW?
NOW!
PSSSS!
SHWIK!
BOOM!

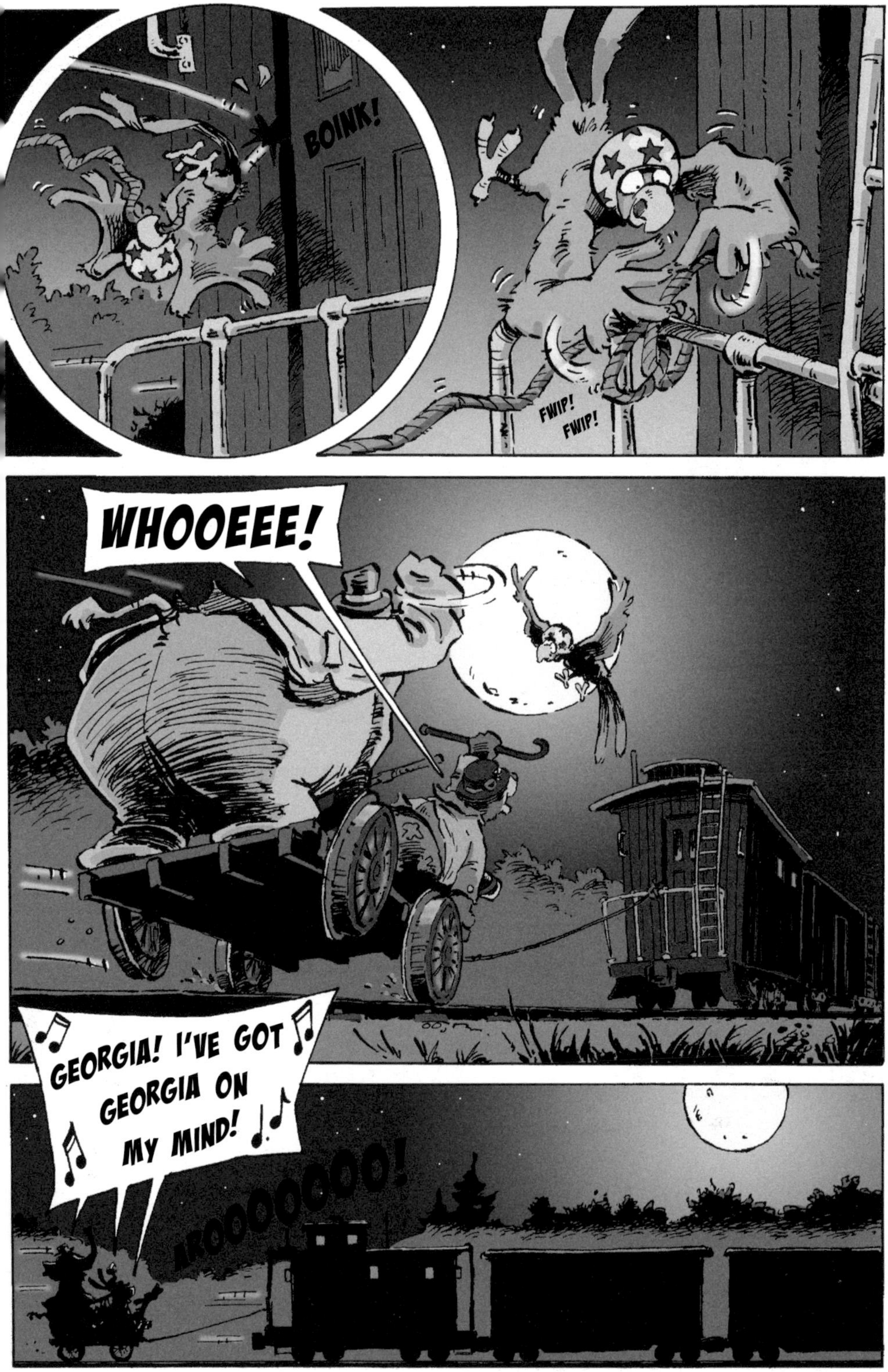
BOINK!
FWIP! FWIP!
WHOOEEE!
GEORGIA! I'VE GOT GEORGIA ON MY MIND!
AROOOOOOOO!

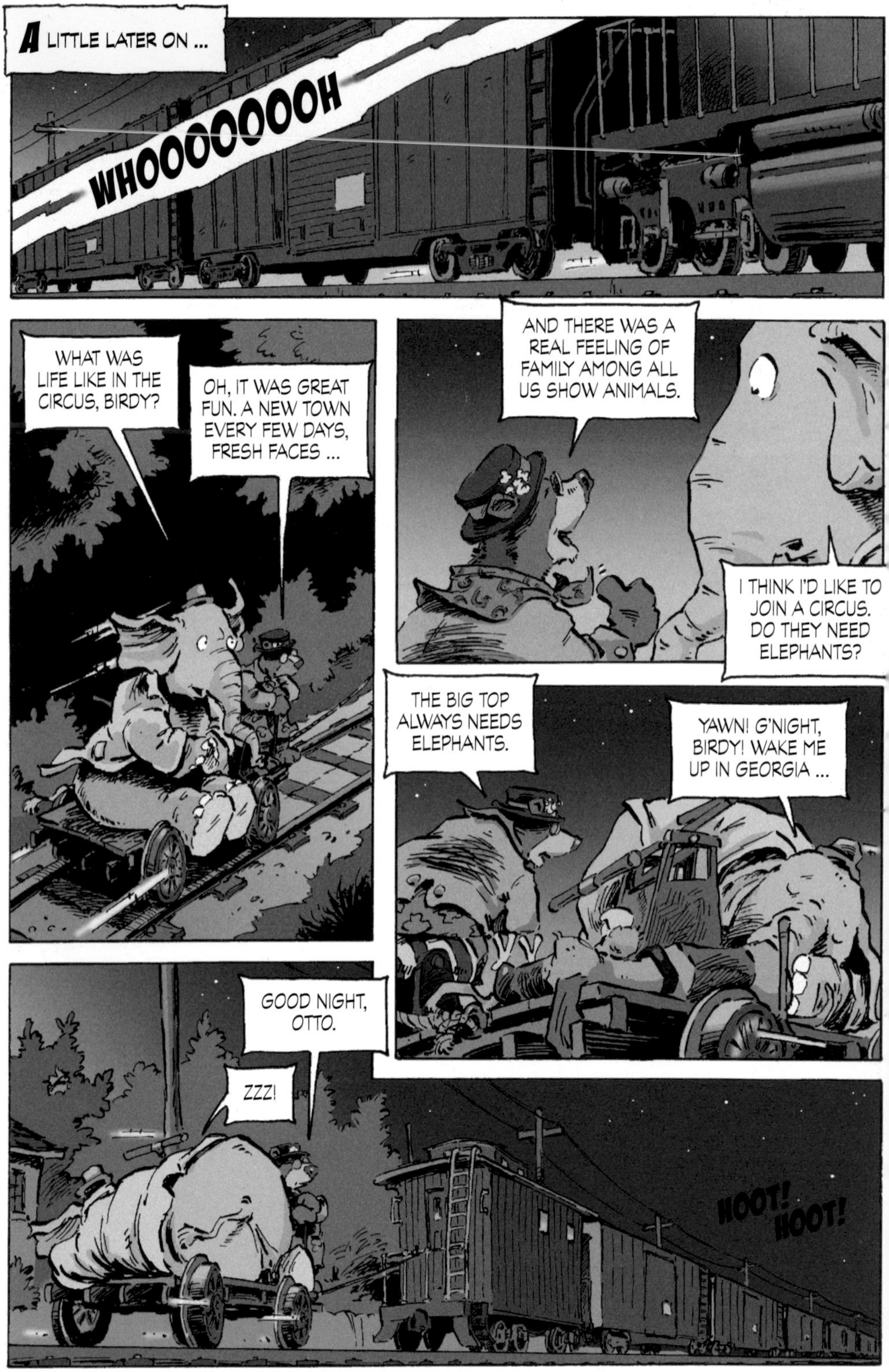
A LITTLE LATER ON ...
WHOOOOOOOH
WHAT WAS LIFE LIKE IN THE CIRCUS, BIRDY?
OH, IT WAS GREAT FUN. A NEW TOWN EVERY FEW DAYS, FRESH FACES ...
AND THERE WAS A REAL FEELING OF FAMILY AMONG ALL US SHOW ANIMALS.
I THINK I'D LIKE TO JOIN A CIRCUS. DO THEY NEED ELEPHANTS?
THE BIG TOP ALWAYS NEEDS ELEPHANTS.
YAWN! G'NIGHT, BIRDY! WAKE ME UP IN GEORGIA ...
GOOD NIGHT, OTTO.
ZZZ!
HOOT! HOOT!

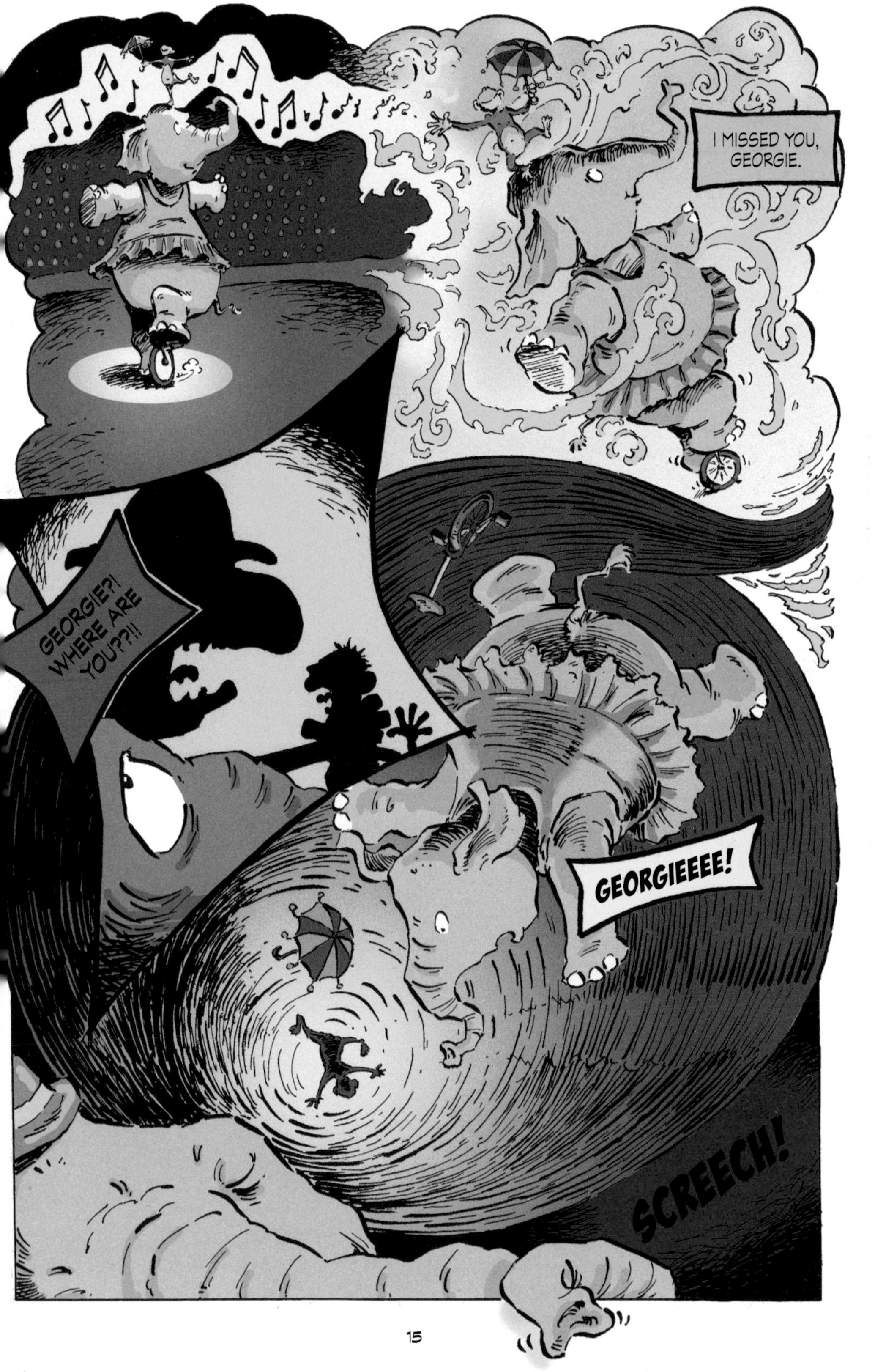
I MISSED YOU, GEORGIE.
GEORGIE?! WHERE ARE YOU??!!
GEORGIEEEE!
SCREECH!

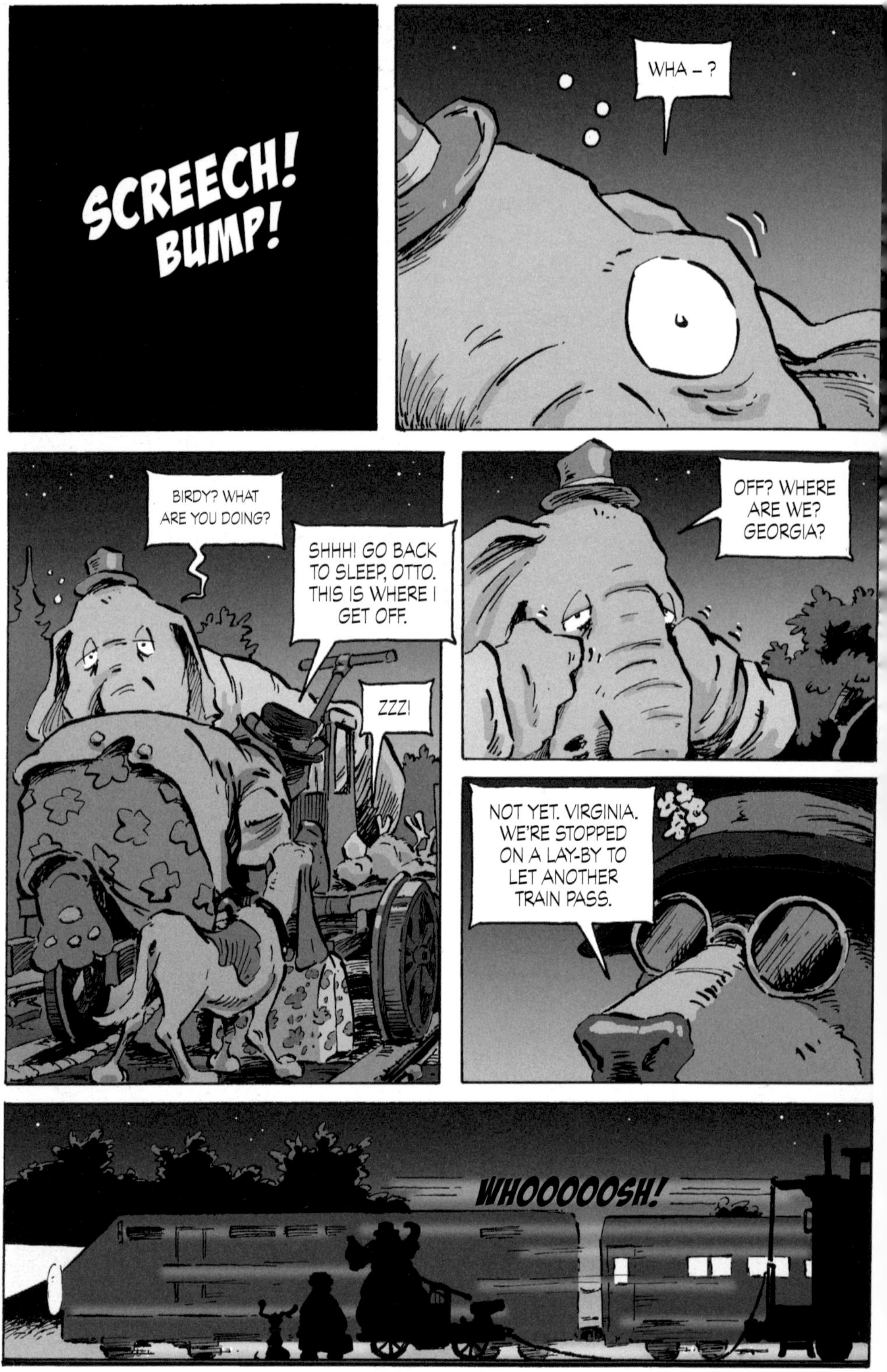
SCREECH! BUMP!
WHA – ?
BIRDY? WHAT ARE YOU DOING?
SHHH! GO BACK TO SLEEP, OTTO. THIS IS WHERE I GET OFF.
ZZZ!
OFF? WHERE ARE WE? GEORGIA?
NOT YET. VIRGINIA. WE'RE STOPPED ON A LAY-BY TO LET ANOTHER TRAIN PASS.
WHOOOOOSH!

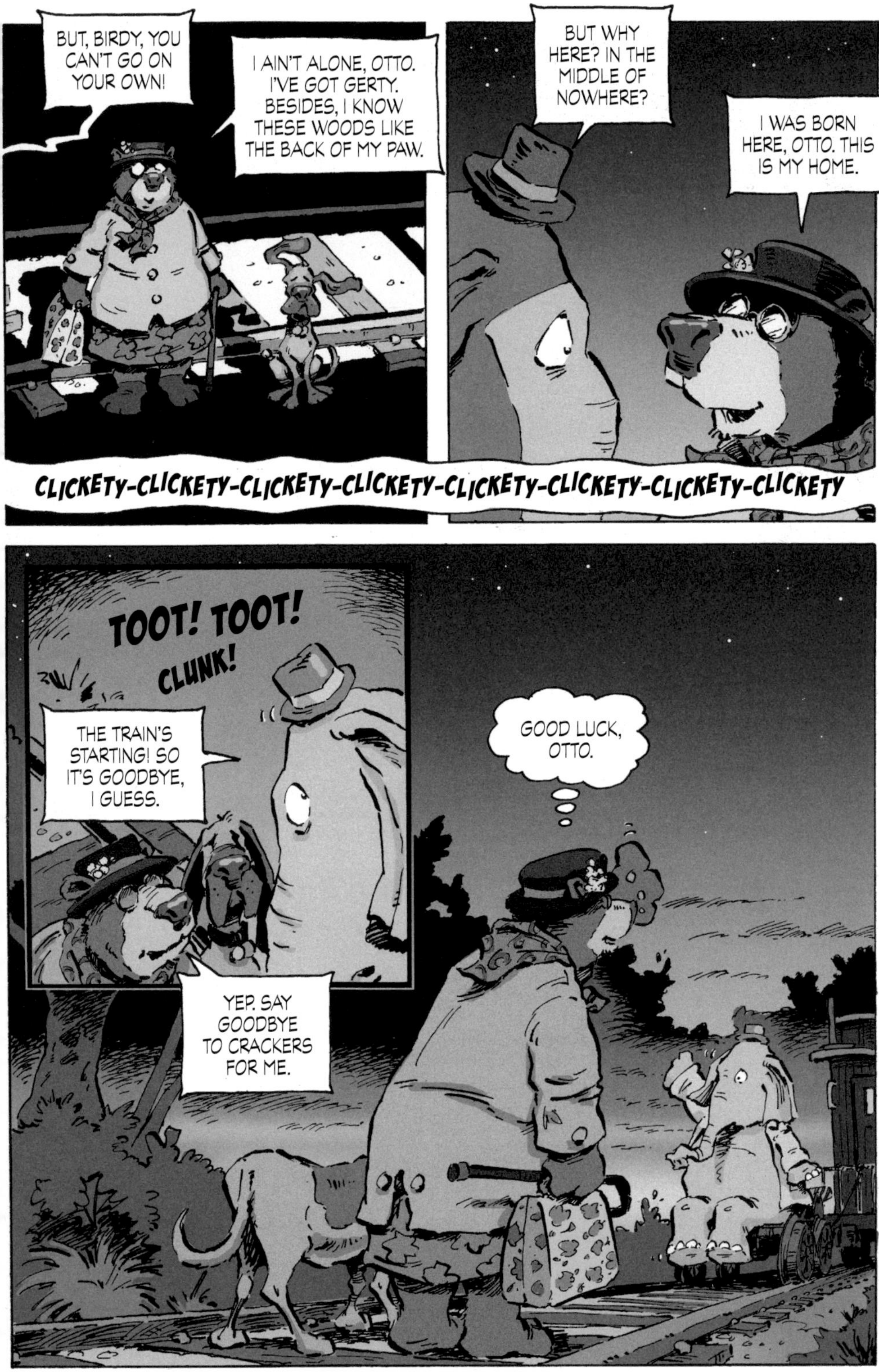
BUT, BIRDY, YOU CAN'T GO ON YOUR OWN!
I AIN'T ALONE, OTTO. I'VE GOT GERTY. BESIDES, I KNOW THESE WOODS LIKE THE BACK OF MY PAW.
BUT WHY HERE? IN THE MIDDLE OF NOWHERE?
I WAS BORN HERE, OTTO. THIS IS MY HOME.
CLICKETY-CLICKETY-CLICKETY-CLICKETY-CLICKETY-CLICKETY-CLICKETY-CLICKETY
TOOT! TOOT!
CLUNK!
THE TRAIN'S STARTING! SO IT'S GOODBYE, I GUESS.
YEP. SAY GOODBYE TO CRACKERS FOR ME.
GOOD LUCK, OTTO.

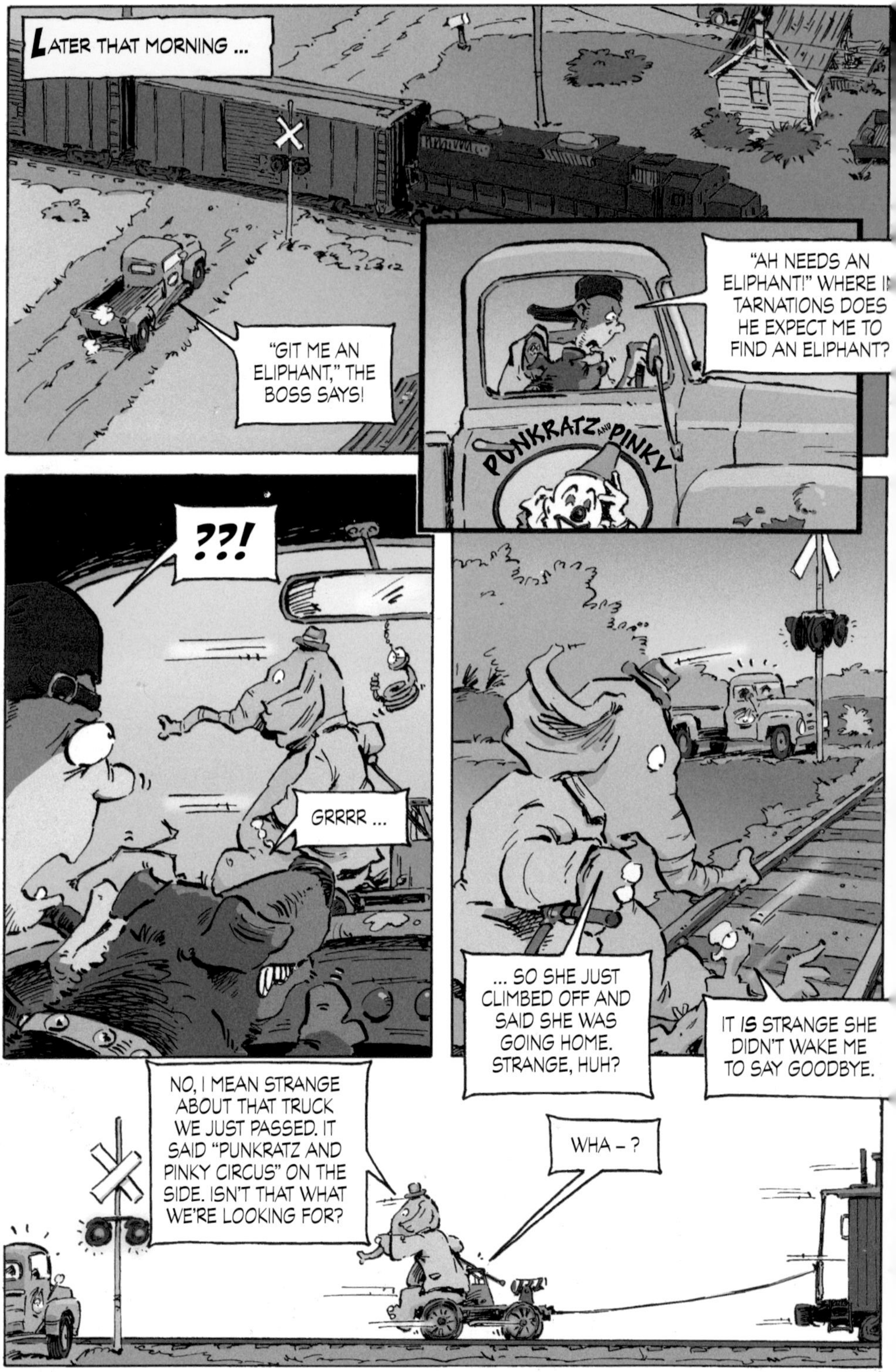
LATER THAT MORNING ...
"GIT ME AN ELIPHANT," THE BOSS SAYS!
"AH NEEDS AN ELIPHANT!" WHERE IN TARNATIONS DOES HE EXPECT ME TO FIND AN ELIPHANT?
PUNKRATZ AND PINKY
??!
GRRRR ...
... SO SHE JUST CLIMBED OFF AND SAID SHE WAS GOING HOME. STRANGE, HUH?
IT IS STRANGE SHE DIDN'T WAKE ME TO SAY GOODBYE.
NO, I MEAN STRANGE ABOUT THAT TRUCK WE JUST PASSED. IT SAID "PUNKRATZ AND PINKY CIRCUS" ON THE SIDE. ISN'T THAT WHAT WE'RE LOOKING FOR?
WHA – ?

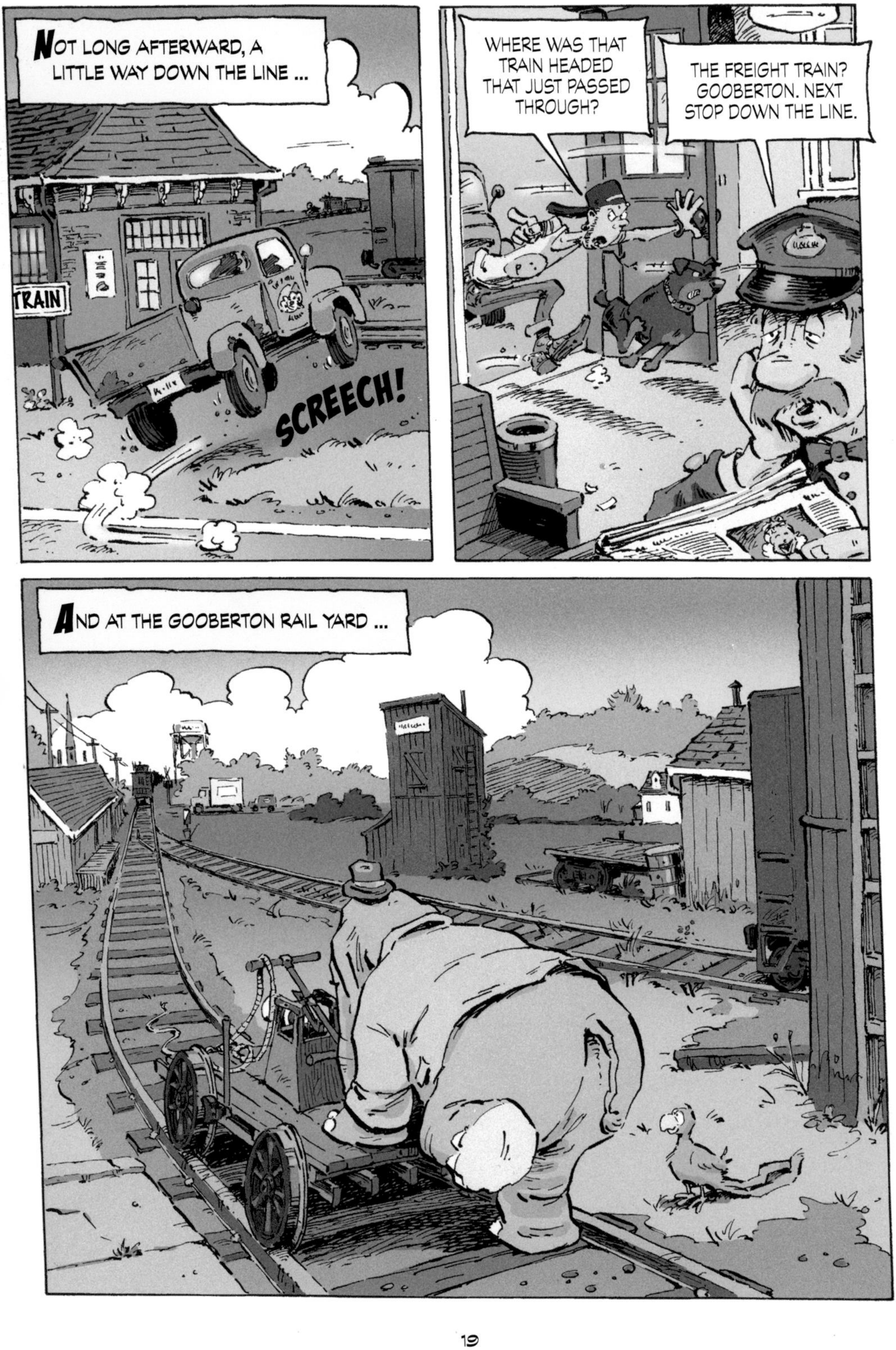
NOT LONG AFTERWARD, A LITTLE WAY DOWN THE LINE ...
TRAIN
SCREECH!
WHERE WAS THAT TRAIN HEADED THAT JUST PASSED THROUGH?
THE FREIGHT TRAIN? GOOBERTON. NEXT STOP DOWN THE LINE.
AND AT THE GOOBERTON RAIL YARD ...

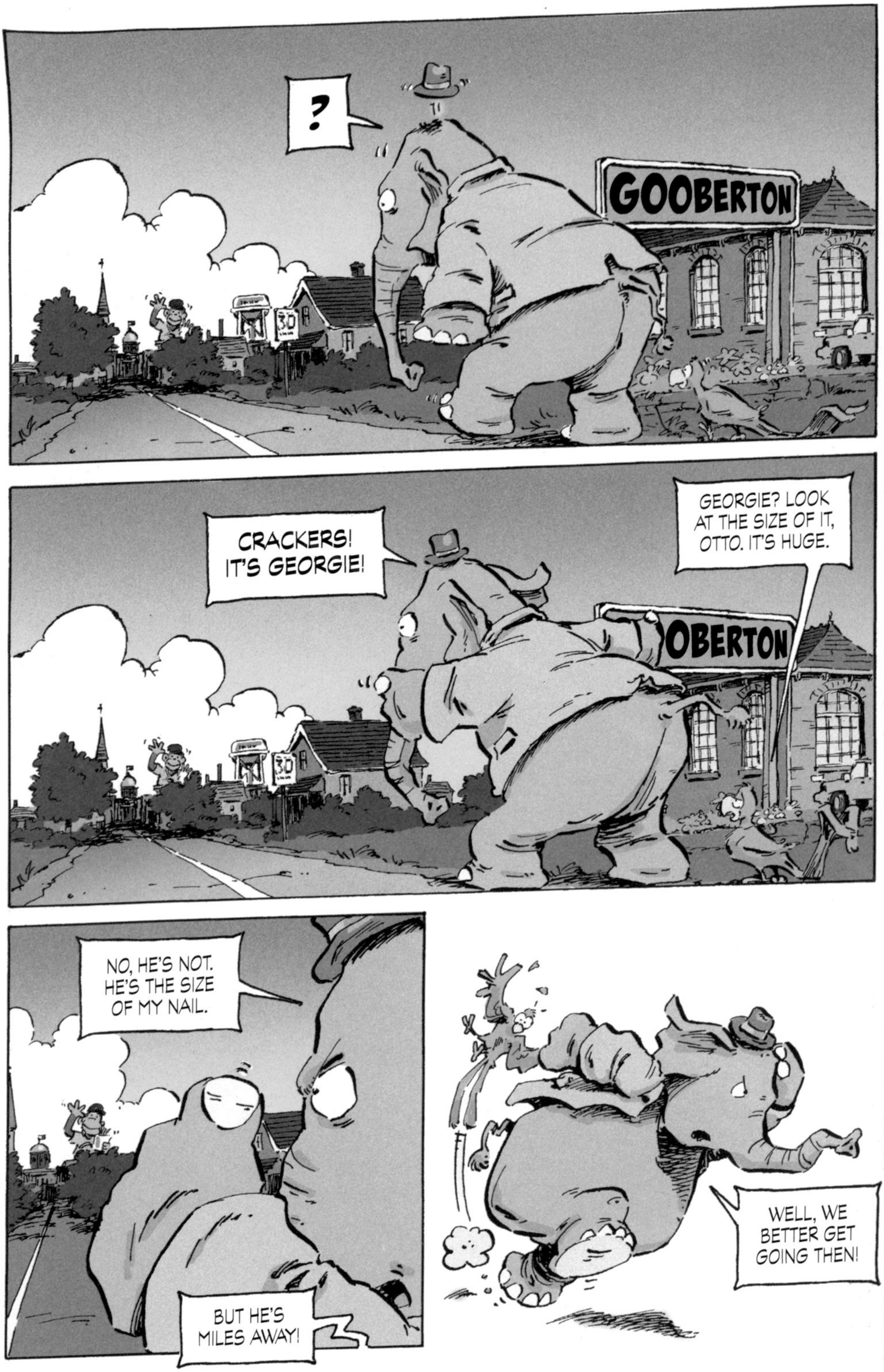
?
GOOBERTON
CRACKERS! IT'S GEORGIE!
GEORGIE? LOOK AT THE SIZE OF IT, OTTO. IT'S HUGE.
OBERTON
NO, HE'S NOT. HE'S THE SIZE OF MY NAIL.
BUT HE'S MILES AWAY!
WELL, WE BETTER GET GOING THEN!

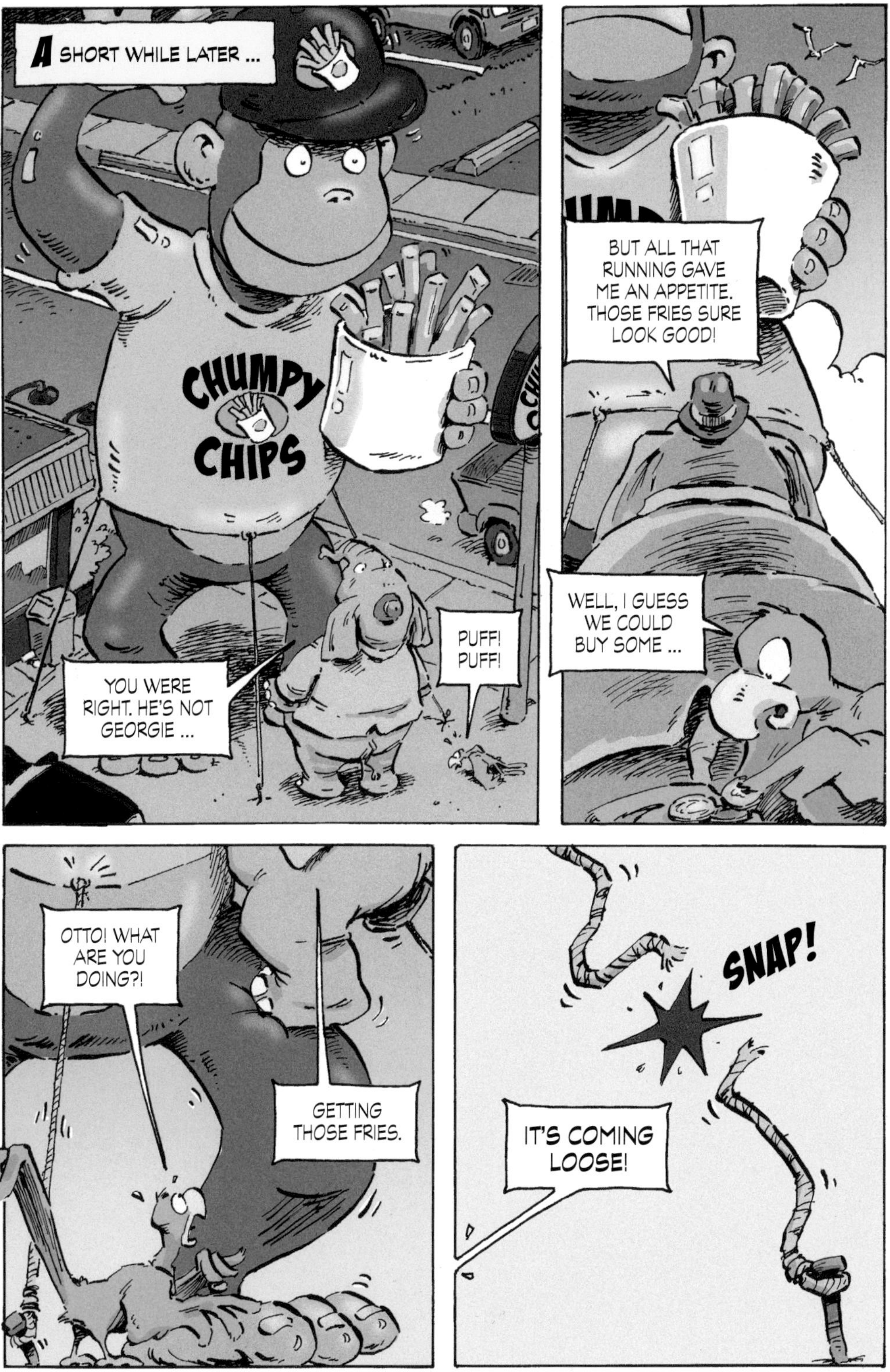
A SHORT WHILE LATER ...
CHUMPY CHIPS
YOU WERE RIGHT. HE'S NOT GEORGIE ...
PUFF! PUFF!
BUT ALL THAT RUNNING GAVE ME AN APPETITE. THOSE FRIES SURE LOOK GOOD!
WELL, I GUESS WE COULD BUY SOME ...
OTTO! WHAT ARE YOU DOING?!
GETTING THOSE FRIES.
SNAP!
IT'S COMING LOOSE!

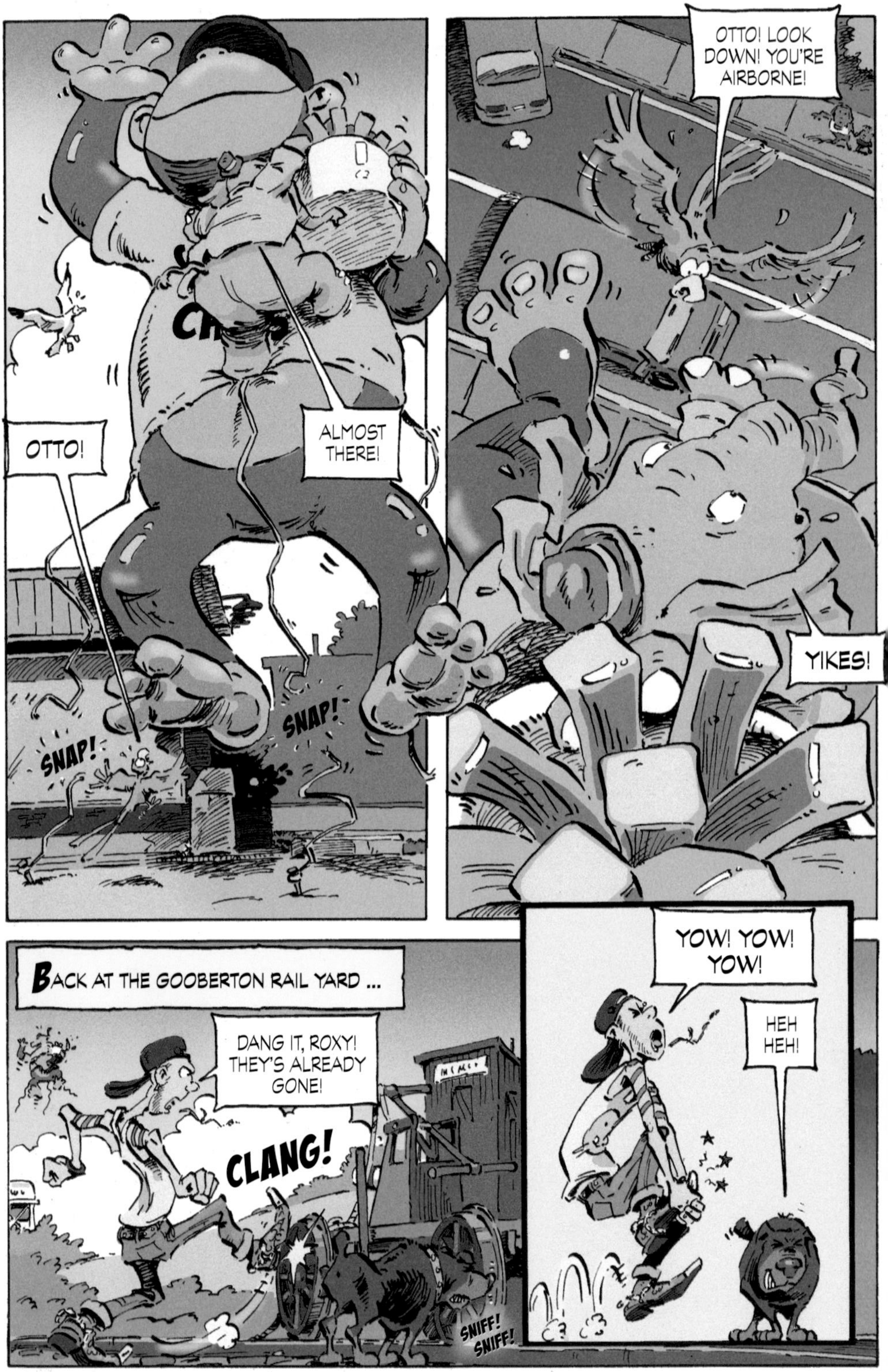
ALMOST THERE!
OTTO!
SNAP!
SNAP!
OTTO! LOOK DOWN! YOU'RE AIRBORNE!
YIKES!
BACK AT THE GOOBERTON RAIL YARD ...
DANG IT, ROXY! THEY'S ALREADY GONE!
CLANG!
SNIFF! SNIFF!
YOW! YOW! YOW!
HEH HEH!

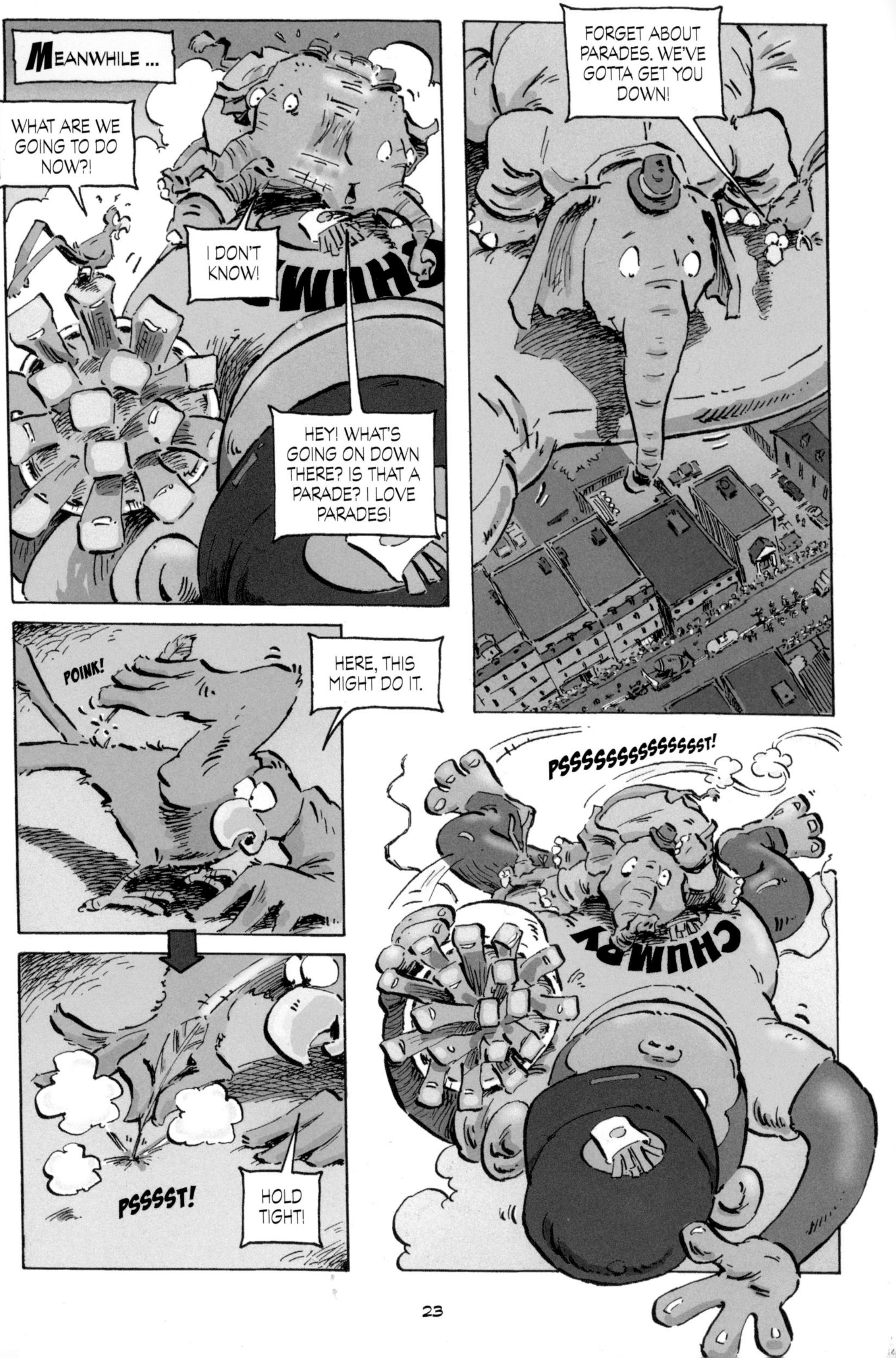
MEANWHILE ...
WHAT ARE WE GOING TO DO NOW?!
I DON'T KNOW!
CHUMPY
HEY! WHAT'S GOING ON DOWN THERE? IS THAT A PARADE? I LOVE PARADES!
FORGET ABOUT PARADES. WE'VE GOTTA GET YOU DOWN!
POINK!
HERE, THIS MIGHT DO IT.
PSSSST!
HOLD TIGHT!
PSSSSSSSSSSSSSST!
CHUMPY

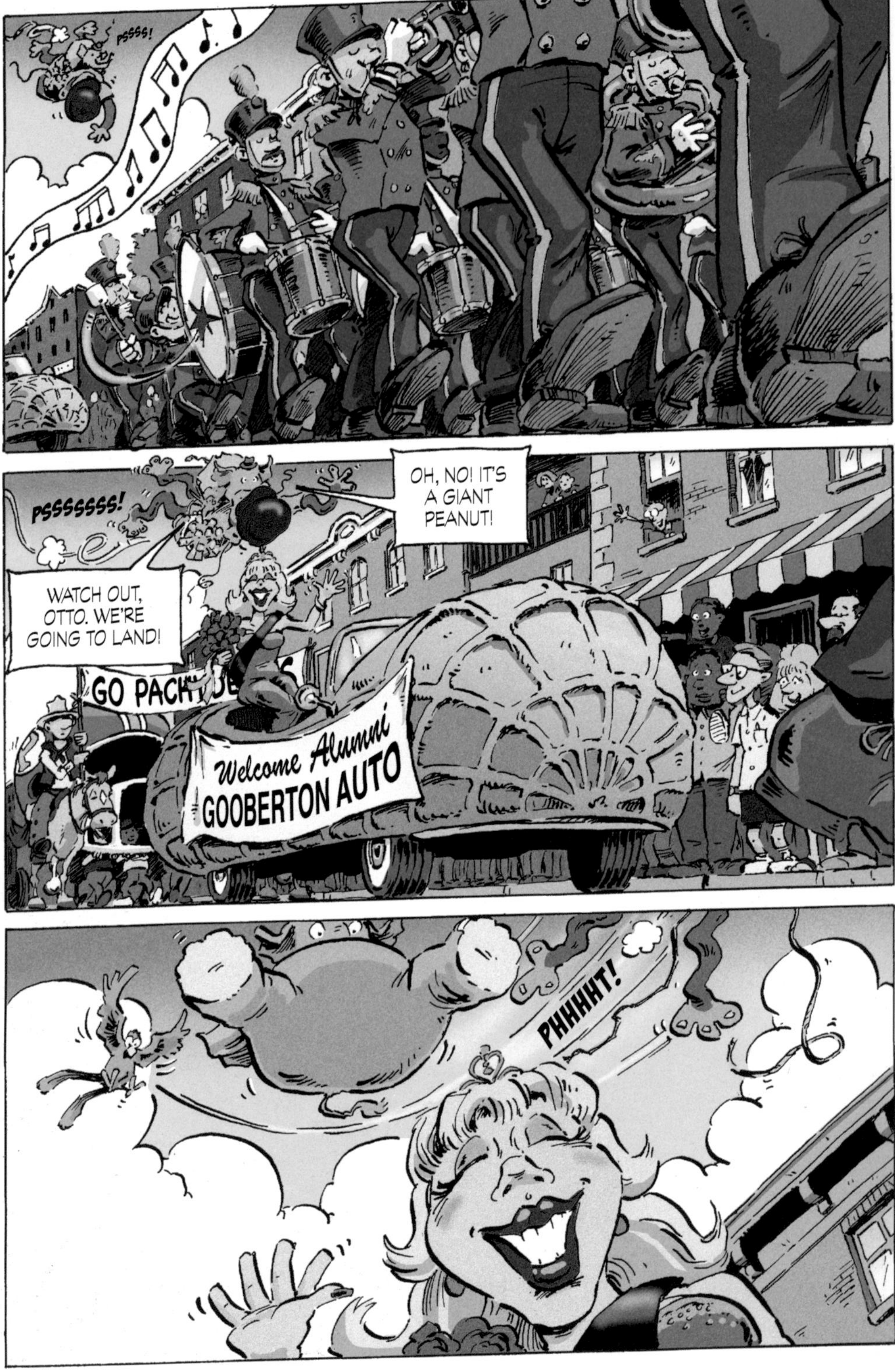
PSSSS!
PSSSSSSS!
OH, NO! IT'S A GIANT PEANUT!
WATCH OUT, OTTO. WE'RE GOING TO LAND!
GO PACH
Welcome Alumni
GOOBERTON AUTO
PHHHHT!

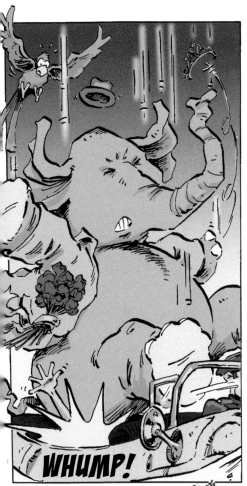

WHUMP!

FWIP!

FWIP!

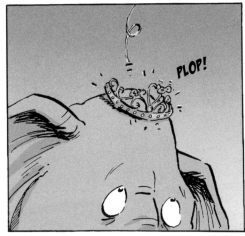

PLOP!

IT'S OKAY. IT'S A FAKE PEANUT.

PAK ATTACK!

Welcome Alumni GOOBERTON AUTO

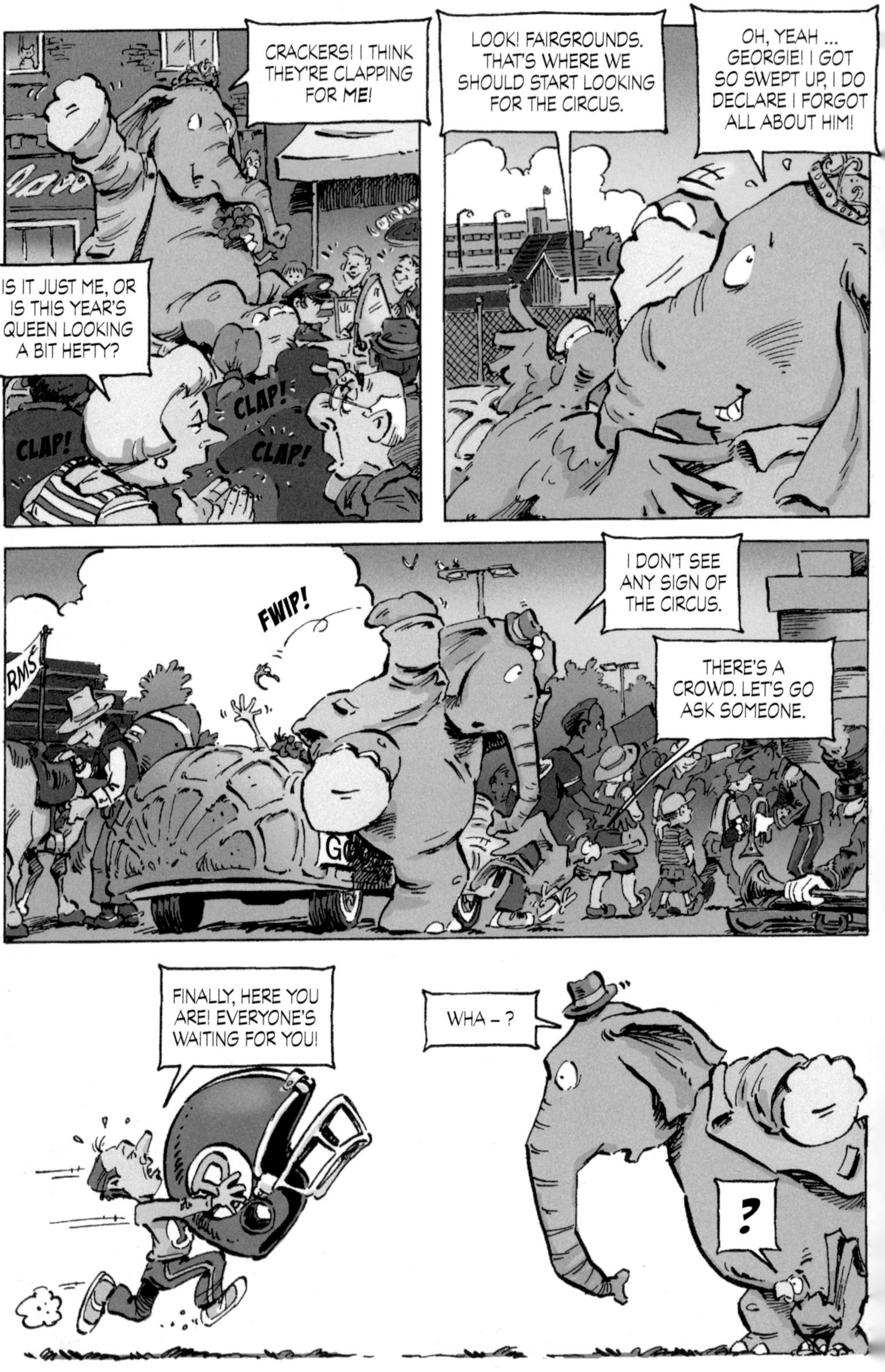
CRACKERS! I THINK THEY'RE CLAPPING FOR ME!
IS IT JUST ME, OR IS THIS YEAR'S QUEEN LOOKING A BIT HEFTY?
CLAP!
CLAP!
CLAP!
LOOK! FAIRGROUNDS. THAT'S WHERE WE SHOULD START LOOKING FOR THE CIRCUS.
OH, YEAH ... GEORGIE! I GOT SO SWEPT UP, I DO DECLARE I FORGOT ALL ABOUT HIM!
FWIP!
I DON'T SEE ANY SIGN OF THE CIRCUS.
THERE'S A CROWD. LET'S GO ASK SOMEONE.
FINALLY, HERE YOU ARE! EVERYONE'S WAITING FOR YOU!
WHA – ?
?

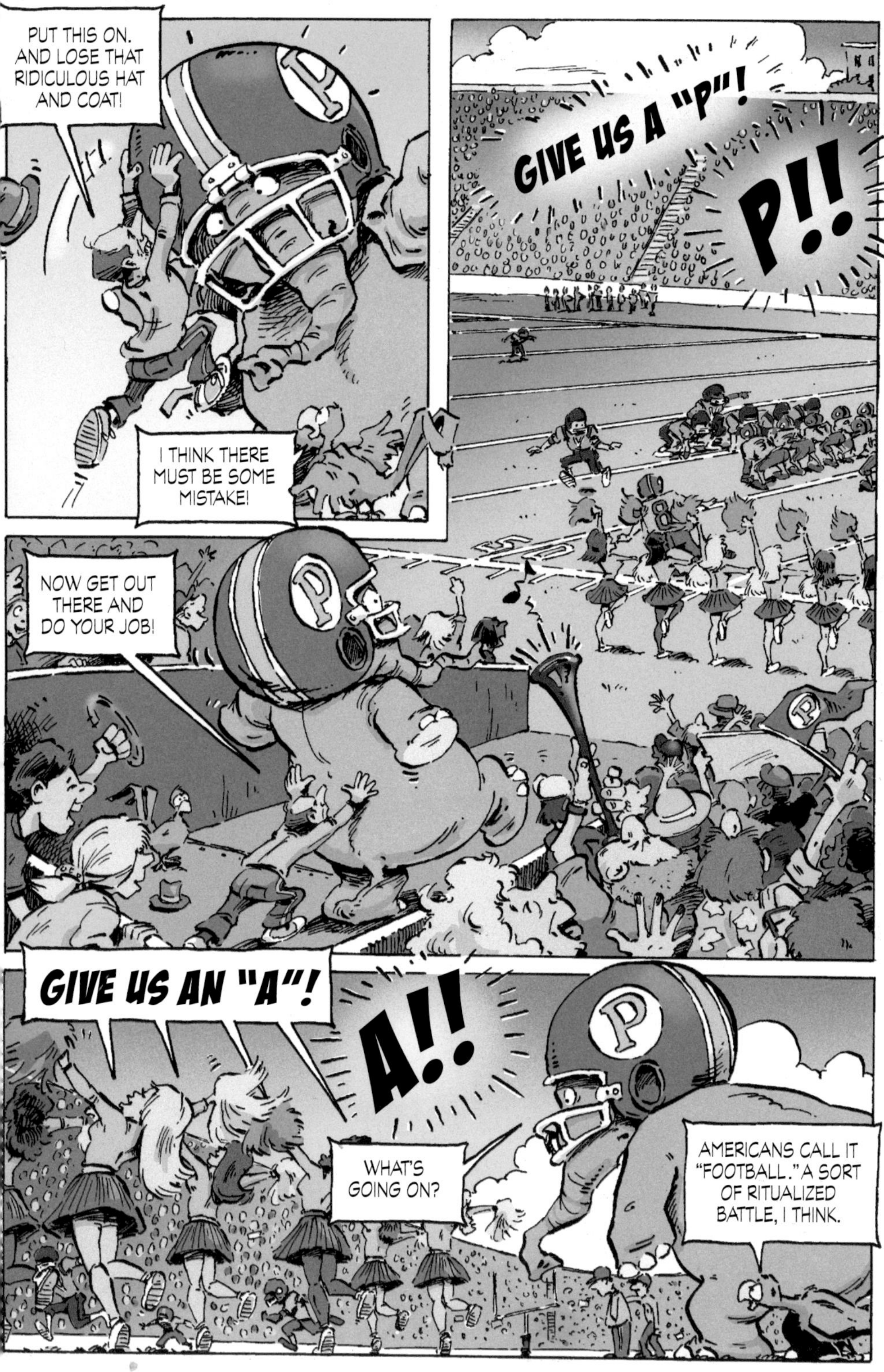
PUT THIS ON. AND LOSE THAT RIDICULOUS HAT AND COAT!
I THINK THERE MUST BE SOME MISTAKE!
GIVE US A "P"!
P!!
NOW GET OUT THERE AND DO YOUR JOB!
GIVE US AN "A"!
A!!
WHAT'S GOING ON?
AMERICANS CALL IT "FOOTBALL." A SORT OF RITUALIZED BATTLE, I THINK.

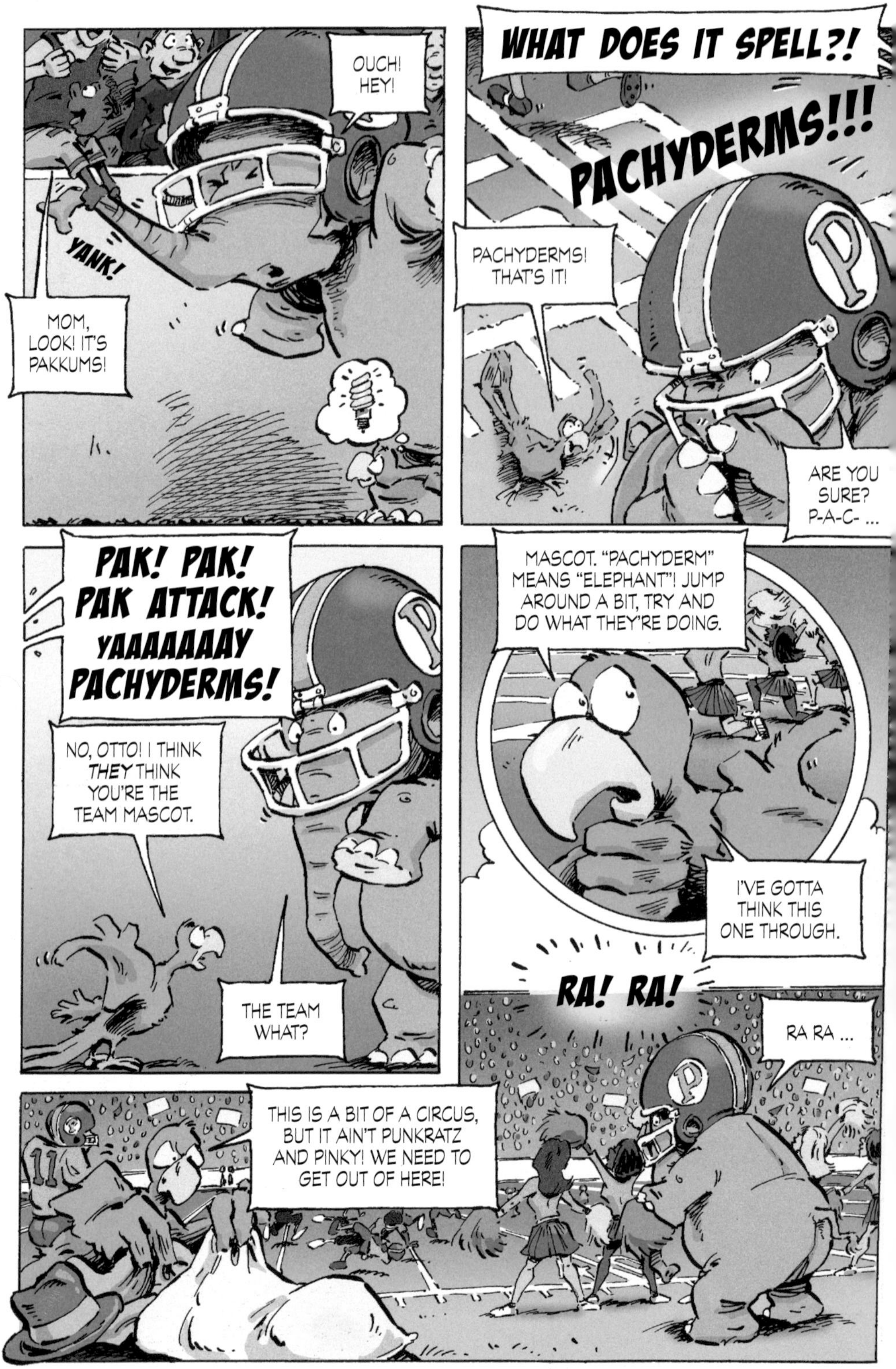
OUCH! HEY!
YANK!
MOM, LOOK! IT'S PAKKUMS!
WHAT DOES IT SPELL?!
PACHYDERMS!!!
PACHYDERMS! THAT'S IT!
ARE YOU SURE? P-A-C- ...
PAK! PAK! PAK ATTACK! YAAAAAAAY PACHYDERMS!
NO, OTTO! I THINK *THEY* THINK YOU'RE THE TEAM MASCOT.
THE TEAM WHAT?
MASCOT. "PACHYDERM" MEANS "ELEPHANT"! JUMP AROUND A BIT, TRY AND DO WHAT THEY'RE DOING.
I'VE GOTTA THINK THIS ONE THROUGH.
RA! RA!
RA RA ...
THIS IS A BIT OF A CIRCUS, BUT IT AIN'T PUNKRATZ AND PINKY! WE NEED TO GET OUT OF HERE!

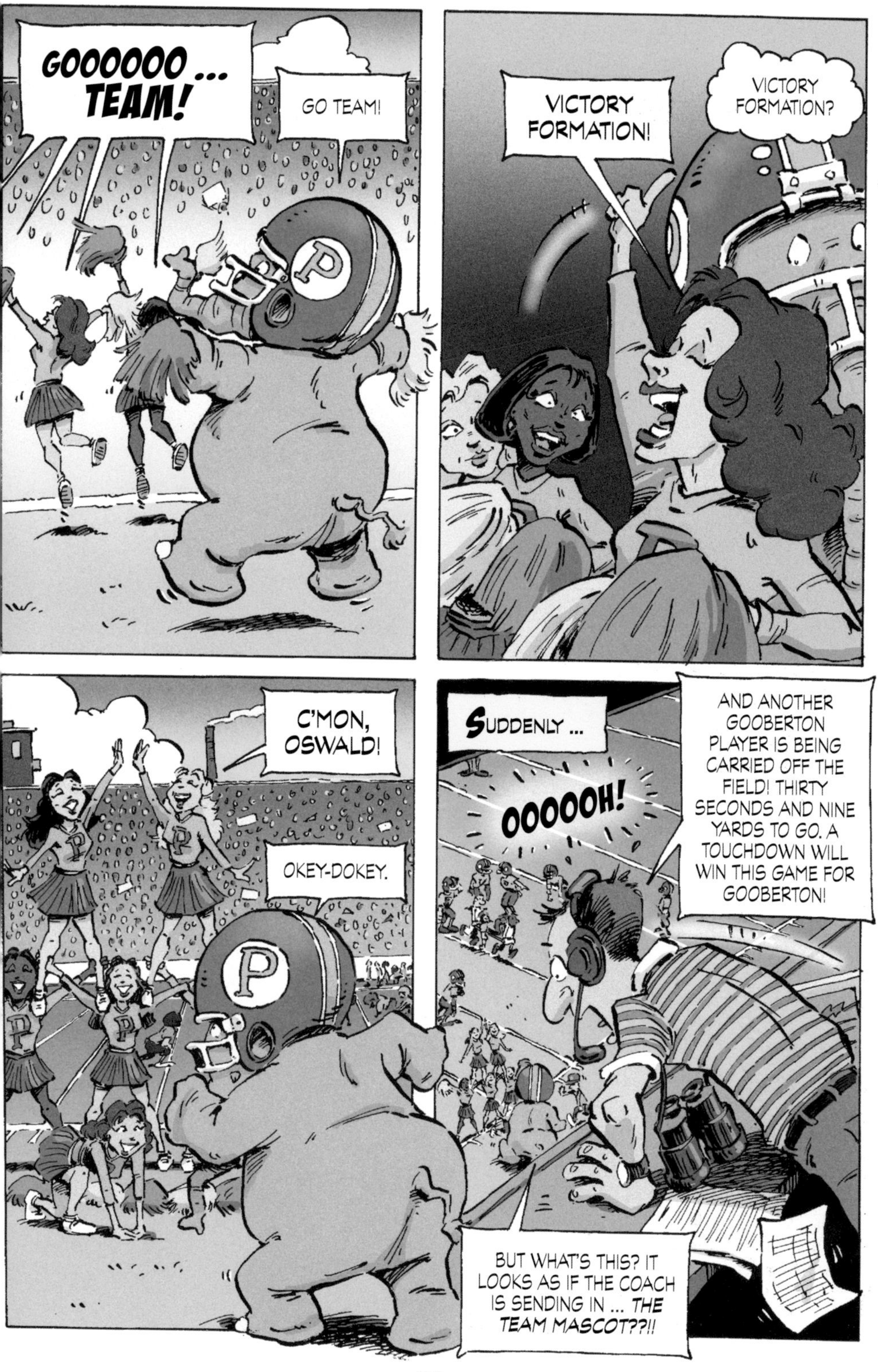
GOOOOOO ... TEAM!
GO TEAM!
VICTORY FORMATION!
VICTORY FORMATION?
C'MON, OSWALD!
OKEY-DOKEY.
SUDDENLY ...
OOOOOH!
AND ANOTHER GOOBERTON PLAYER IS BEING CARRIED OFF THE FIELD! THIRTY SECONDS AND NINE YARDS TO GO. A TOUCHDOWN WILL WIN THIS GAME FOR GOOBERTON!
BUT WHAT'S THIS? IT LOOKS AS IF THE COACH IS SENDING IN ... *THE TEAM MASCOT??!!*

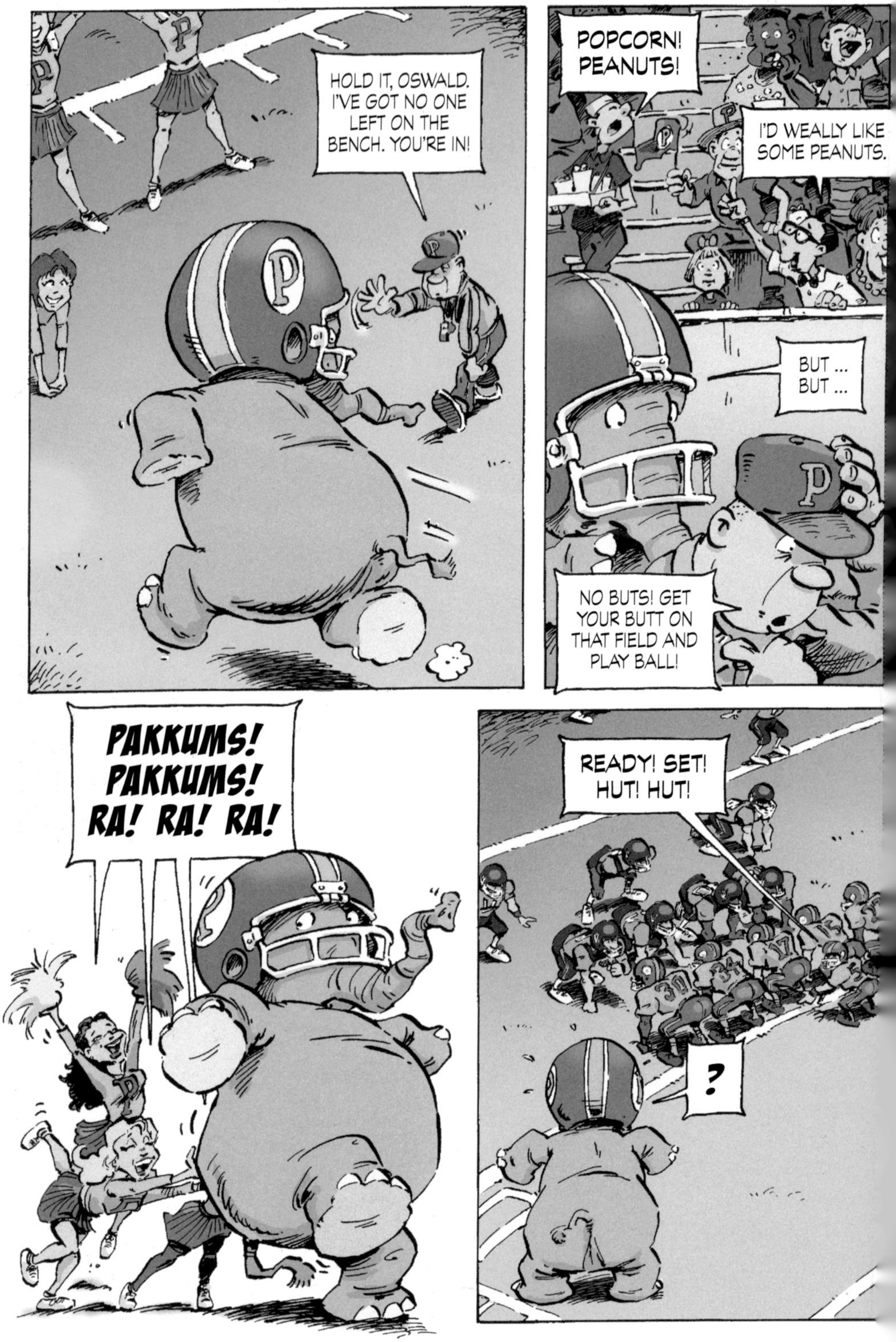
HOLD IT, OSWALD. I'VE GOT NO ONE LEFT ON THE BENCH. YOU'RE IN!
POPCORN! PEANUTS!
I'D WEALLY LIKE SOME PEANUTS.
BUT ... BUT ...
NO BUTS! GET YOUR BUTT ON THAT FIELD AND PLAY BALL!
PAKKUMS! PAKKUMS! RA! RA! RA!
READY! SET! HUT! HUT!
?

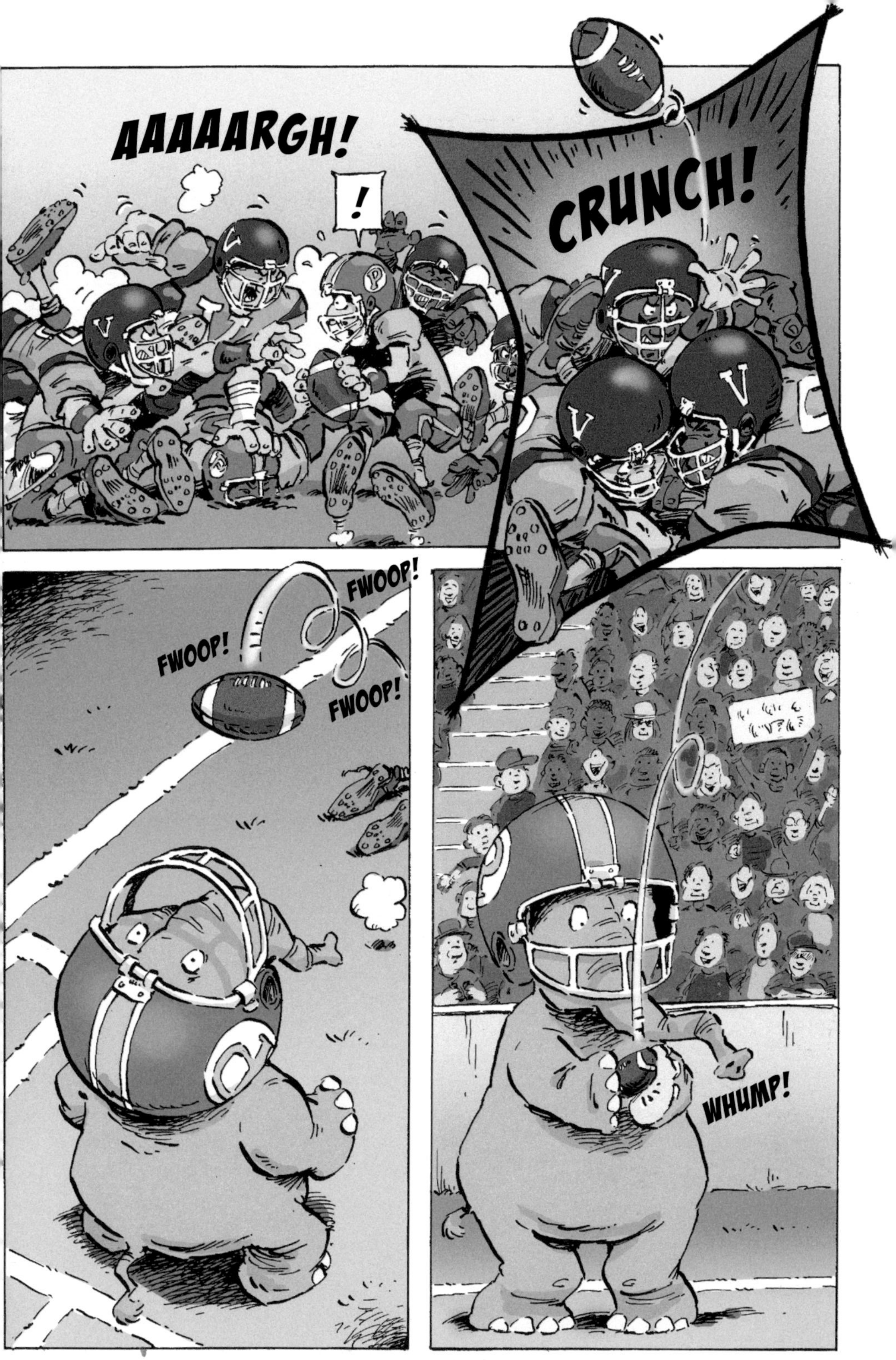
AAAAARGH!
!
CRUNCH!
FWOOP!
FWOOP!
FWOOP!
WHUMP!

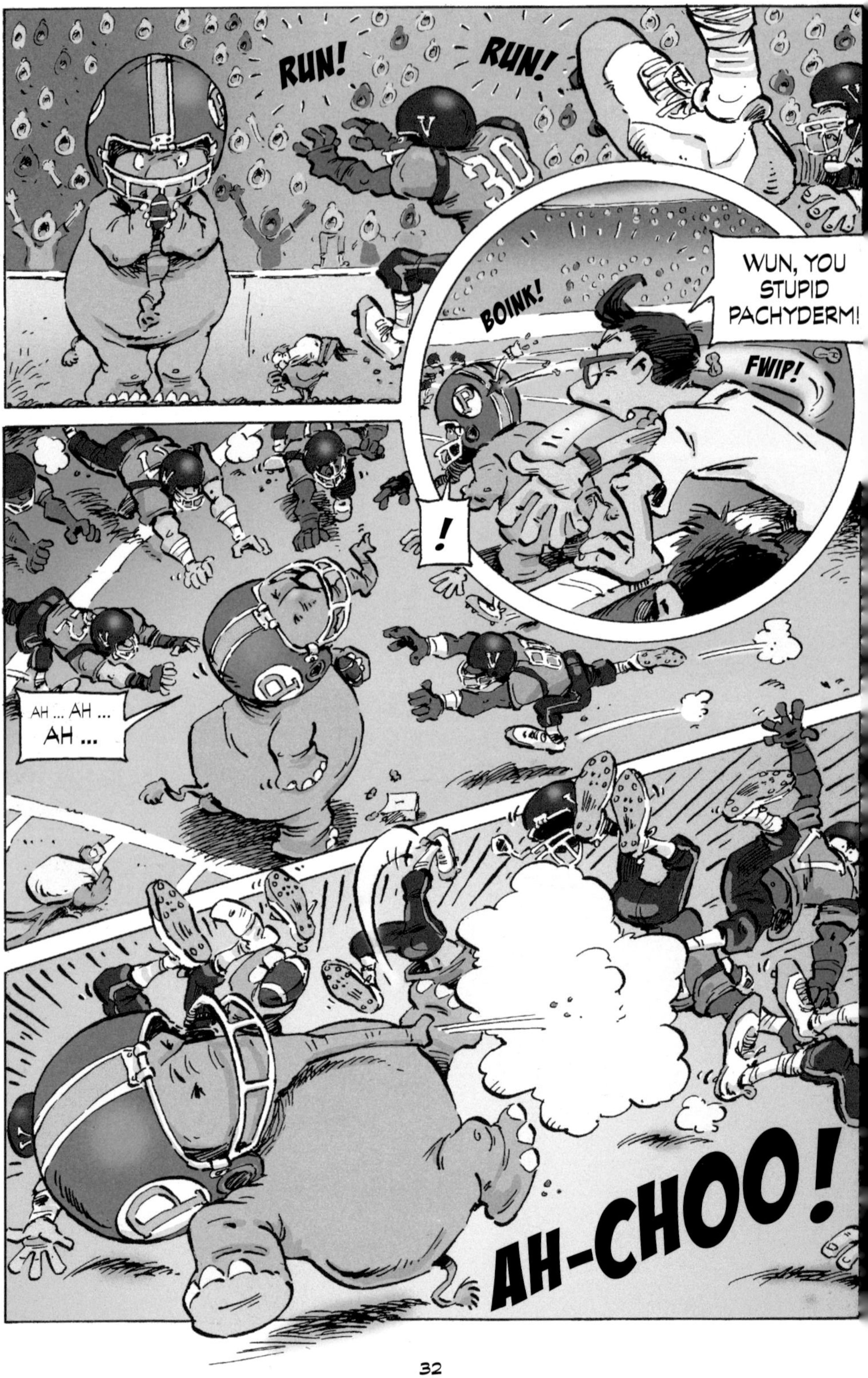
RUN!
RUN!
BOINK!
WUN, YOU STUPID PACHYDERM!
FWIP!
!
AH ... AH ... AH ...
AH-CHOO!

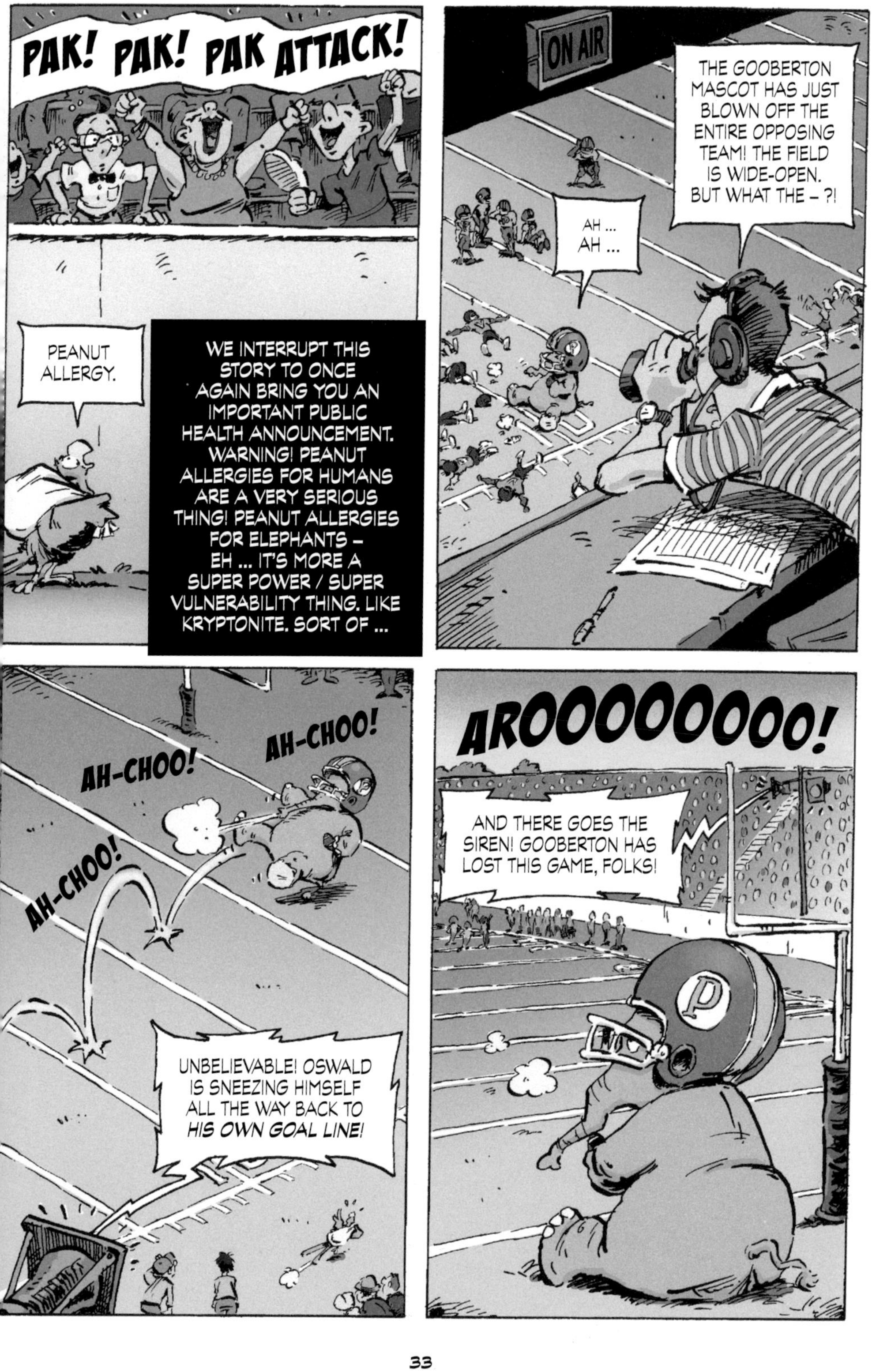
PAK! PAK! PAK ATTACK!
PEANUT ALLERGY.
WE INTERRUPT THIS STORY TO ONCE AGAIN BRING YOU AN IMPORTANT PUBLIC HEALTH ANNOUNCEMENT. WARNING! PEANUT ALLERGIES FOR HUMANS ARE A VERY SERIOUS THING! PEANUT ALLERGIES FOR ELEPHANTS – EH ... IT'S MORE A SUPER POWER / SUPER VULNERABILITY THING. LIKE KRYPTONITE. SORT OF ...
ON AIR
THE GOOBERTON MASCOT HAS JUST BLOWN OFF THE ENTIRE OPPOSING TEAM! THE FIELD IS WIDE-OPEN. BUT WHAT THE – ?!
AH ... AH ...
AH-CHOO!
AH-CHOO!
AH-CHOO!
UNBELIEVABLE! OSWALD IS SNEEZING HIMSELF ALL THE WAY BACK TO HIS OWN GOAL LINE!
AROOOOOOOOO!
AND THERE GOES THE SIREN! GOOBERTON HAS LOST THIS GAME, FOLKS!

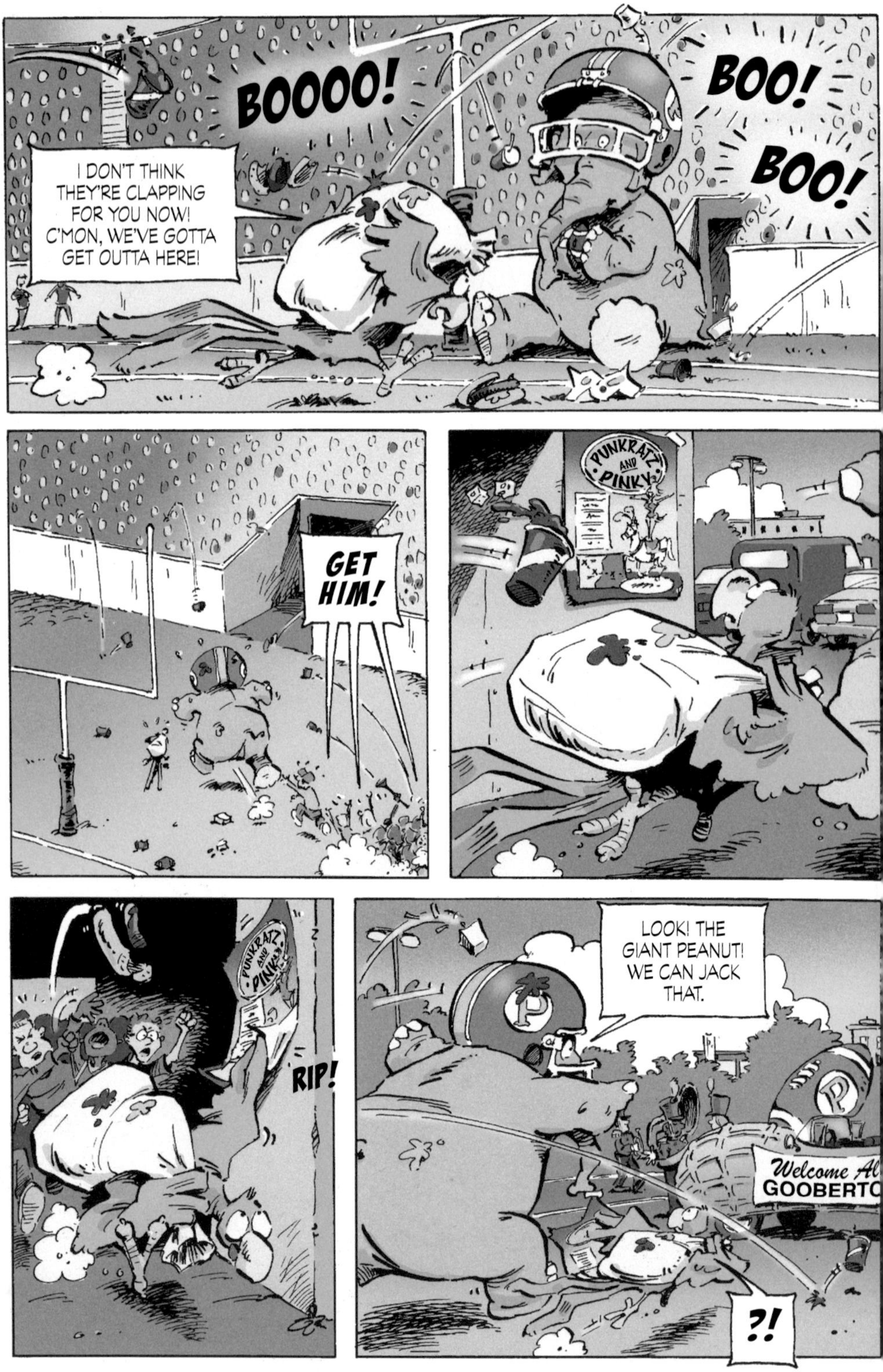
BOOOO!
BOO!
BOO!
I DON'T THINK THEY'RE CLAPPING FOR YOU NOW! C'MON, WE'VE GOTTA GET OUTTA HERE!
GET HIM!
PUNKRATZ AND PINKY
RIP!
LOOK! THE GIANT PEANUT! WE CAN JACK THAT.
?!

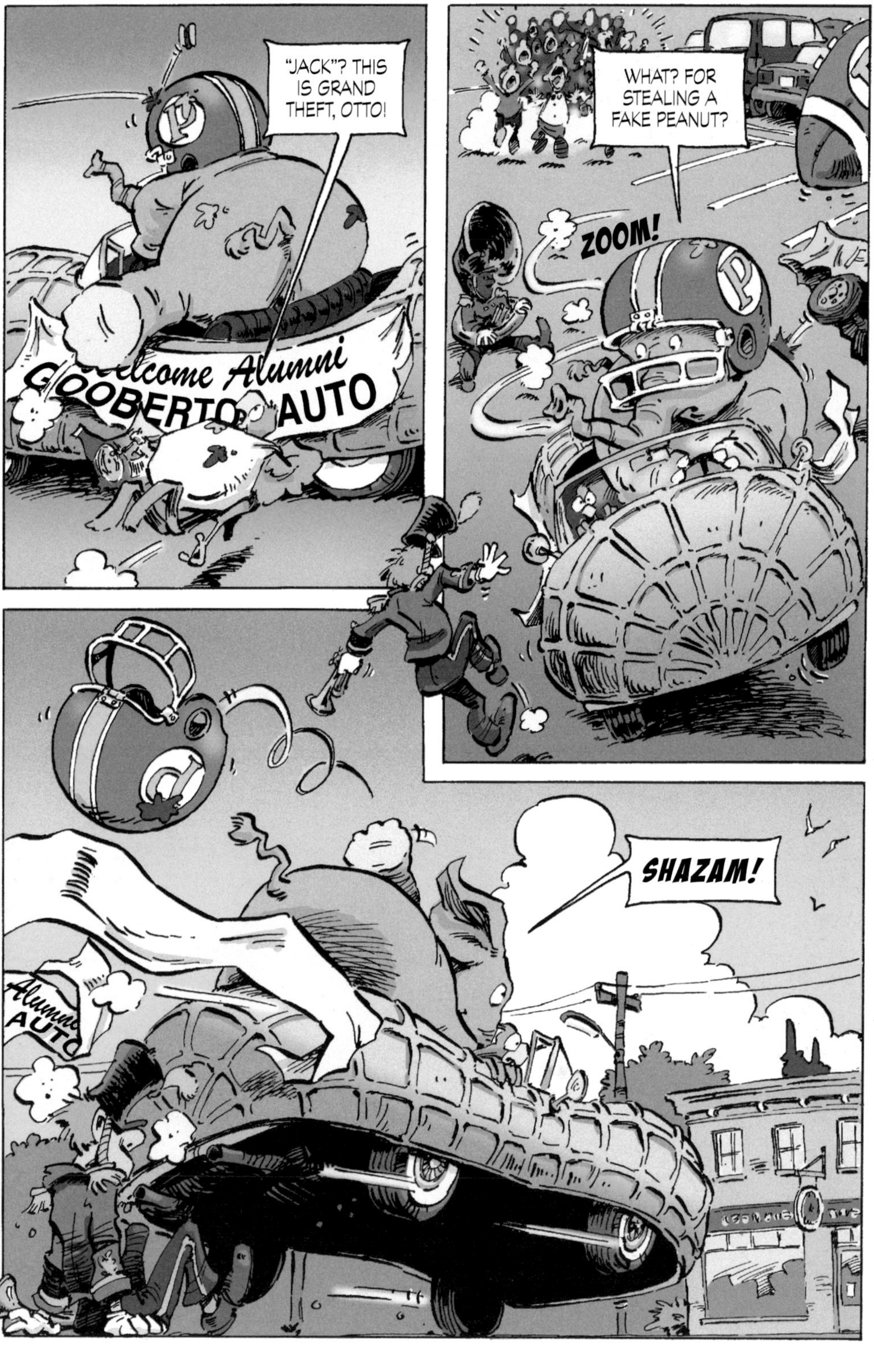
"JACK"? THIS IS GRAND THEFT, OTTO!
Welcome Alumni
GOOBERTO AUTO
WHAT? FOR STEALING A FAKE PEANUT?
ZOOM!
SHAZAM!

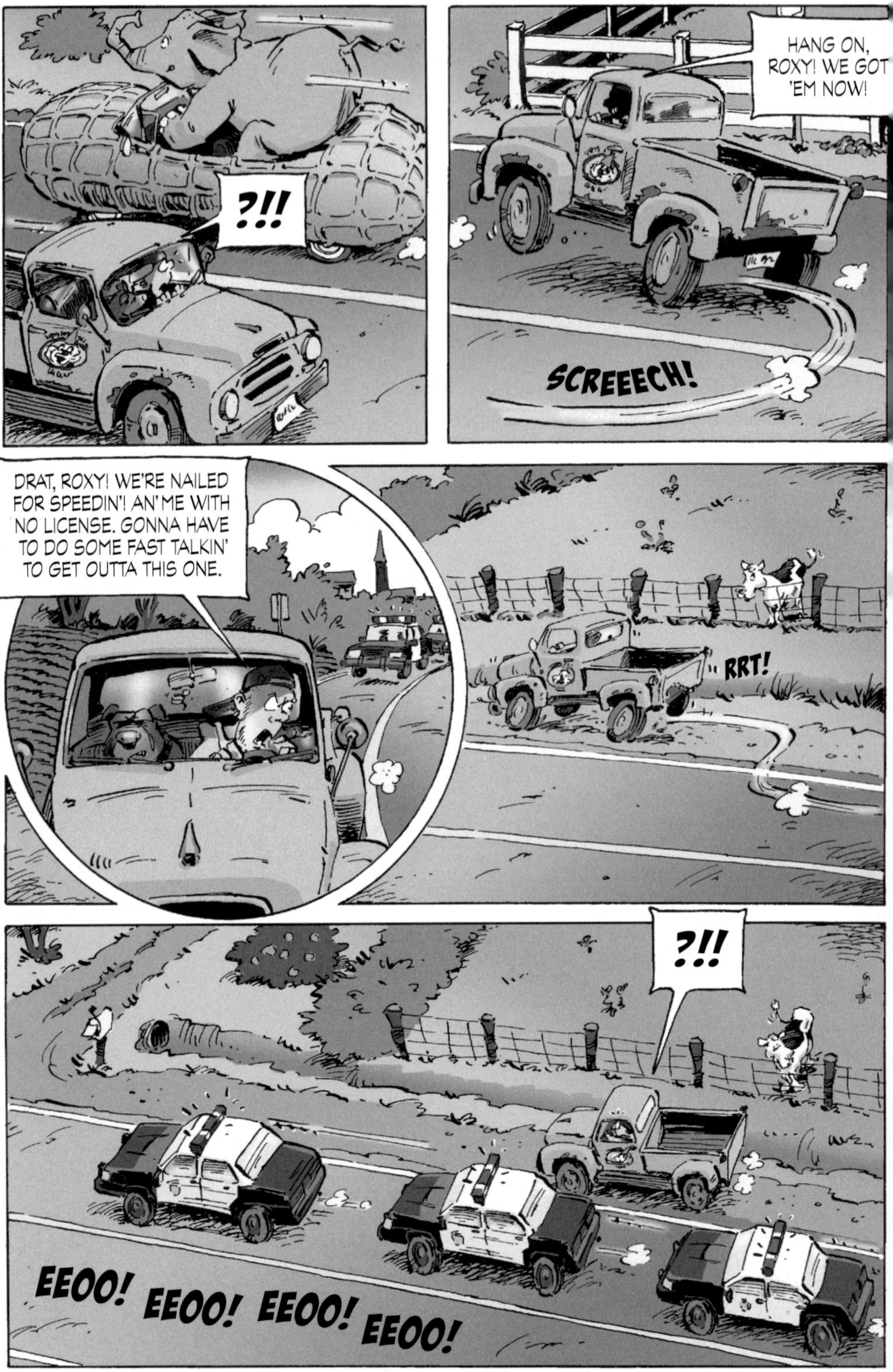
?!!
HANG ON, ROXY! WE GOT 'EM NOW!
SCREEECH!
DRAT, ROXY! WE'RE NAILED FOR SPEEDIN'! AN' ME WITH NO LICENSE. GONNA HAVE TO DO SOME FAST TALKIN' TO GET OUTTA THIS ONE.
RRT!
?!!
EEOO! EEOO! EEOO! EEOO!

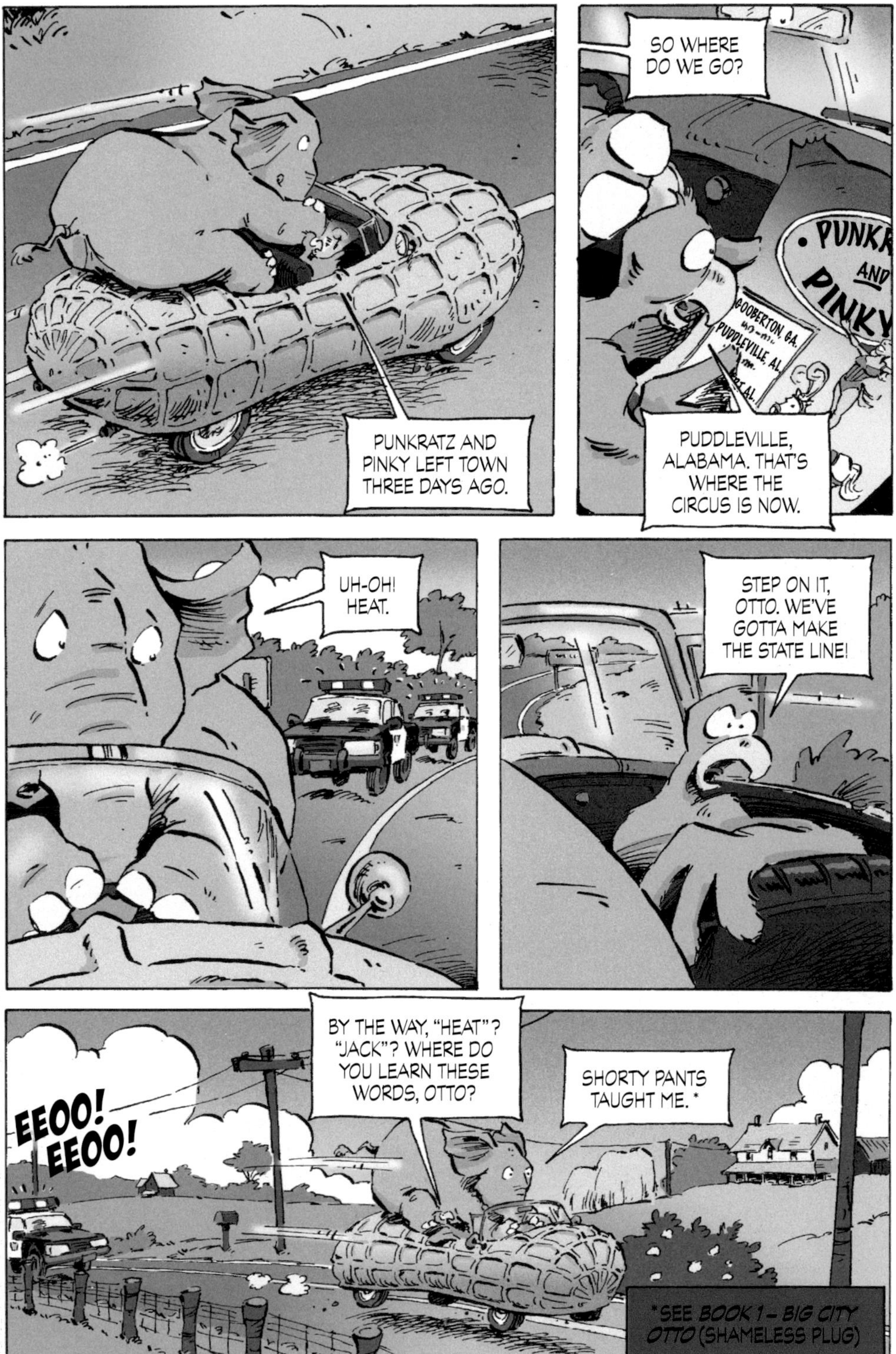
PUNKRATZ AND PINKY LEFT TOWN THREE DAYS AGO.
SO WHERE DO WE GO?
PUNKRATZ AND PINKY
GOOBERTON, GA.
PUDDLEVILLE, AL.
PUDDLEVILLE, ALABAMA. THAT'S WHERE THE CIRCUS IS NOW.
UH-OH! HEAT.
STEP ON IT, OTTO. WE'VE GOTTA MAKE THE STATE LINE!
EEOO! EEOO!
BY THE WAY, "HEAT"? "JACK"? WHERE DO YOU LEARN THESE WORDS, OTTO?
SHORTY PANTS TAUGHT ME. *
*SEE *BOOK 1 – BIG CITY OTTO* (SHAMELESS PLUG)

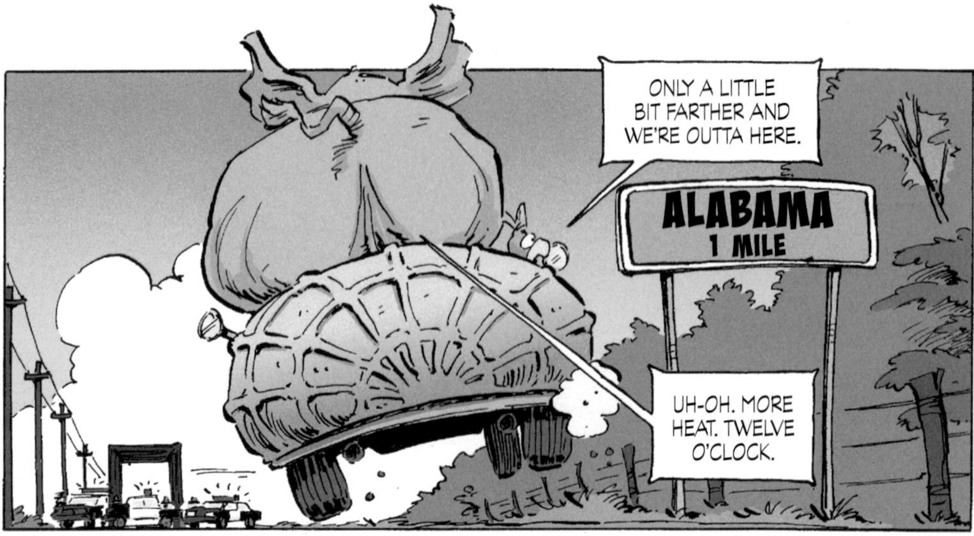
ONLY A LITTLE BIT FARTHER AND WE'RE OUTTA HERE.
ALABAMA
1 MILE
UH-OH. MORE HEAT. TWELVE O'CLOCK.

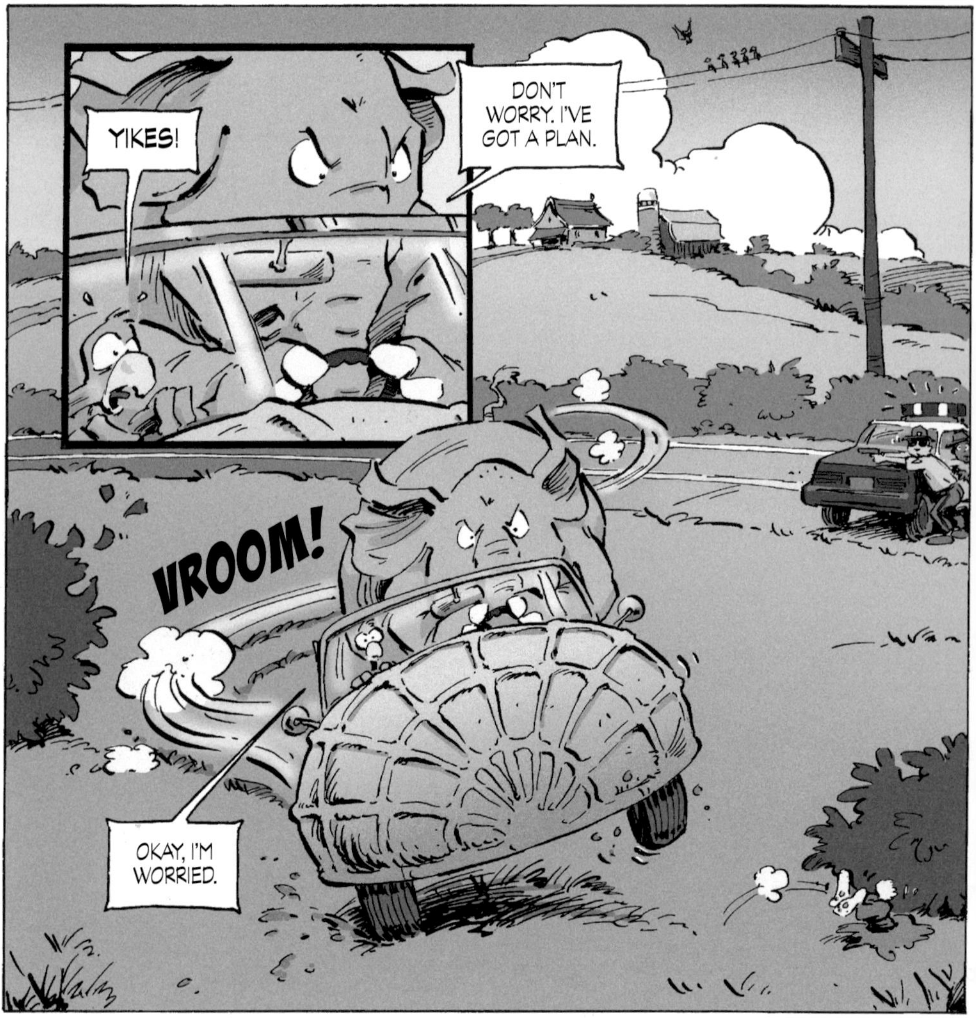
YIKES!
DON'T WORRY. I'VE GOT A PLAN.
VROOM!
OKAY, I'M WORRIED.

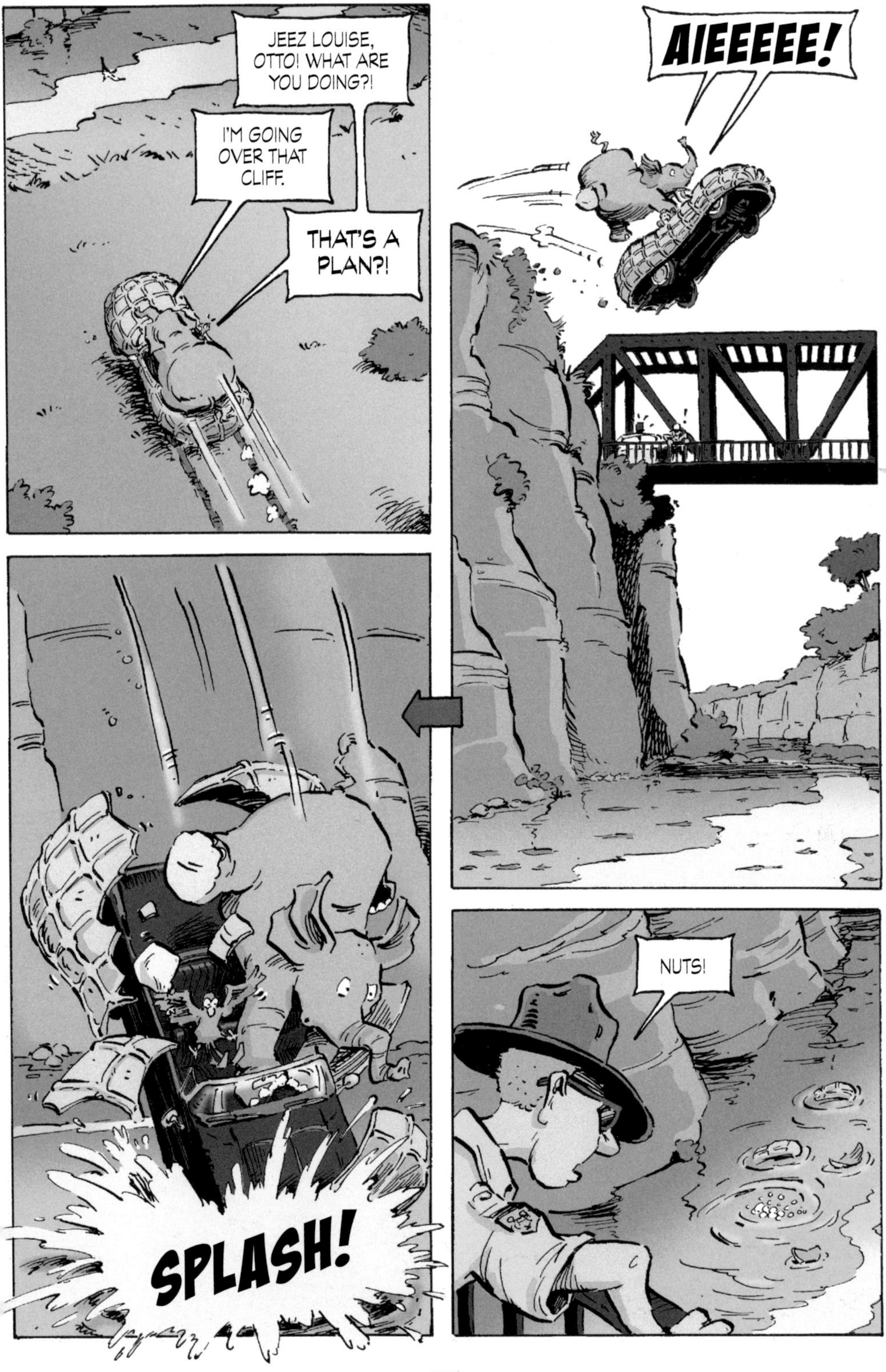
JEEZ LOUISE, OTTO! WHAT ARE YOU DOING?!
I'M GOING OVER THAT CLIFF.
THAT'S A PLAN?!
AIEEEEE!
SPLASH!
NUTS!

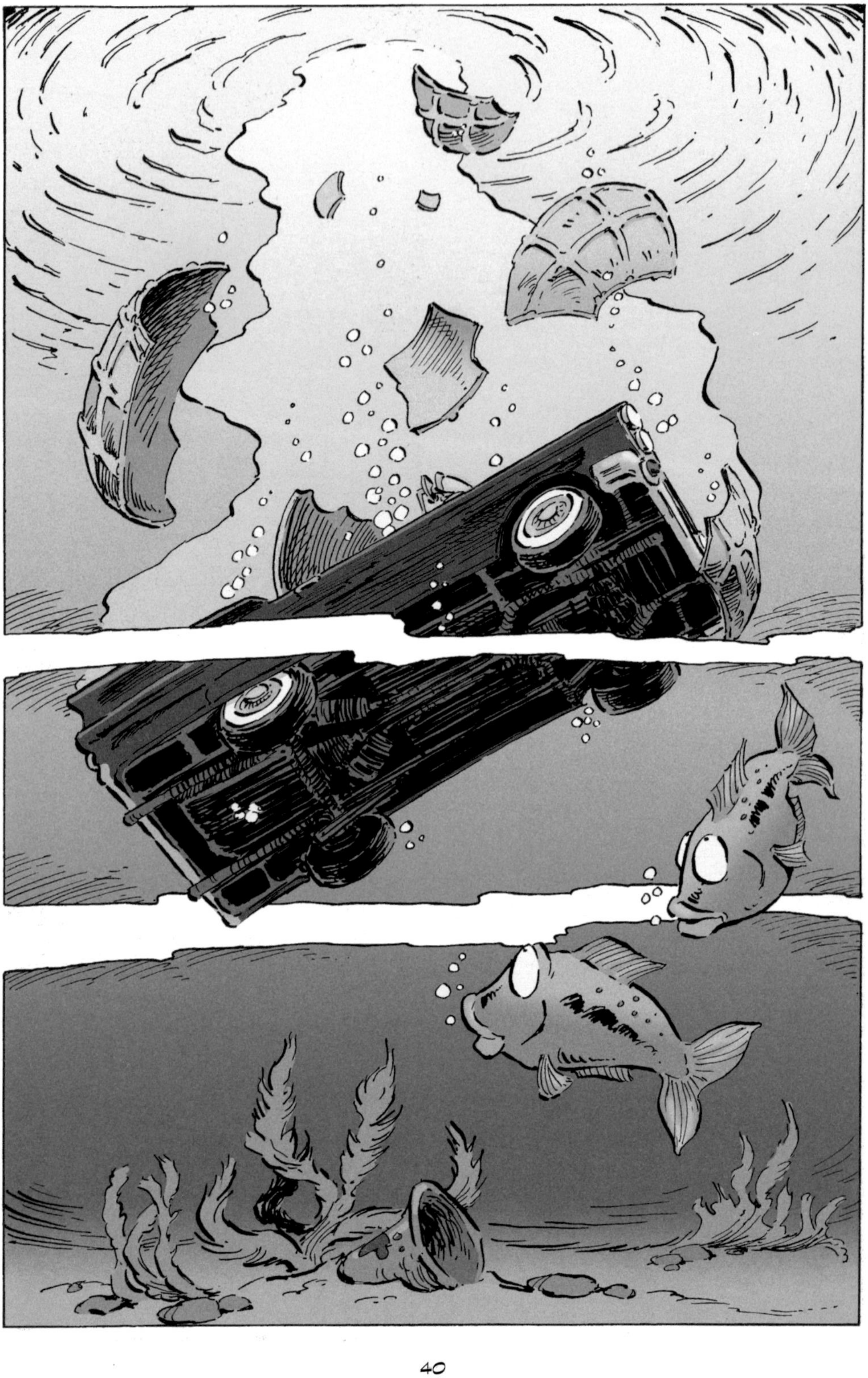

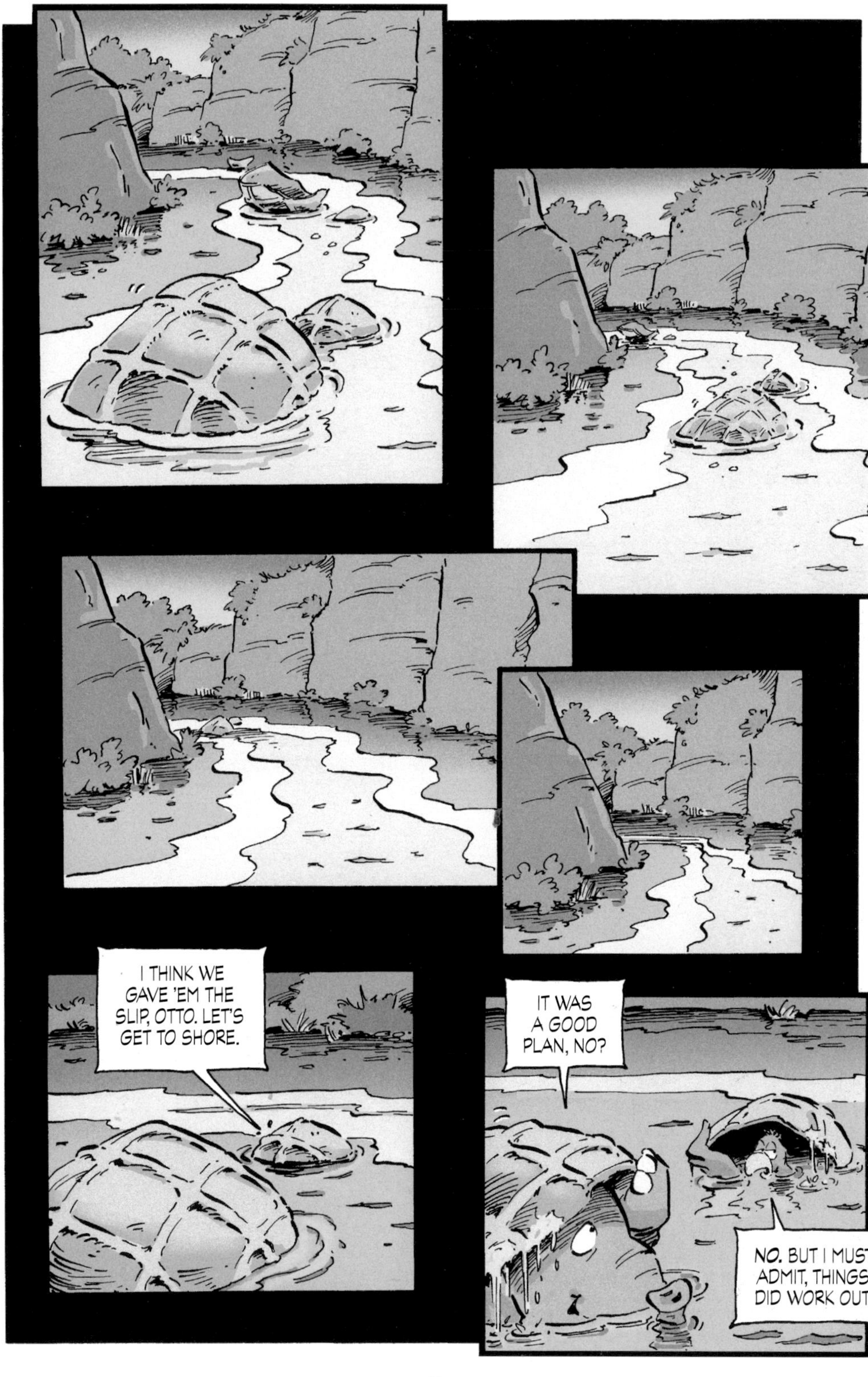
I THINK WE GAVE 'EM THE SLIP, OTTO. LET'S GET TO SHORE.
IT WAS A GOOD PLAN, NO?
NO. BUT I MUST ADMIT, THINGS DID WORK OUT.

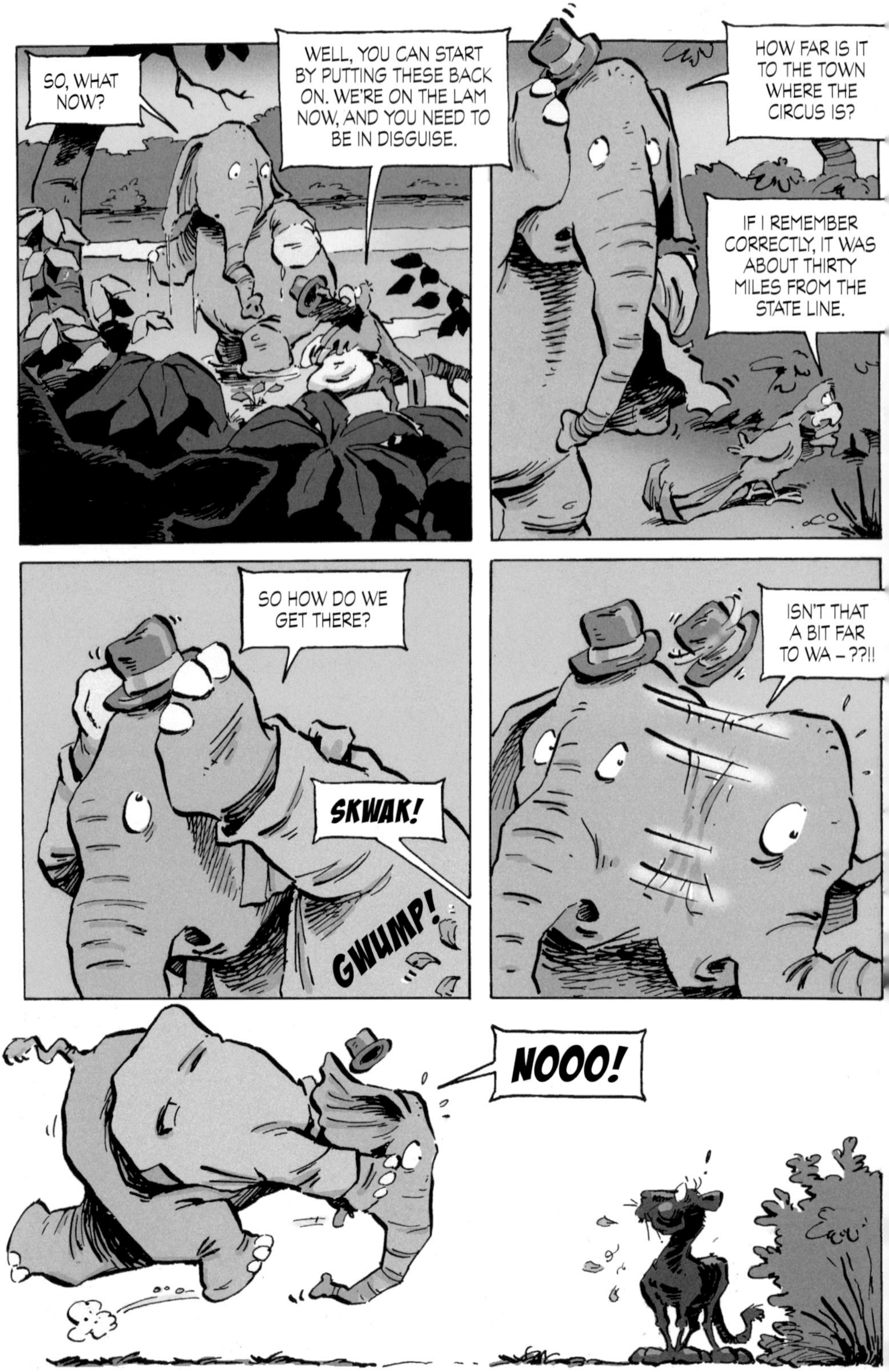
SO, WHAT NOW?
WELL, YOU CAN START BY PUTTING THESE BACK ON. WE'RE ON THE LAM NOW, AND YOU NEED TO BE IN DISGUISE.
HOW FAR IS IT TO THE TOWN WHERE THE CIRCUS IS?
IF I REMEMBER CORRECTLY, IT WAS ABOUT THIRTY MILES FROM THE STATE LINE.
SO HOW DO WE GET THERE?
SKWAK!
GWUMP!
ISN'T THAT A BIT FAR TO WA – ??!!
NOOO!

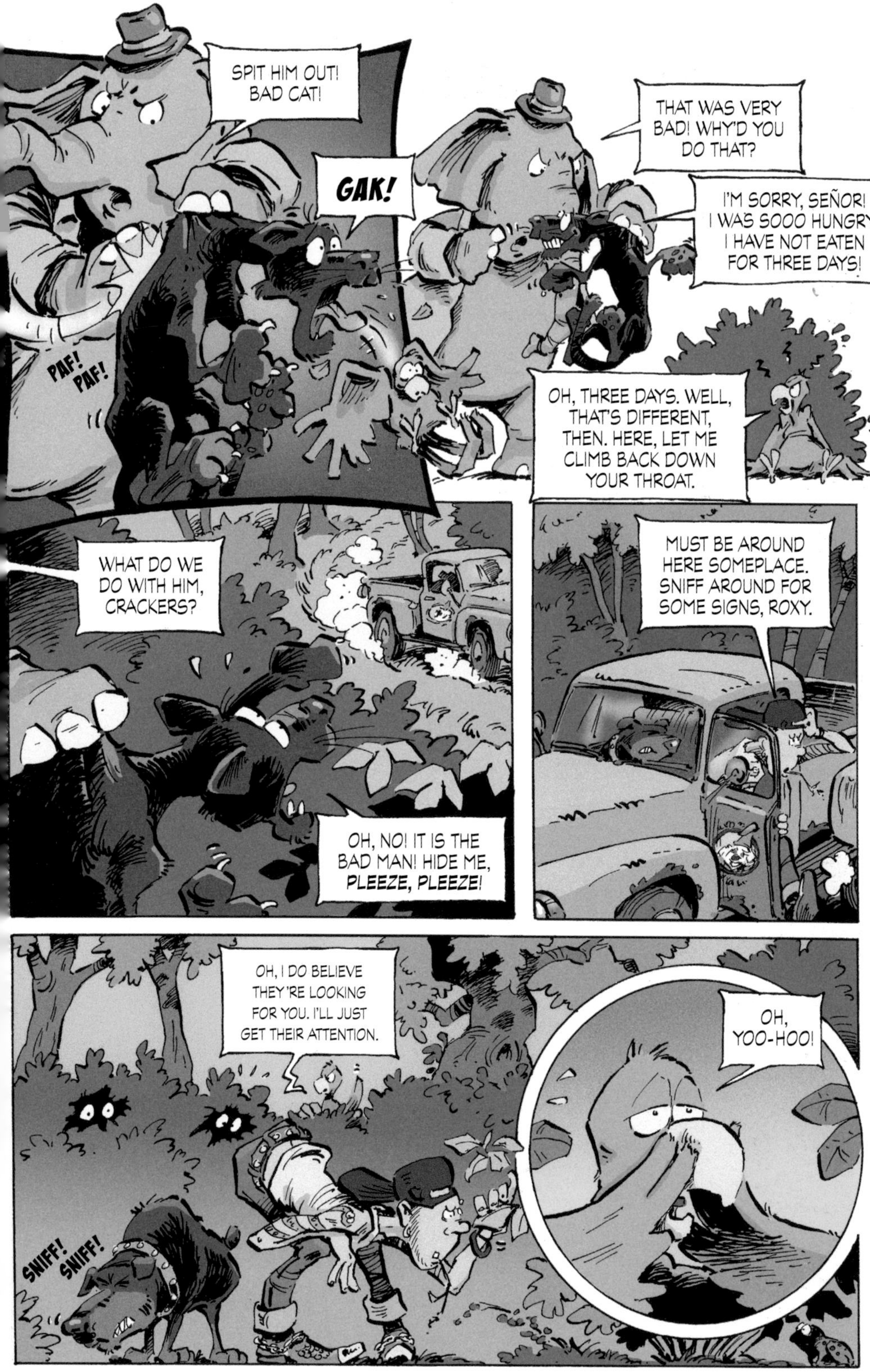
SPIT HIM OUT! BAD CAT!
GAK!
PAF! PAF!
THAT WAS VERY BAD! WHY'D YOU DO THAT?
I'M SORRY, SEÑOR! I WAS SOOO HUNGRY! I HAVE NOT EATEN FOR THREE DAYS!
OH, THREE DAYS. WELL, THAT'S DIFFERENT, THEN. HERE, LET ME CLIMB BACK DOWN YOUR THROAT.
WHAT DO WE DO WITH HIM, CRACKERS?
OH, NO! IT IS THE BAD MAN! HIDE ME, PLEEZE, PLEEZE!
MUST BE AROUND HERE SOMEPLACE. SNIFF AROUND FOR SOME SIGNS, ROXY.
OH, I DO BELIEVE THEY'RE LOOKING FOR YOU. I'LL JUST GET THEIR ATTENTION.
OH, YOO-HOO!
SNIFF! SNIFF!

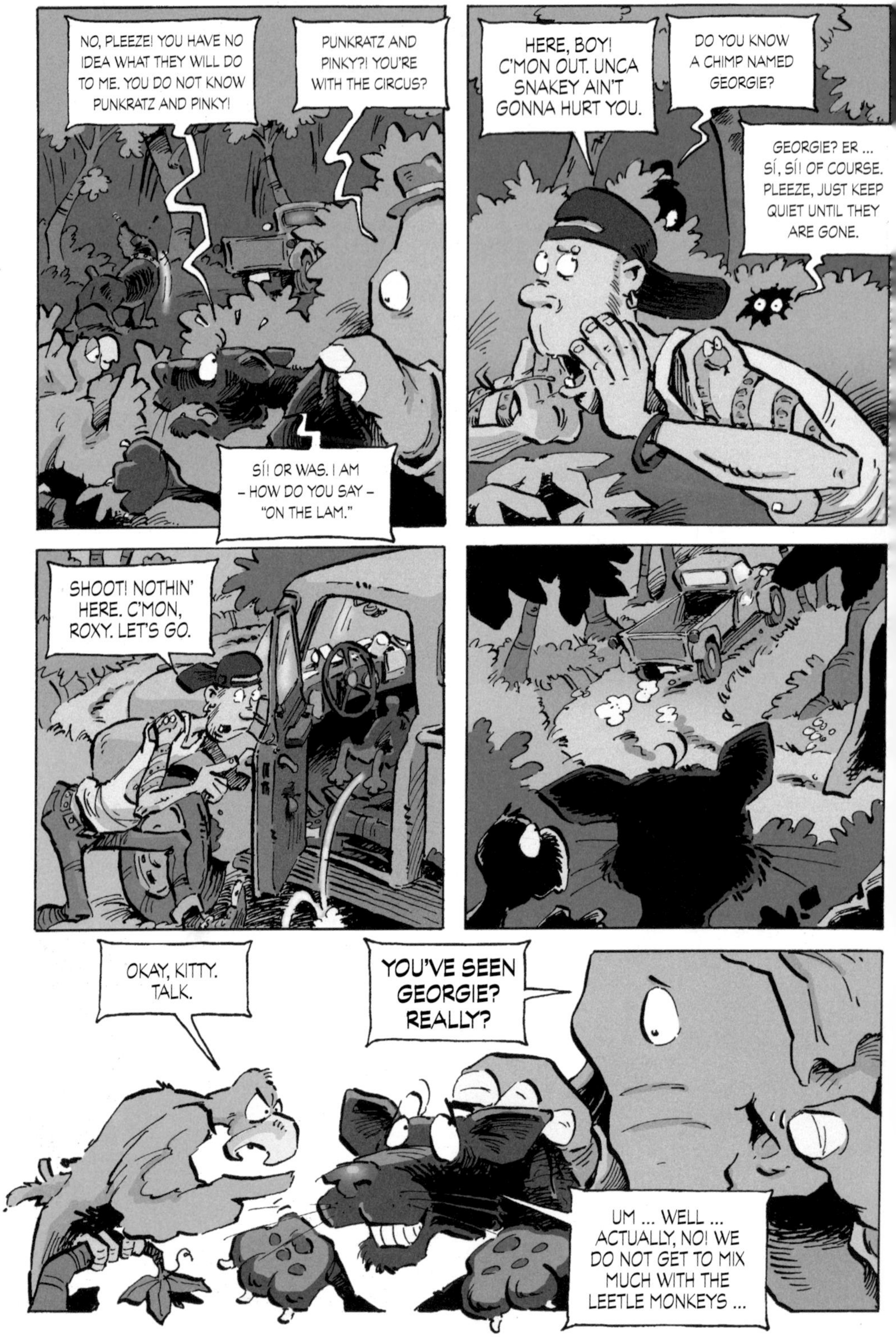
NO, PLEEZE! YOU HAVE NO IDEA WHAT THEY WILL DO TO ME. YOU DO NOT KNOW PUNKRATZ AND PINKY!
PUNKRATZ AND PINKY?! YOU'RE WITH THE CIRCUS?
SÍ! OR WAS. I AM – HOW DO YOU SAY – "ON THE LAM."
HERE, BOY! C'MON OUT. UNCA SNAKEY AIN'T GONNA HURT YOU.
DO YOU KNOW A CHIMP NAMED GEORGIE?
GEORGIE? ER ... SÍ, SÍ! OF COURSE. PLEEZE, JUST KEEP QUIET UNTIL THEY ARE GONE.
SHOOT! NOTHIN' HERE. C'MON, ROXY. LET'S GO.
OKAY, KITTY. TALK.
YOU'VE SEEN GEORGIE? REALLY?
UM ... WELL ... ACTUALLY, NO! WE DO NOT GET TO MIX MUCH WITH THE LEETLE MONKEYS ...

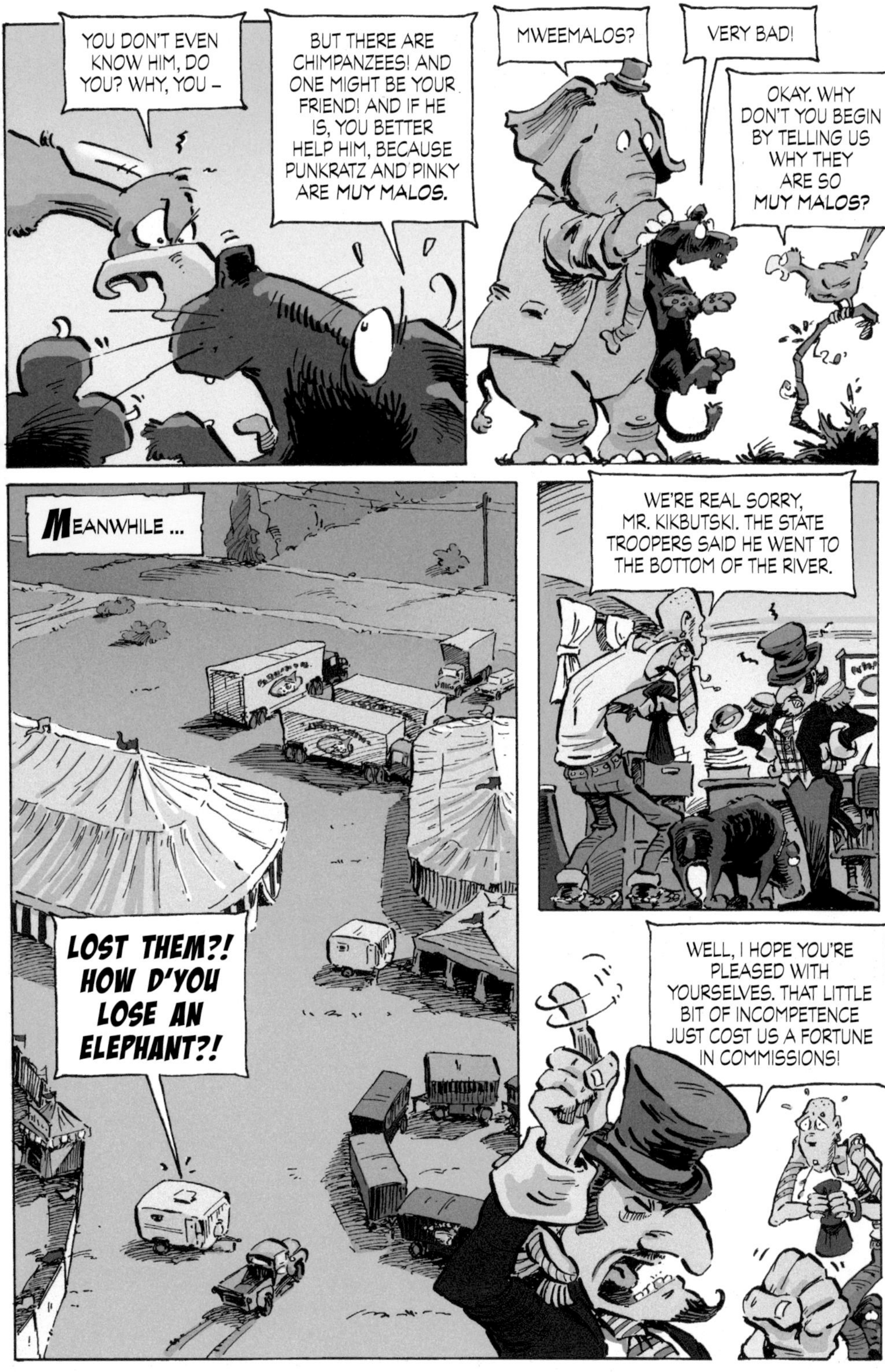

YOU DON'T EVEN KNOW HIM, DO YOU? WHY, YOU –
BUT THERE ARE CHIMPANZEES! AND ONE MIGHT BE YOUR FRIEND! AND IF HE IS, YOU BETTER HELP HIM, BECAUSE PUNKRATZ AND PINKY ARE *MUY MALOS.*
MWEEMALOS?
VERY BAD!
OKAY. WHY DON'T YOU BEGIN BY TELLING US WHY THEY ARE SO *MUY MALOS?*
MEANWHILE ...
LOST THEM?! HOW D'YOU LOSE AN ELEPHANT?!
WE'RE REAL SORRY, MR. KIKBUTSKI. THE STATE TROOPERS SAID HE WENT TO THE BOTTOM OF THE RIVER.
WELL, I HOPE YOU'RE PLEASED WITH YOURSELVES. THAT LITTLE BIT OF INCOMPETENCE JUST COST US A FORTUNE IN COMMISSIONS!

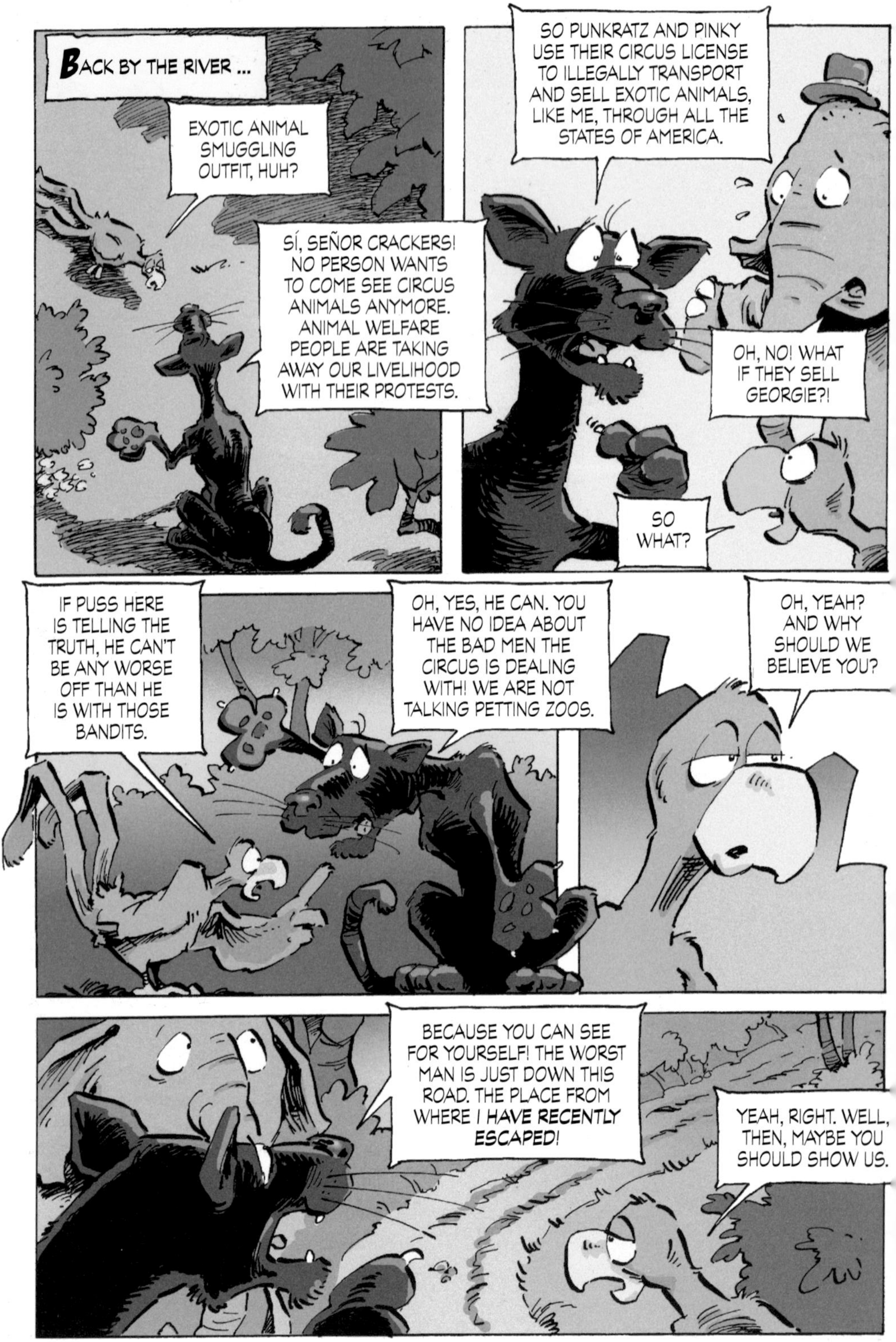
BACK BY THE RIVER ...
EXOTIC ANIMAL SMUGGLING OUTFIT, HUH?
SÍ, SEÑOR CRACKERS! NO PERSON WANTS TO COME SEE CIRCUS ANIMALS ANYMORE. ANIMAL WELFARE PEOPLE ARE TAKING AWAY OUR LIVELIHOOD WITH THEIR PROTESTS.
SO PUNKRATZ AND PINKY USE THEIR CIRCUS LICENSE TO ILLEGALLY TRANSPORT AND SELL EXOTIC ANIMALS, LIKE ME, THROUGH ALL THE STATES OF AMERICA.
OH, NO! WHAT IF THEY SELL GEORGIE?!
SO WHAT?
IF PUSS HERE IS TELLING THE TRUTH, HE CAN'T BE ANY WORSE OFF THAN HE IS WITH THOSE BANDITS.
OH, YES, HE CAN. YOU HAVE NO IDEA ABOUT THE BAD MEN THE CIRCUS IS DEALING WITH! WE ARE NOT TALKING PETTING ZOOS.
OH, YEAH? AND WHY SHOULD WE BELIEVE YOU?
BECAUSE YOU CAN SEE FOR YOURSELF! THE WORST MAN IS JUST DOWN THIS ROAD. THE PLACE FROM WHERE I HAVE RECENTLY ESCAPED!
YEAH, RIGHT. WELL, THEN, MAYBE YOU SHOULD SHOW US.

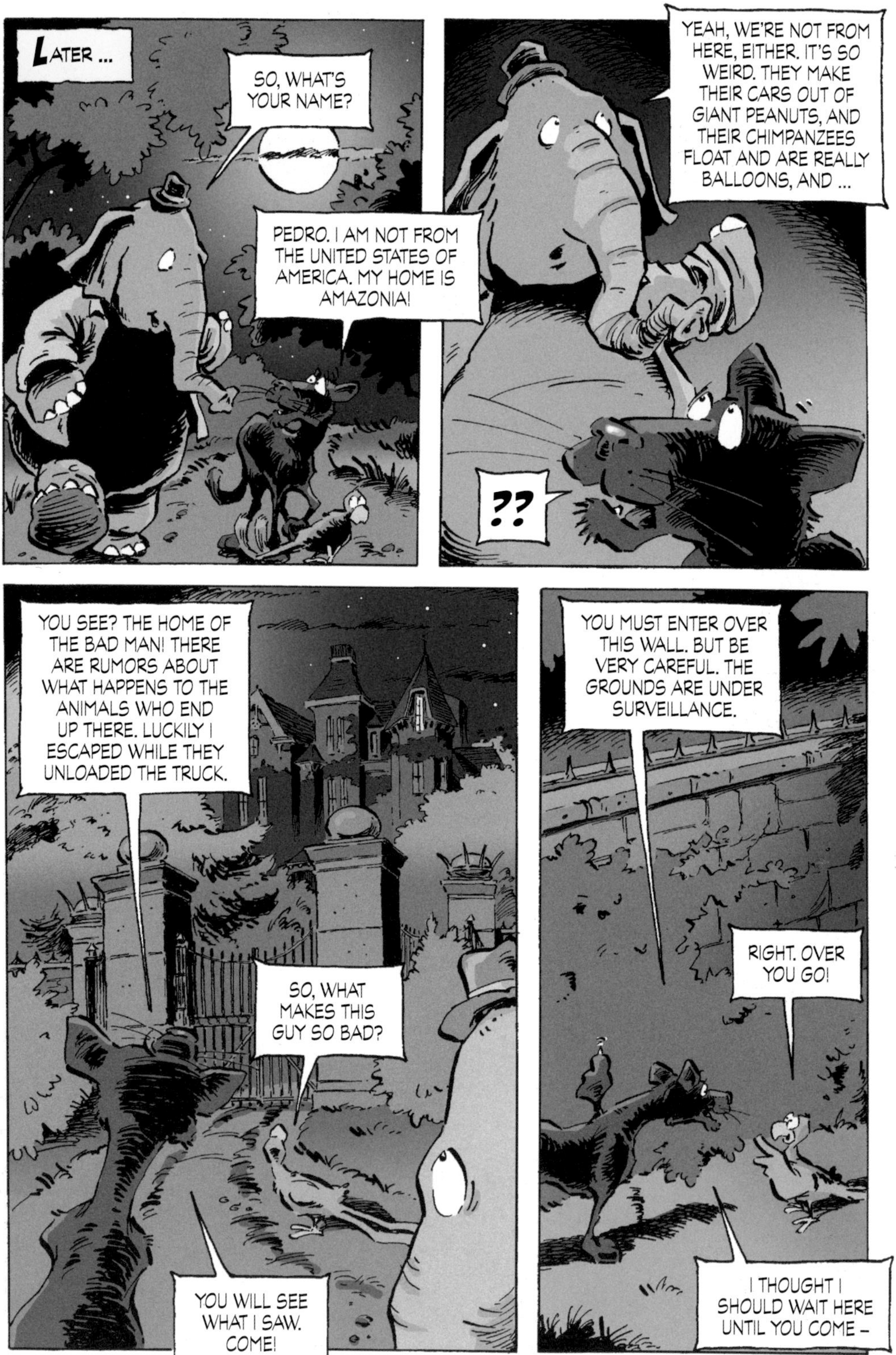
LATER ...
SO, WHAT'S YOUR NAME?
PEDRO. I AM NOT FROM THE UNITED STATES OF AMERICA. MY HOME IS AMAZONIA!
YEAH, WE'RE NOT FROM HERE, EITHER. IT'S SO WEIRD. THEY MAKE THEIR CARS OUT OF GIANT PEANUTS, AND THEIR CHIMPANZEES FLOAT AND ARE REALLY BALLOONS, AND ...
??
YOU SEE? THE HOME OF THE BAD MAN! THERE ARE RUMORS ABOUT WHAT HAPPENS TO THE ANIMALS WHO END UP THERE. LUCKILY I ESCAPED WHILE THEY UNLOADED THE TRUCK.
SO, WHAT MAKES THIS GUY SO BAD?
YOU WILL SEE WHAT I SAW. COME!
YOU MUST ENTER OVER THIS WALL. BUT BE VERY CAREFUL. THE GROUNDS ARE UNDER SURVEILLANCE.
RIGHT. OVER YOU GO!
I THOUGHT I SHOULD WAIT HERE UNTIL YOU COME –

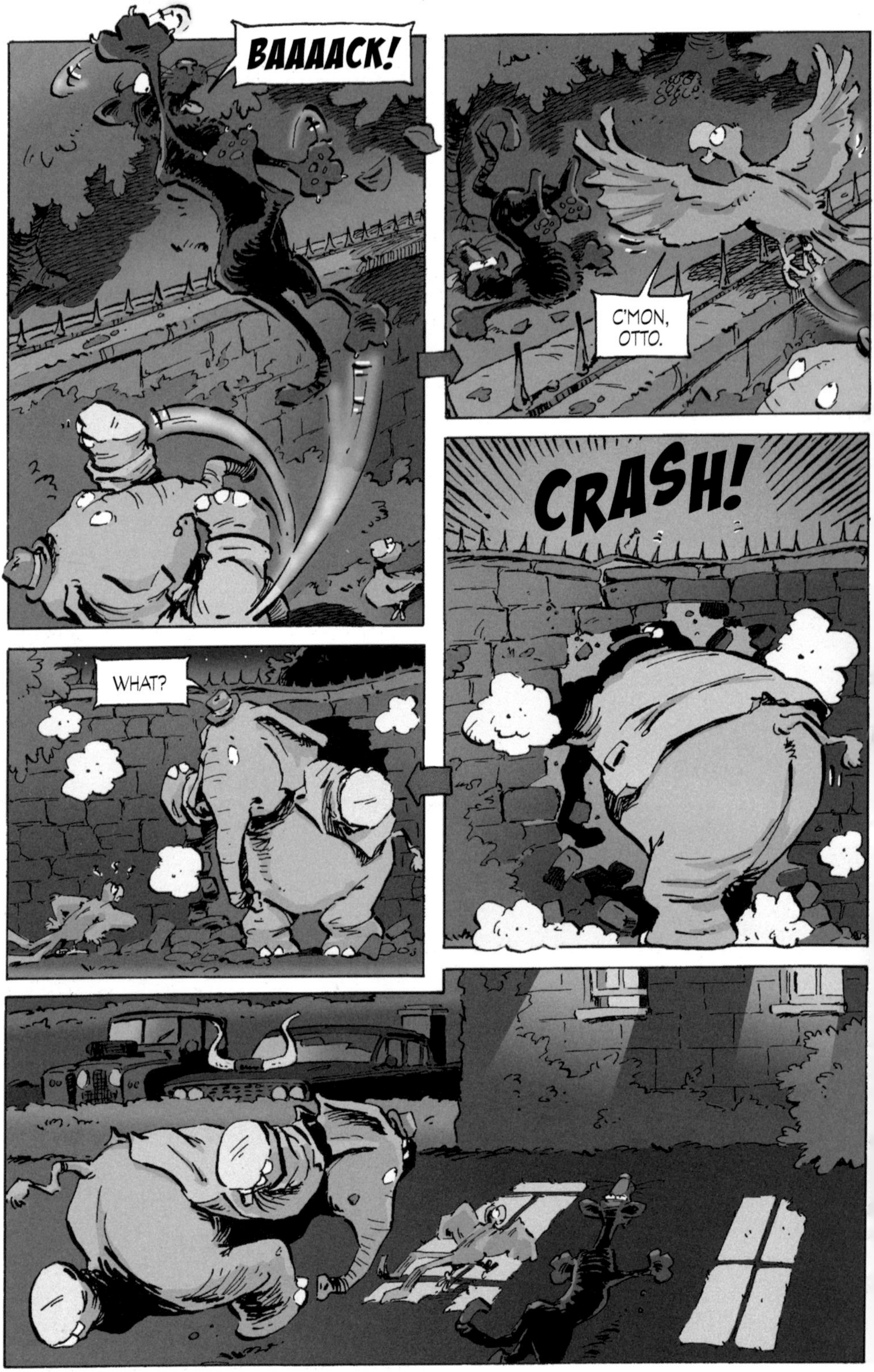
BAAAACK!
C'MON, OTTO.
CRASH!
WHAT?

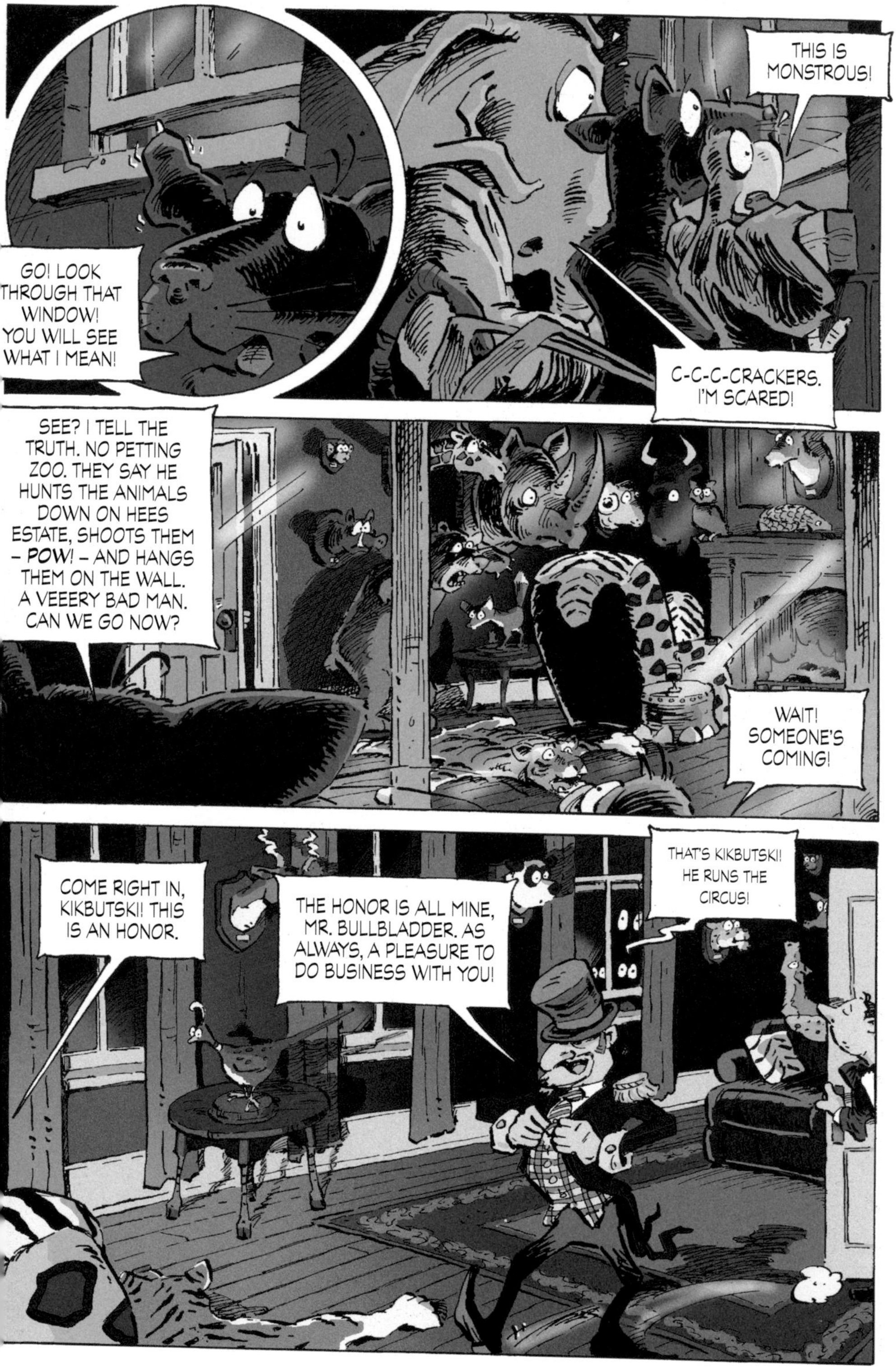
THIS IS MONSTROUS!
GO! LOOK THROUGH THAT WINDOW! YOU WILL SEE WHAT I MEAN!
C-C-C-CRACKERS. I'M SCARED!
SEE? I TELL THE TRUTH. NO PETTING ZOO. THEY SAY HE HUNTS THE ANIMALS DOWN ON HEES ESTATE, SHOOTS THEM – **POW**! – AND HANGS THEM ON THE WALL. A VEEERY BAD MAN. CAN WE GO NOW?
WAIT! SOMEONE'S COMING!
COME RIGHT IN, KIKBUTSKI! THIS IS AN HONOR.
THE HONOR IS ALL MINE, MR. BULLBLADDER. AS ALWAYS, A PLEASURE TO DO BUSINESS WITH YOU!
THAT'S KIKBUTSKI! HE RUNS THE CIRCUS!

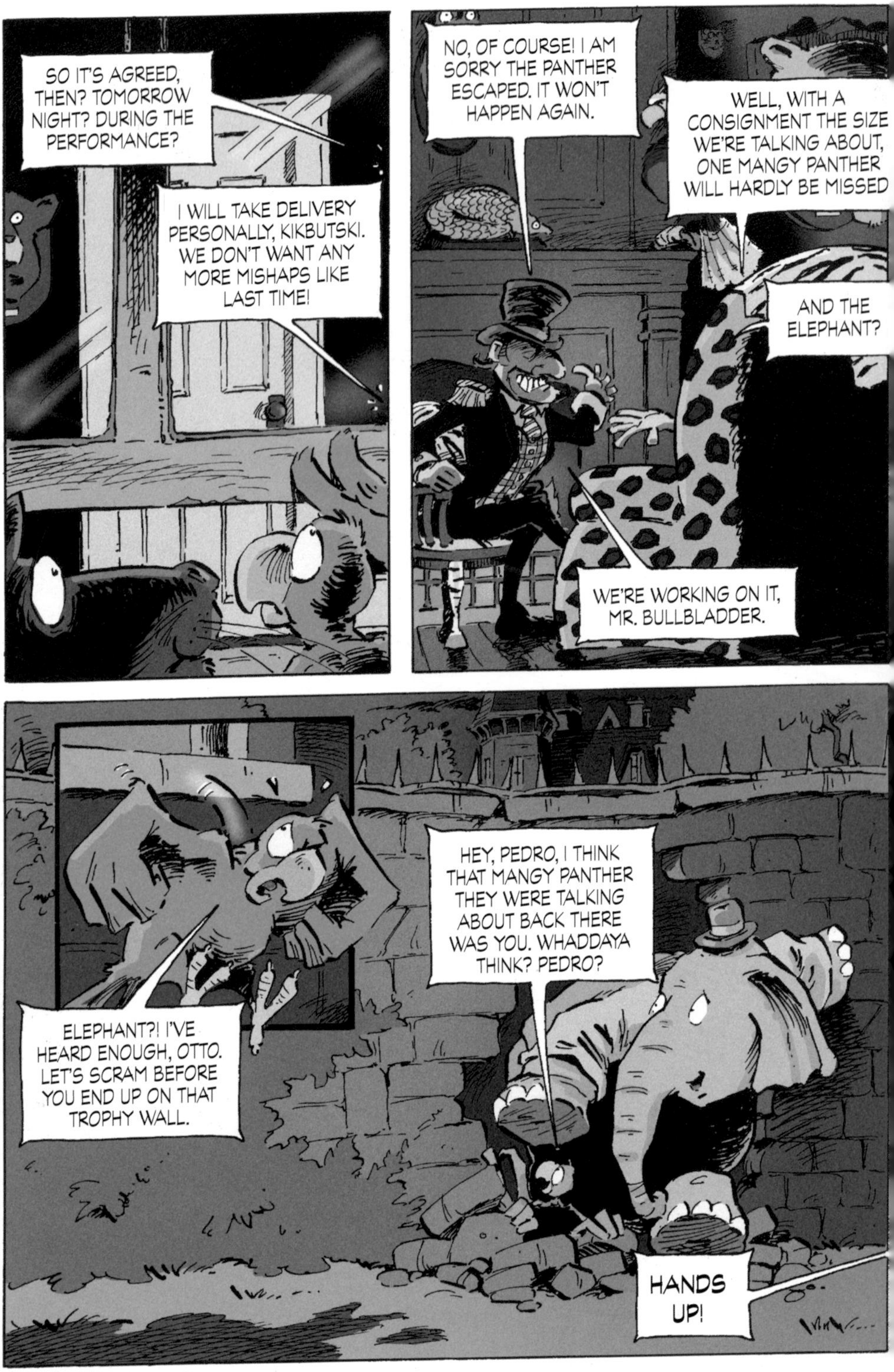
SO IT'S AGREED, THEN? TOMORROW NIGHT? DURING THE PERFORMANCE?
I WILL TAKE DELIVERY PERSONALLY, KIKBUTSKI. WE DON'T WANT ANY MORE MISHAPS LIKE LAST TIME!
NO, OF COURSE! I AM SORRY THE PANTHER ESCAPED. IT WON'T HAPPEN AGAIN.
WELL, WITH A CONSIGNMENT THE SIZE WE'RE TALKING ABOUT, ONE MANGY PANTHER WILL HARDLY BE MISSED
AND THE ELEPHANT?
WE'RE WORKING ON IT, MR. BULLBLADDER.
ELEPHANT?! I'VE HEARD ENOUGH, OTTO. LET'S SCRAM BEFORE YOU END UP ON THAT TROPHY WALL.
HEY, PEDRO, I THINK THAT MANGY PANTHER THEY WERE TALKING ABOUT BACK THERE WAS YOU. WHADDAYA THINK? PEDRO?
HANDS UP!

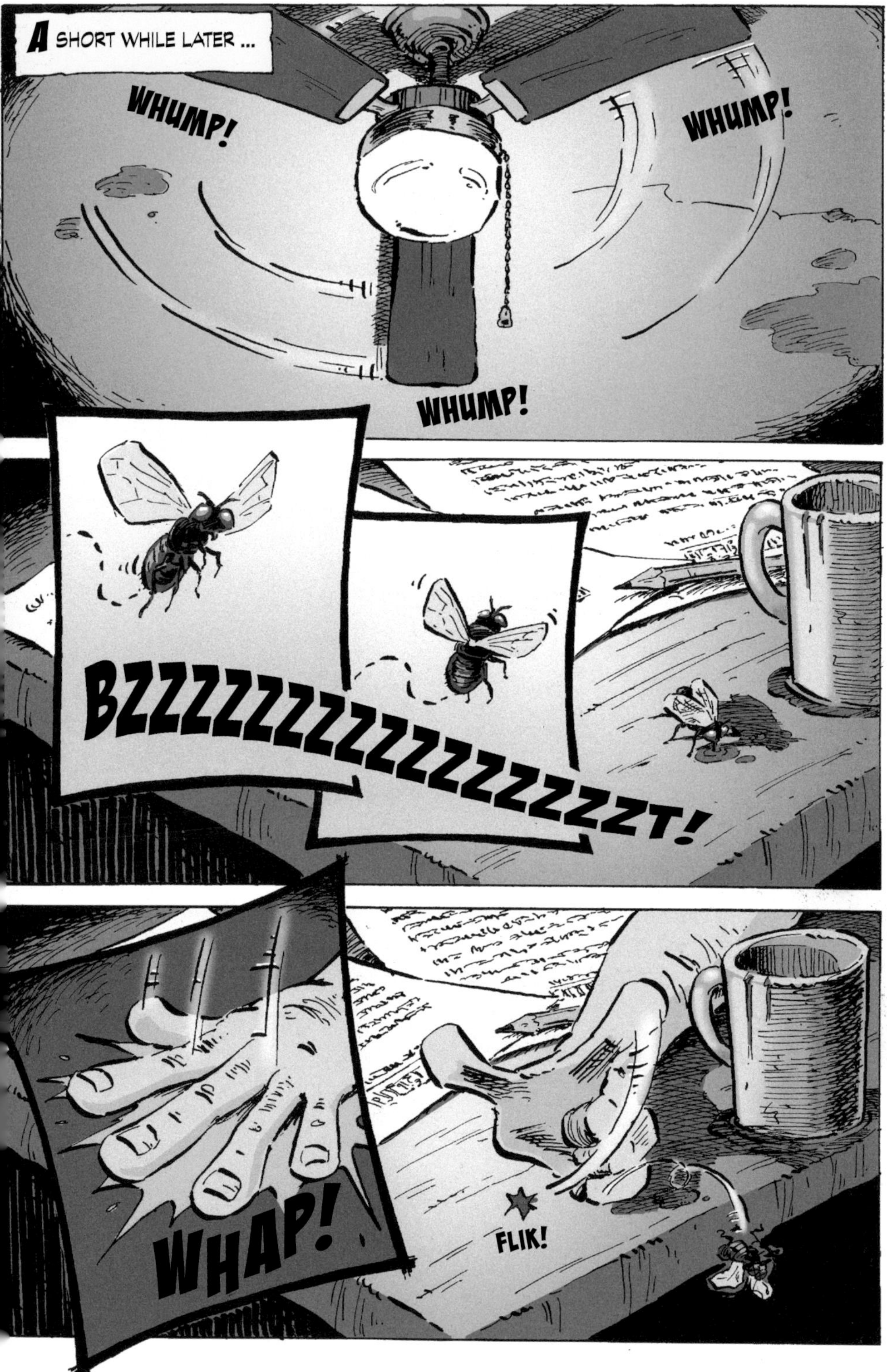
A SHORT WHILE LATER ...
WHUMP!
WHUMP!
WHUMP!
BZZZZZZZZZZZZZZZZZZZT!
WHAP!
FLIK!

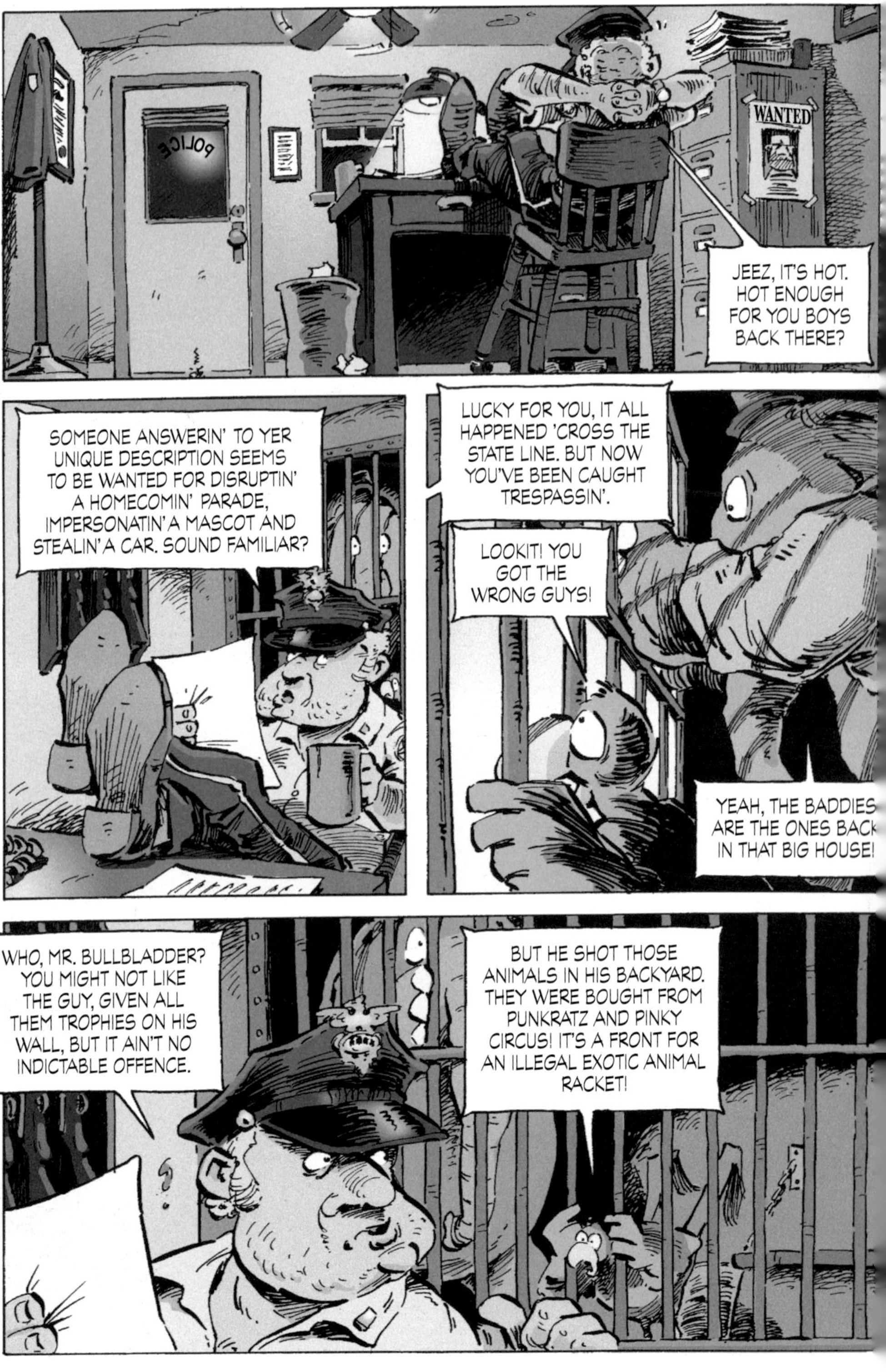
POLICE
WANTED
JEEZ, IT'S HOT. HOT ENOUGH FOR YOU BOYS BACK THERE?
SOMEONE ANSWERIN' TO YER UNIQUE DESCRIPTION SEEMS TO BE WANTED FOR DISRUPTIN' A HOMECOMIN' PARADE, IMPERSONATIN' A MASCOT AND STEALIN' A CAR. SOUND FAMILIAR?
LUCKY FOR YOU, IT ALL HAPPENED 'CROSS THE STATE LINE. BUT NOW YOU'VE BEEN CAUGHT TRESPASSIN'.
LOOKIT! YOU GOT THE WRONG GUYS!
YEAH, THE BADDIES ARE THE ONES BACK IN THAT BIG HOUSE!
WHO, MR. BULLBLADDER? YOU MIGHT NOT LIKE THE GUY, GIVEN ALL THEM TROPHIES ON HIS WALL, BUT IT AIN'T NO INDICTABLE OFFENCE.
BUT HE SHOT THOSE ANIMALS IN HIS BACKYARD. THEY WERE BOUGHT FROM PUNKRATZ AND PINKY CIRCUS! IT'S A FRONT FOR AN ILLEGAL EXOTIC ANIMAL RACKET!

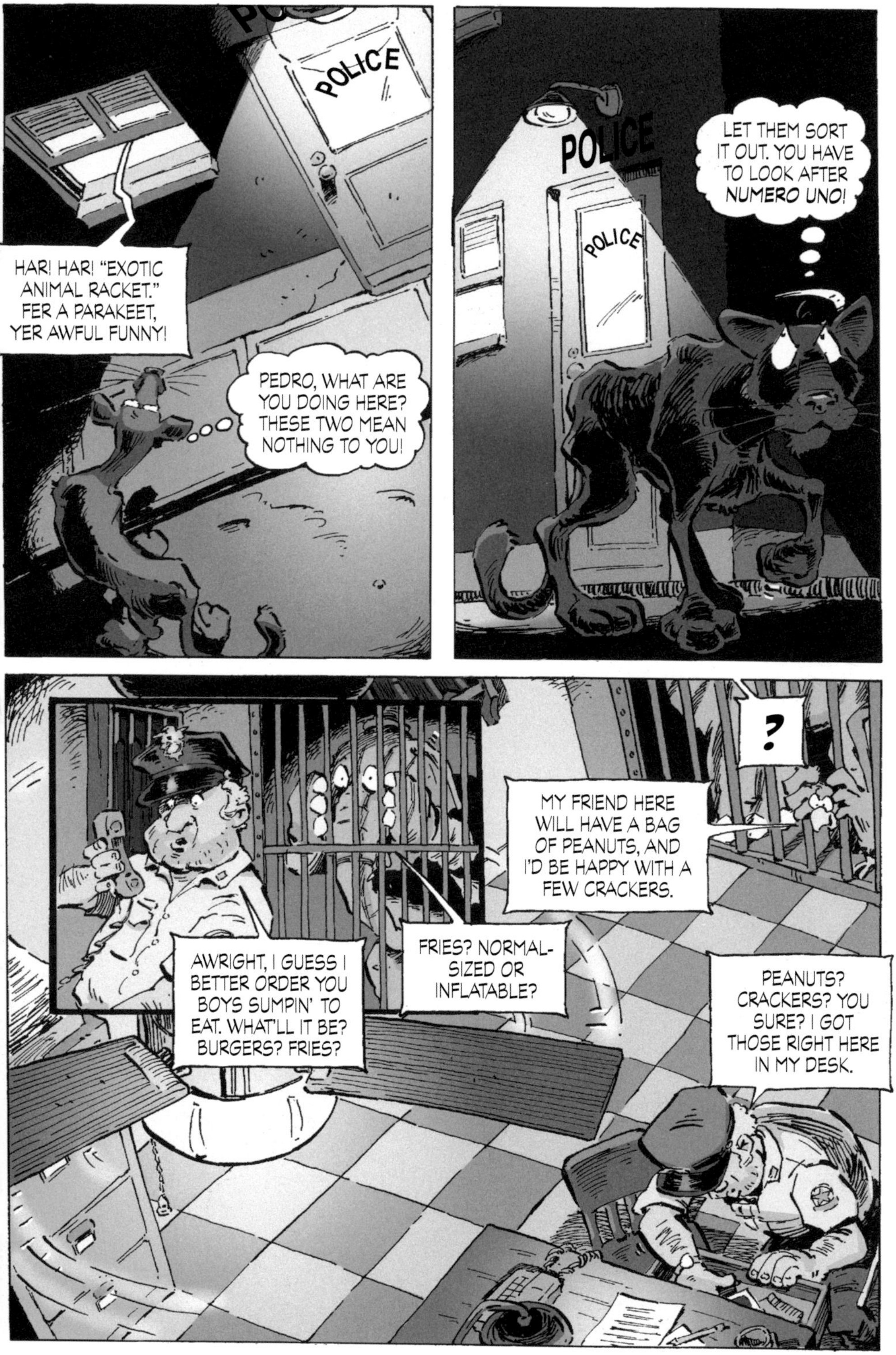
POLICE
POLICE
HAR! HAR! "EXOTIC ANIMAL RACKET." FER A PARAKEET, YER AWFUL FUNNY!
PEDRO, WHAT ARE YOU DOING HERE? THESE TWO MEAN NOTHING TO YOU!
POLICE
POLICE
LET THEM SORT IT OUT. YOU HAVE TO LOOK AFTER NUMERO UNO!
?
MY FRIEND HERE WILL HAVE A BAG OF PEANUTS, AND I'D BE HAPPY WITH A FEW CRACKERS.
AWRIGHT, I GUESS I BETTER ORDER YOU BOYS SUMPIN' TO EAT. WHAT'LL IT BE? BURGERS? FRIES?
FRIES? NORMAL-SIZED OR INFLATABLE?
PEANUTS? CRACKERS? YOU SURE? I GOT THOSE RIGHT HERE IN MY DESK.

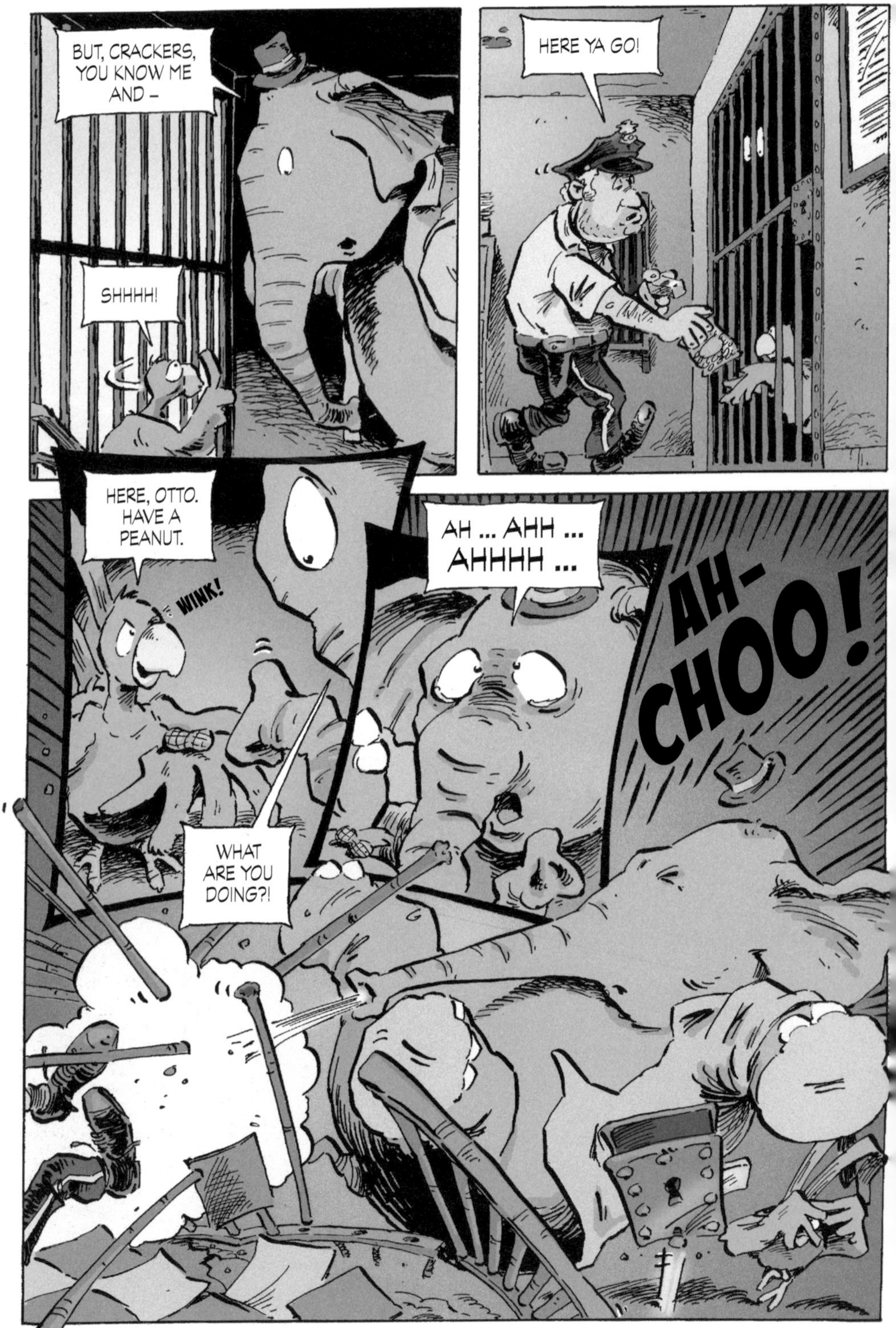
BUT, CRACKERS, YOU KNOW ME AND –
SHHHH!
HERE YA GO!
HERE, OTTO. HAVE A PEANUT.
WINK!
WHAT ARE YOU DOING?!
AH ... AHH ... AHHHH ...
AH-CHOO!

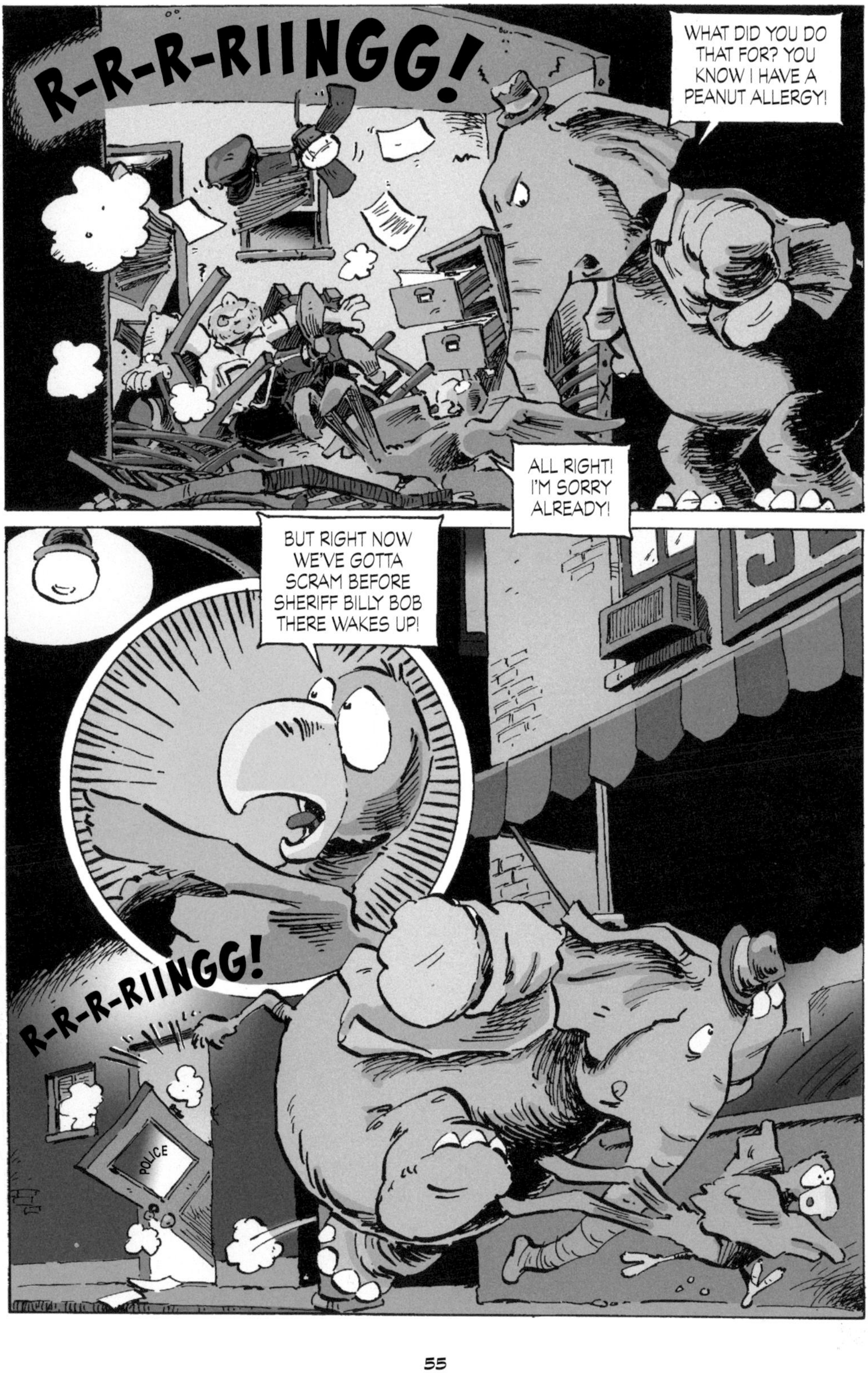
R-R-R-RIINGG!
WHAT DID YOU DO THAT FOR? YOU KNOW I HAVE A PEANUT ALLERGY!
ALL RIGHT! I'M SORRY ALREADY!
BUT RIGHT NOW WE'VE GOTTA SCRAM BEFORE SHERIFF BILLY BOB THERE WAKES UP!
R-R-R-RIINGG!
POLICE

FOLLOW ME!

?!

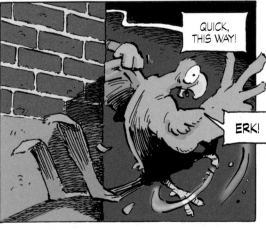

QUICK, THIS WAY!

ERK!

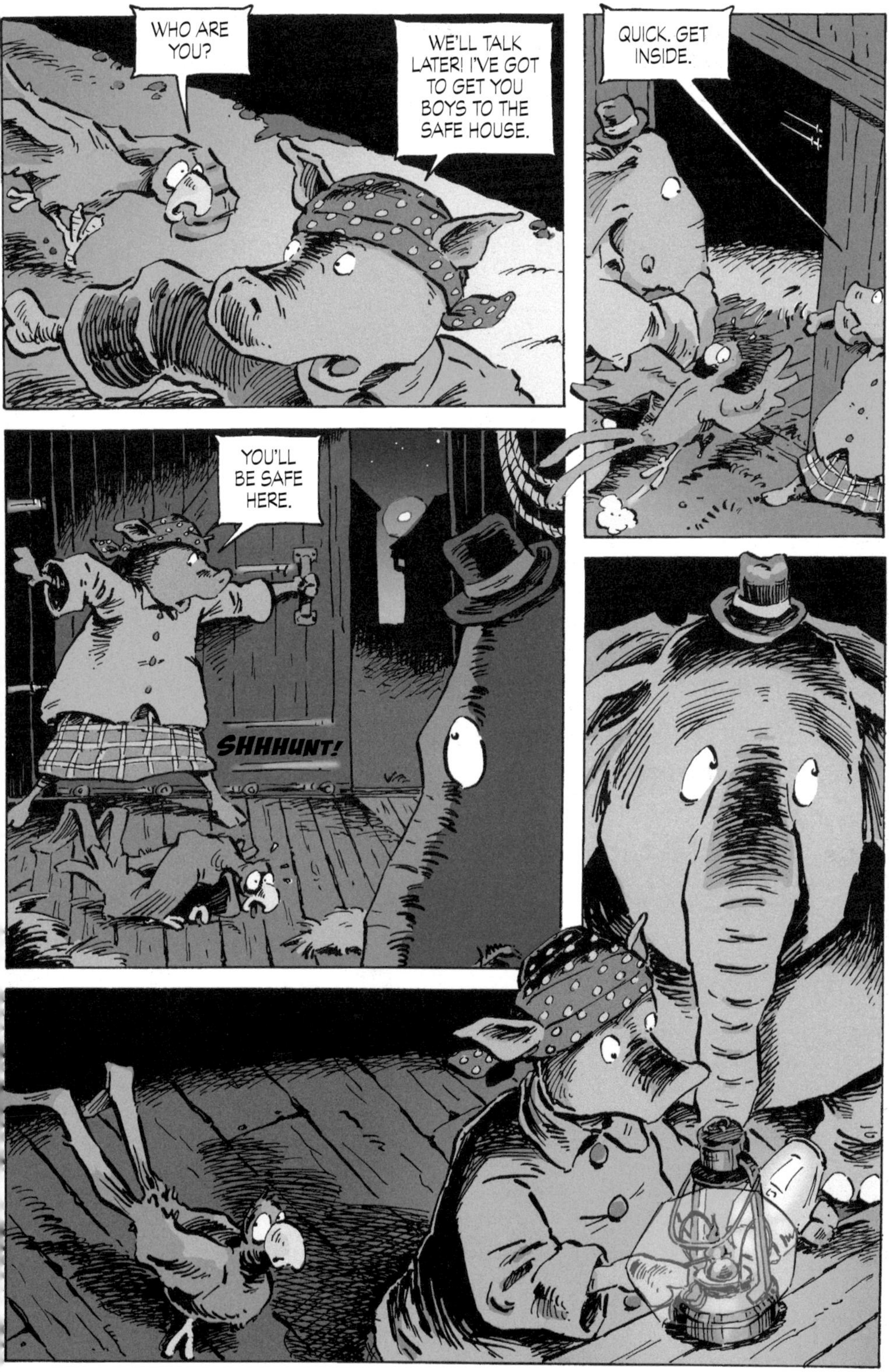
WHO ARE YOU?
WE'LL TALK LATER! I'VE GOT TO GET YOU BOYS TO THE SAFE HOUSE.
QUICK. GET INSIDE.
YOU'LL BE SAFE HERE.
SHHHUNT!

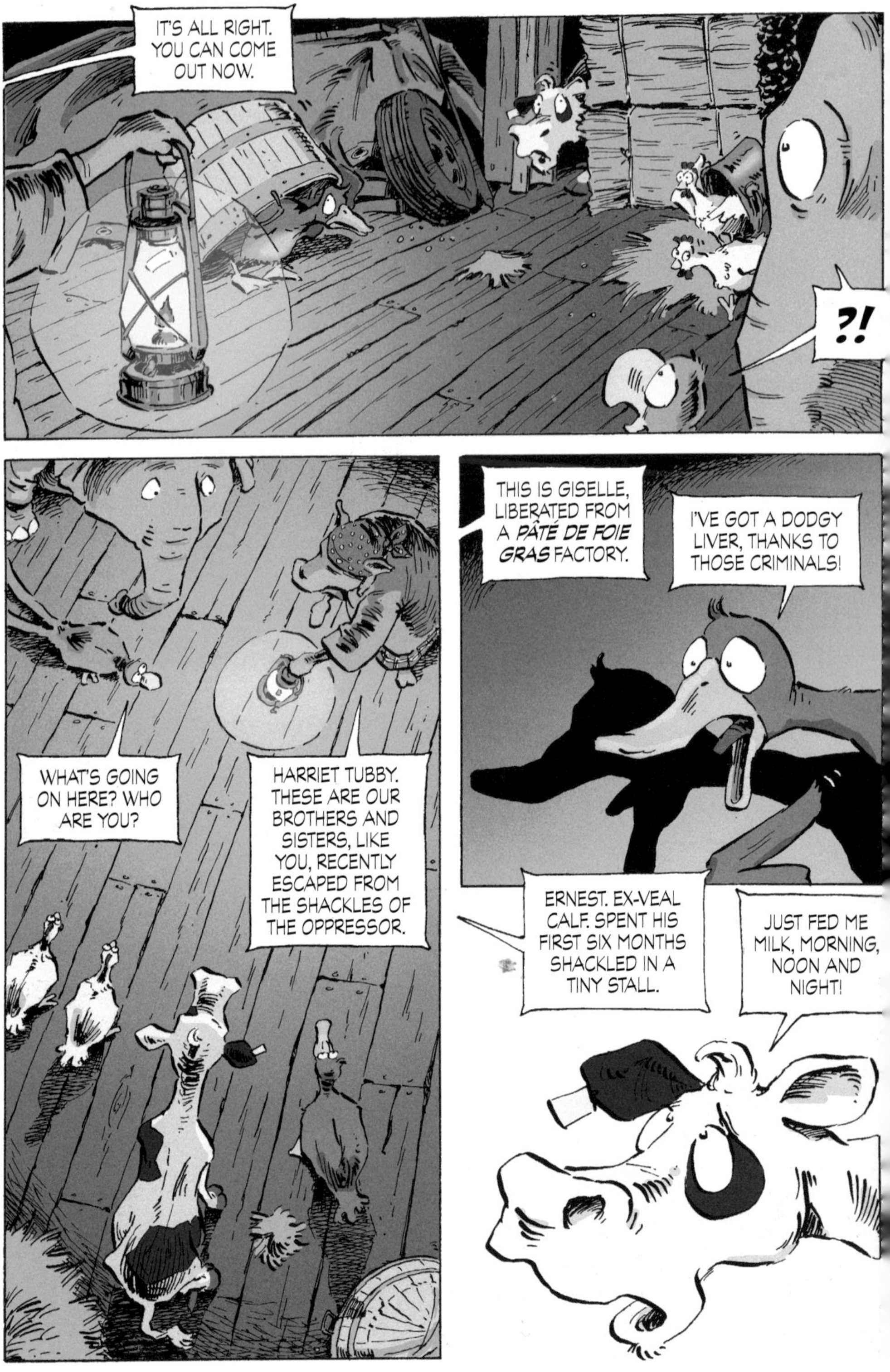
IT'S ALL RIGHT. YOU CAN COME OUT NOW.
?!
WHAT'S GOING ON HERE? WHO ARE YOU?
HARRIET TUBBY. THESE ARE OUR BROTHERS AND SISTERS, LIKE YOU, RECENTLY ESCAPED FROM THE SHACKLES OF THE OPPRESSOR.
THIS IS GISELLE, LIBERATED FROM A *PÂTÉ DE FOIE GRAS* FACTORY.
I'VE GOT A DODGY LIVER, THANKS TO THOSE CRIMINALS!
ERNEST. EX-VEAL CALF. SPENT HIS FIRST SIX MONTHS SHACKLED IN A TINY STALL.
JUST FED ME MILK, MORNING, NOON AND NIGHT!

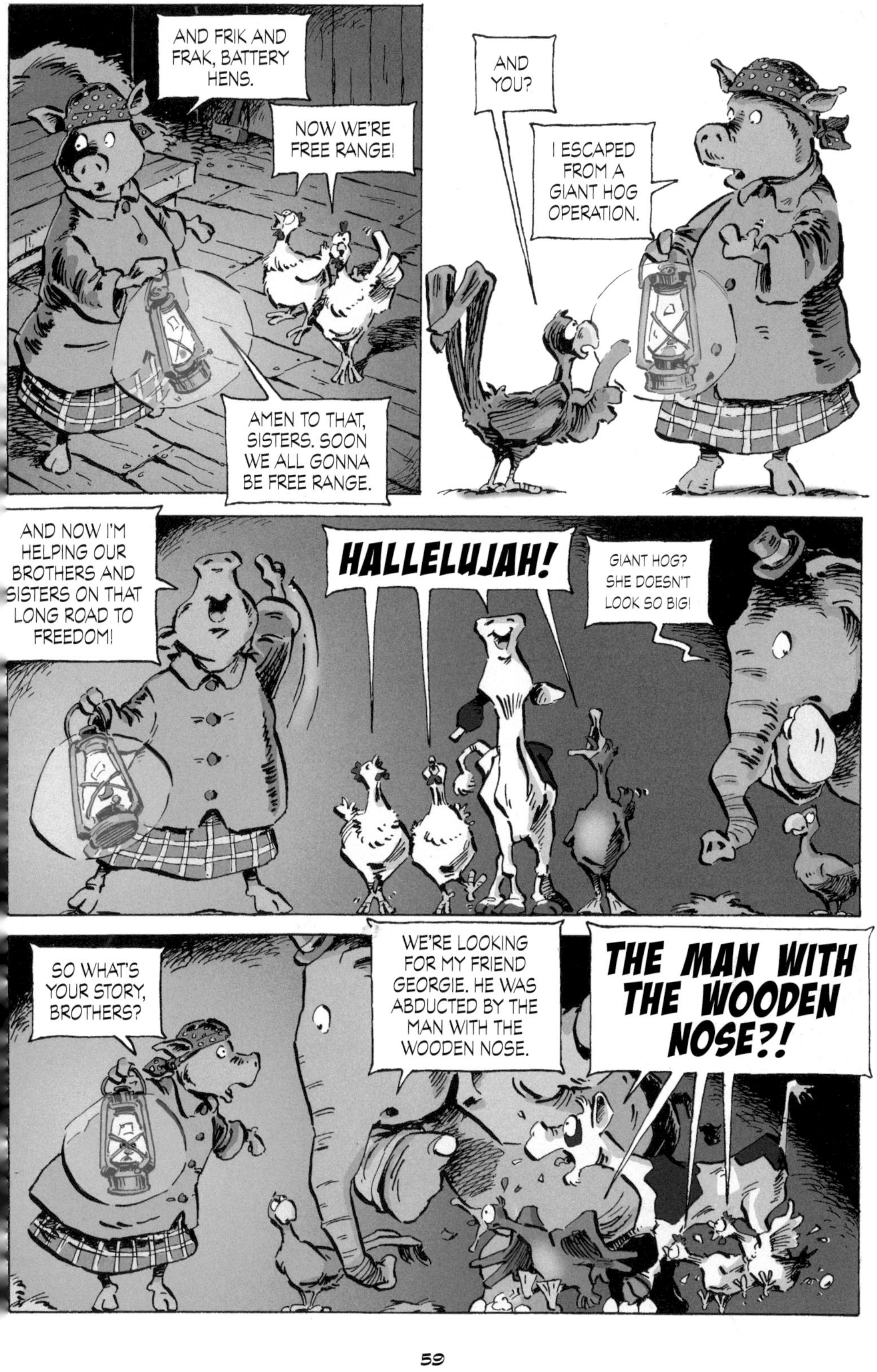
AND FRIK AND FRAK, BATTERY HENS.
NOW WE'RE FREE RANGE!
AMEN TO THAT, SISTERS. SOON WE ALL GONNA BE FREE RANGE.
AND YOU?
I ESCAPED FROM A GIANT HOG OPERATION.
AND NOW I'M HELPING OUR BROTHERS AND SISTERS ON THAT LONG ROAD TO FREEDOM!
HALLELUJAH!
GIANT HOG? SHE DOESN'T LOOK SO BIG!
SO WHAT'S YOUR STORY, BROTHERS?
WE'RE LOOKING FOR MY FRIEND GEORGIE. HE WAS ABDUCTED BY THE MAN WITH THE WOODEN NOSE.
THE MAN WITH THE WOODEN NOSE?!

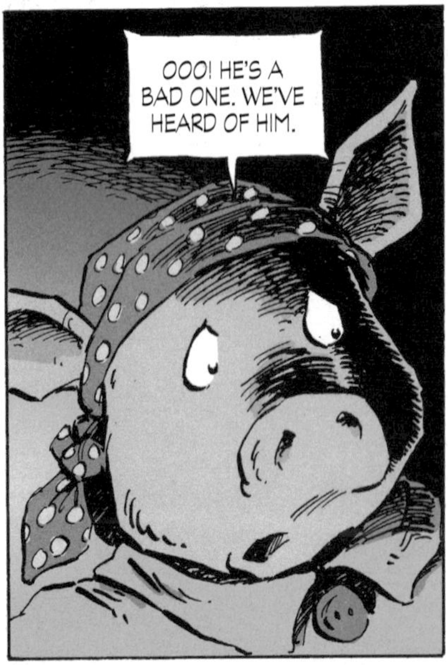
OOO! HE'S A BAD ONE. WE'VE HEARD OF HIM.

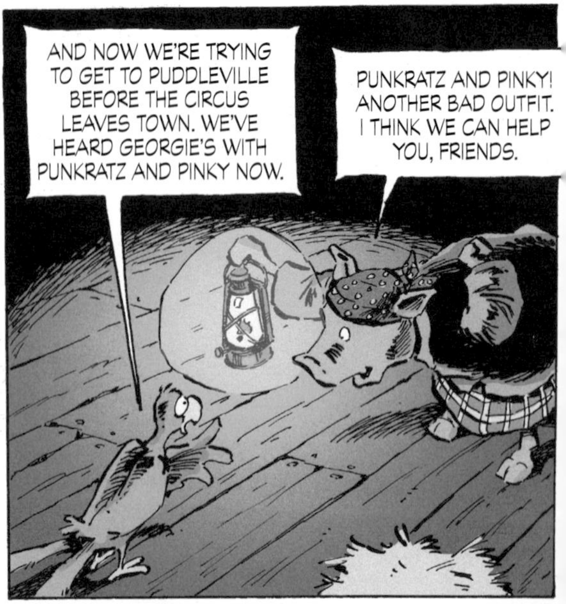
AND NOW WE'RE TRYING TO GET TO PUDDLEVILLE BEFORE THE CIRCUS LEAVES TOWN. WE'VE HEARD GEORGIE'S WITH PUNKRATZ AND PINKY NOW.
PUNKRATZ AND PINKY! ANOTHER BAD OUTFIT. I THINK WE CAN HELP YOU, FRIENDS.

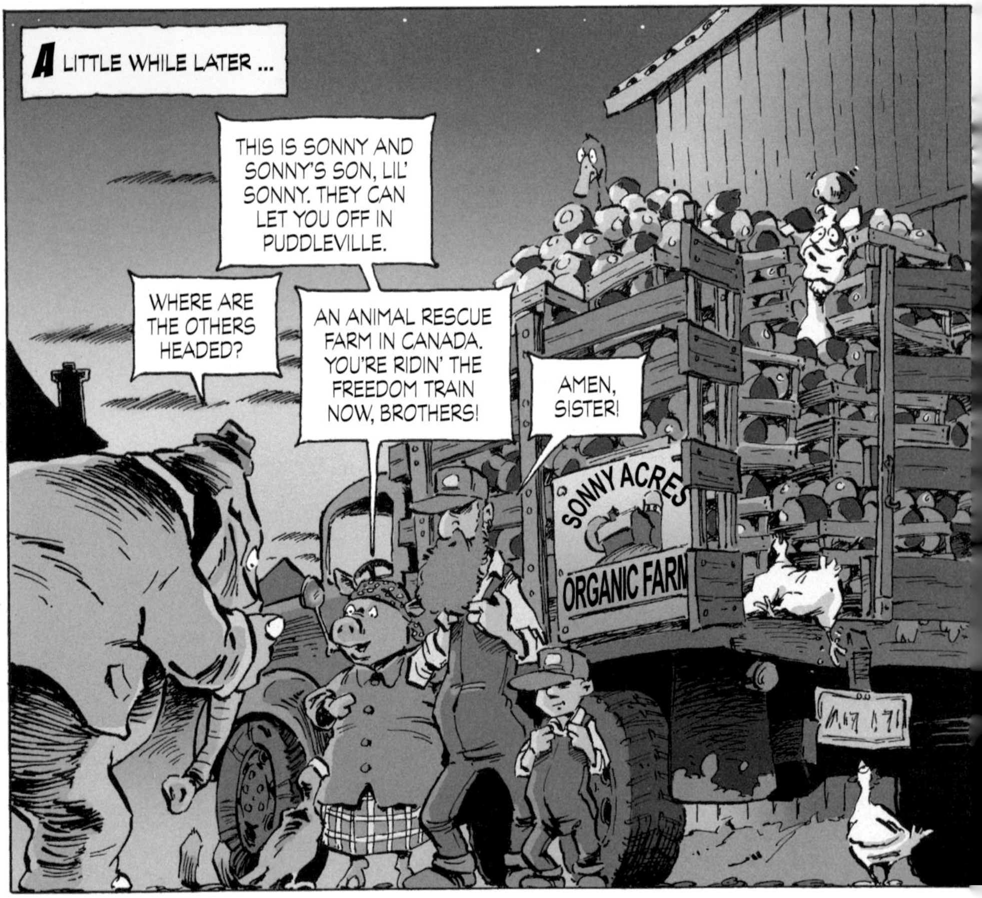
A LITTLE WHILE LATER ...
THIS IS SONNY AND SONNY'S SON, LIL' SONNY. THEY CAN LET YOU OFF IN PUDDLEVILLE.
WHERE ARE THE OTHERS HEADED?
AN ANIMAL RESCUE FARM IN CANADA. YOU'RE RIDIN' THE FREEDOM TRAIN NOW, BROTHERS!
AMEN, SISTER!
SONNY ACRES
ORGANIC FARM

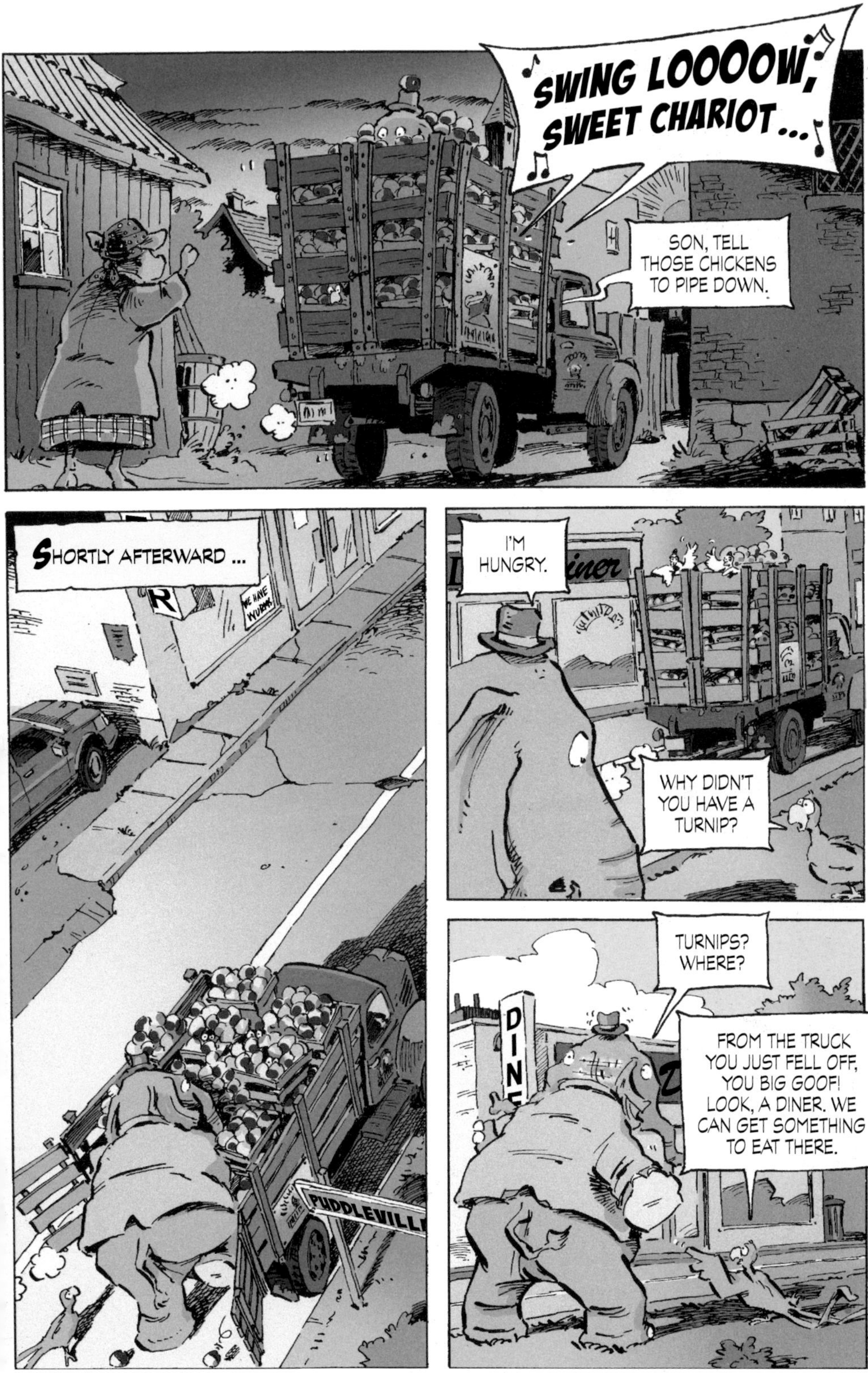
SWING LOOOOW, SWEET CHARIOT...
SON, TELL THOSE CHICKENS TO PIPE DOWN.
SHORTLY AFTERWARD ...
WE HAVE WURMS
PUDDLEVILL
I'M HUNGRY.
WHY DIDN'T YOU HAVE A TURNIP?
TURNIPS? WHERE?
FROM THE TRUCK YOU JUST FELL OFF, YOU BIG GOOF! LOOK, A DINER. WE CAN GET SOMETHING TO EAT THERE.

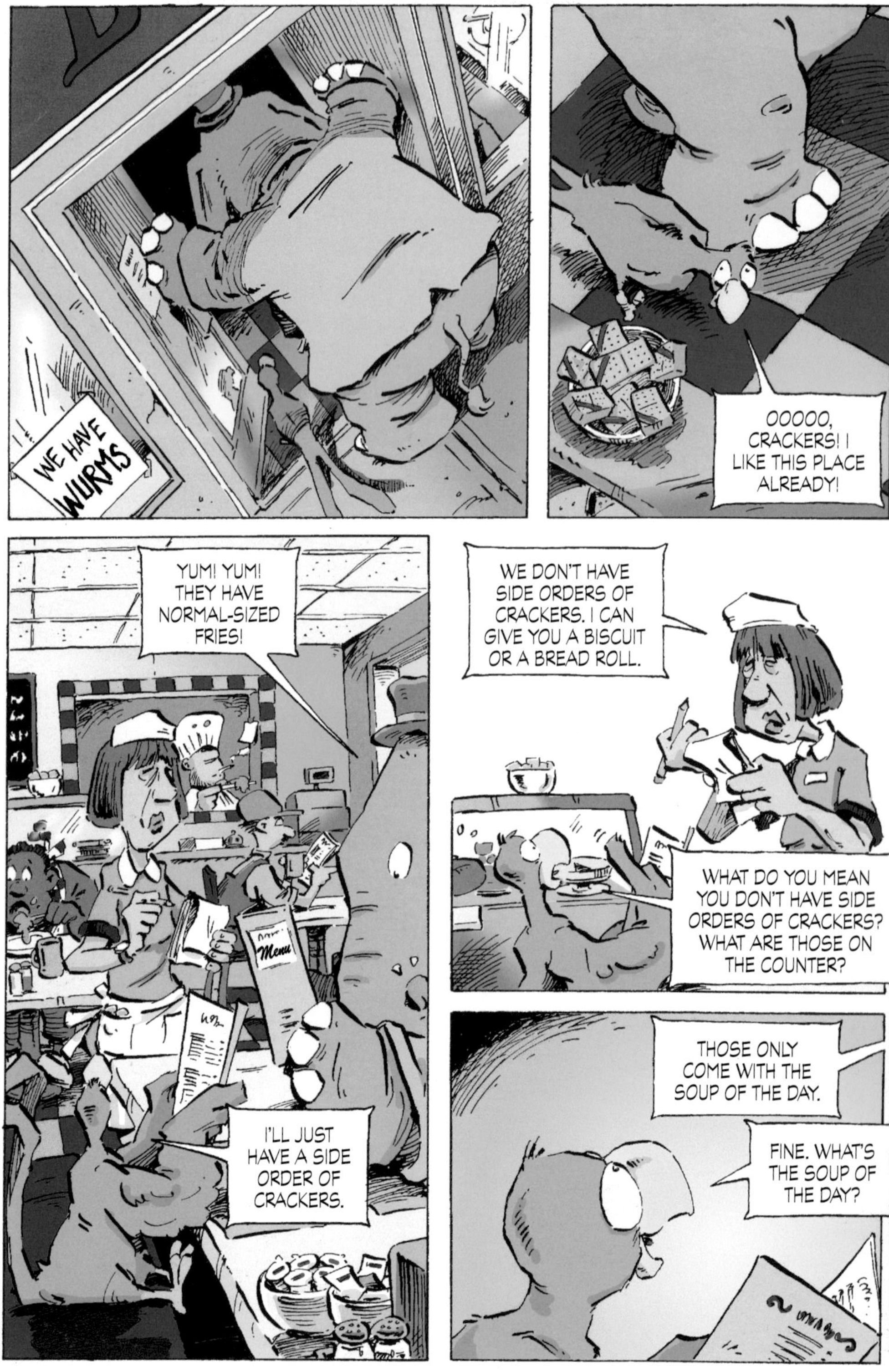
WE HAVE WURMS
OOOOO, CRACKERS! I LIKE THIS PLACE ALREADY!
YUM! YUM! THEY HAVE NORMAL-SIZED FRIES!
I'LL JUST HAVE A SIDE ORDER OF CRACKERS.
Menu
WE DON'T HAVE SIDE ORDERS OF CRACKERS. I CAN GIVE YOU A BISCUIT OR A BREAD ROLL.
WHAT DO YOU MEAN YOU DON'T HAVE SIDE ORDERS OF CRACKERS? WHAT ARE THOSE ON THE COUNTER?
THOSE ONLY COME WITH THE SOUP OF THE DAY.
FINE. WHAT'S THE SOUP OF THE DAY?

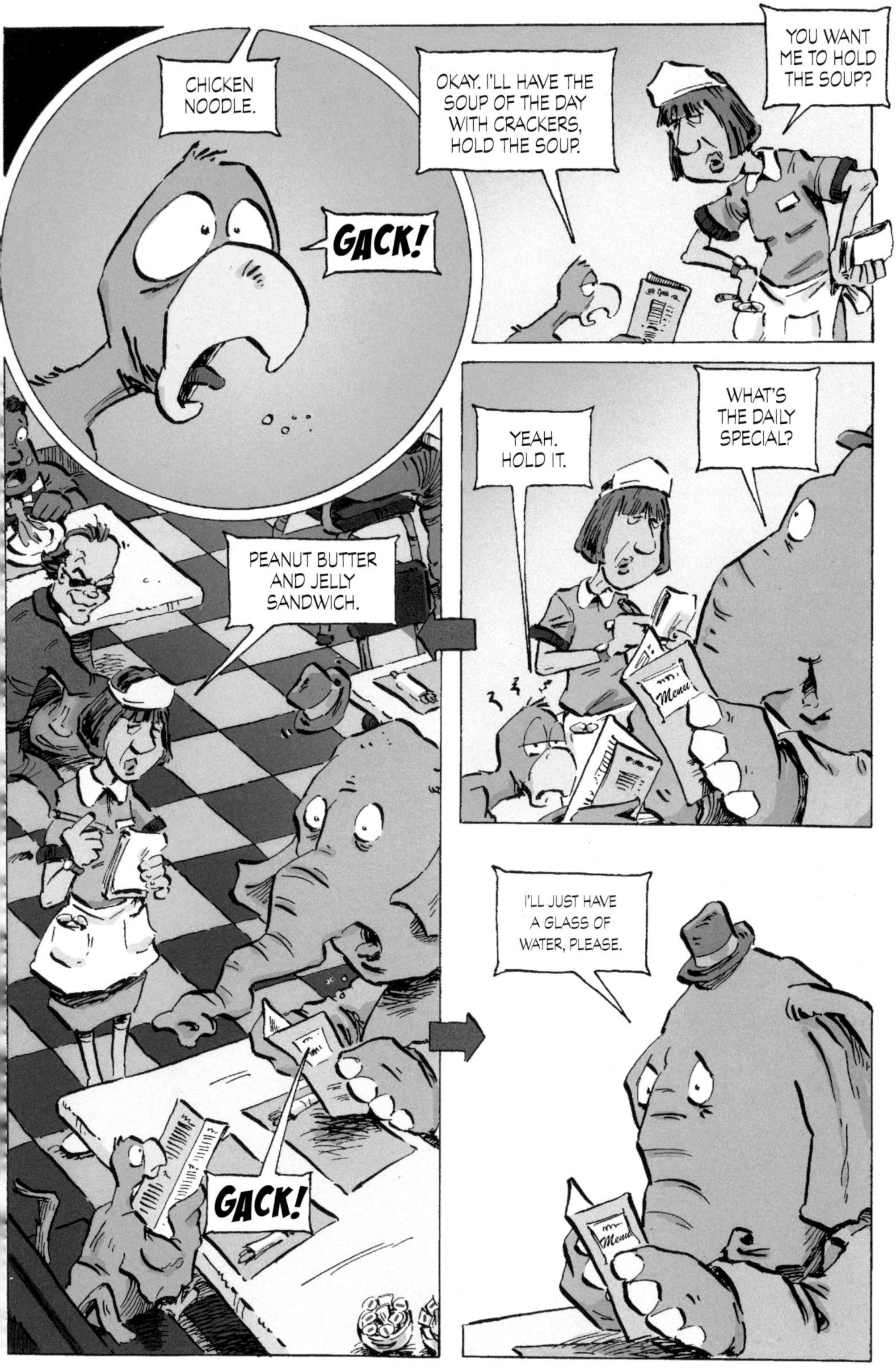
CHICKEN NOODLE.
GACK!
OKAY. I'LL HAVE THE SOUP OF THE DAY WITH CRACKERS, HOLD THE SOUP.
YOU WANT ME TO HOLD THE SOUP?
PEANUT BUTTER AND JELLY SANDWICH.
GACK!
WHAT'S THE DAILY SPECIAL?
YEAH. HOLD IT.
I'LL JUST HAVE A GLASS OF WATER, PLEASE.

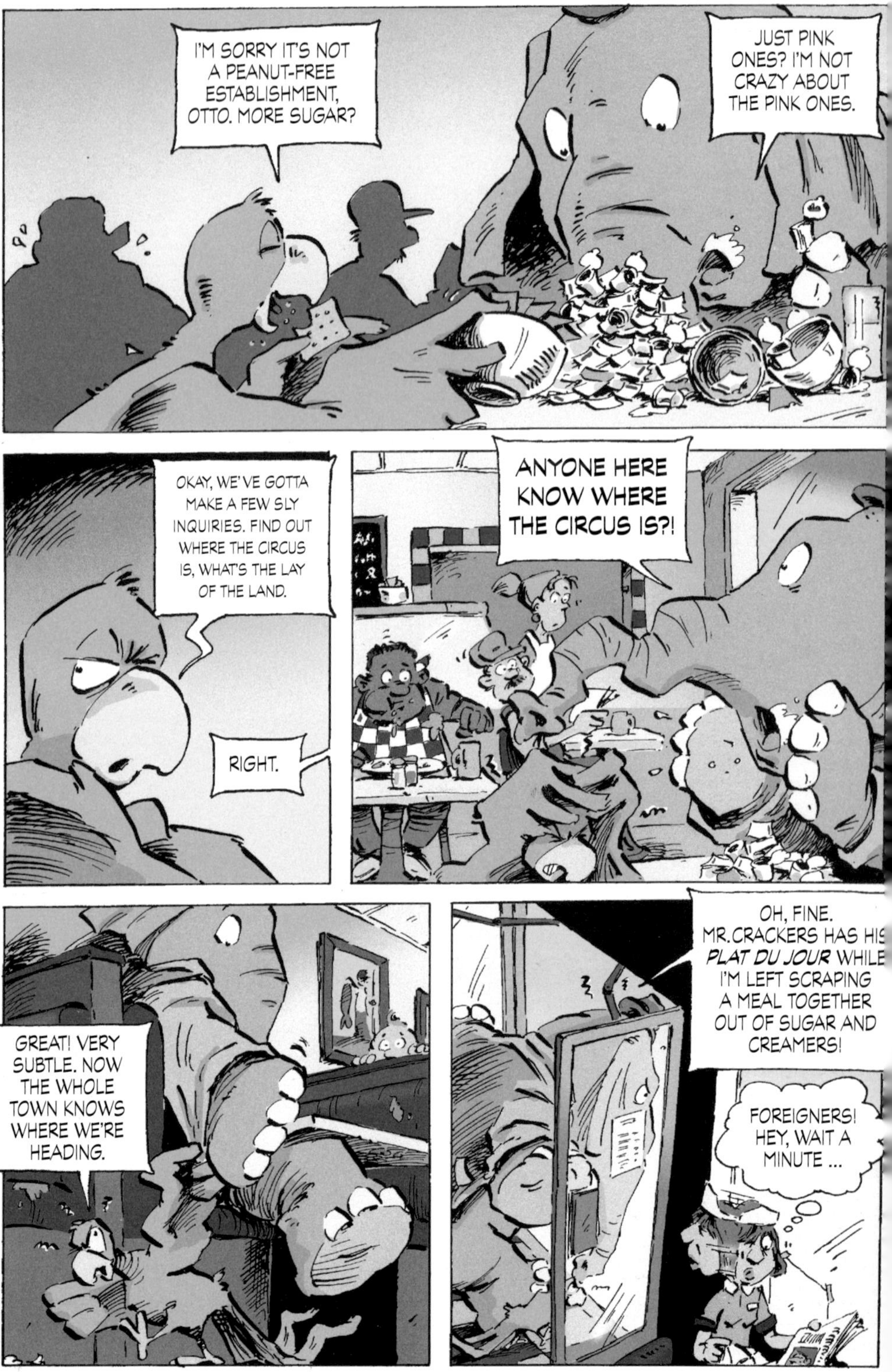
I'M SORRY IT'S NOT A PEANUT-FREE ESTABLISHMENT, OTTO. MORE SUGAR?
JUST PINK ONES? I'M NOT CRAZY ABOUT THE PINK ONES.
OKAY, WE'VE GOTTA MAKE A FEW SLY INQUIRIES. FIND OUT WHERE THE CIRCUS IS, WHAT'S THE LAY OF THE LAND.
RIGHT.
ANYONE HERE KNOW WHERE THE CIRCUS IS?!
GREAT! VERY SUBTLE. NOW THE WHOLE TOWN KNOWS WHERE WE'RE HEADING.
OH, FINE. MR.CRACKERS HAS HIS *PLAT DU JOUR* WHILE I'M LEFT SCRAPING A MEAL TOGETHER OUT OF SUGAR AND CREAMERS!
FOREIGNERS! HEY, WAIT A MINUTE ...

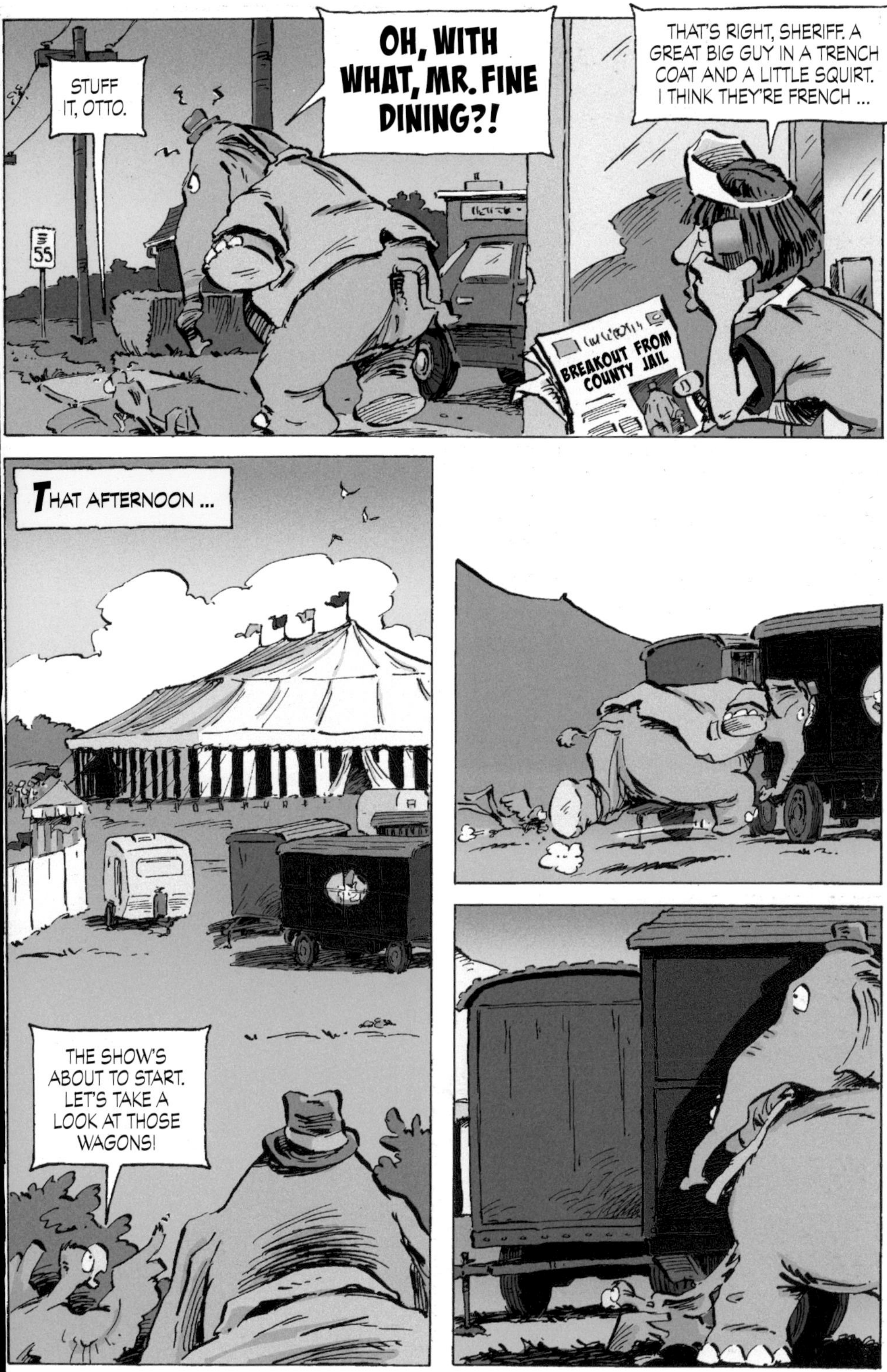
STUFF IT, OTTO.
OH, WITH WHAT, MR. FINE DINING?!
THAT'S RIGHT, SHERIFF. A GREAT BIG GUY IN A TRENCH COAT AND A LITTLE SQUIRT. I THINK THEY'RE FRENCH ...
BREAKOUT FROM COUNTY JAIL
THAT AFTERNOON ...
THE SHOW'S ABOUT TO START. LET'S TAKE A LOOK AT THOSE WAGONS!

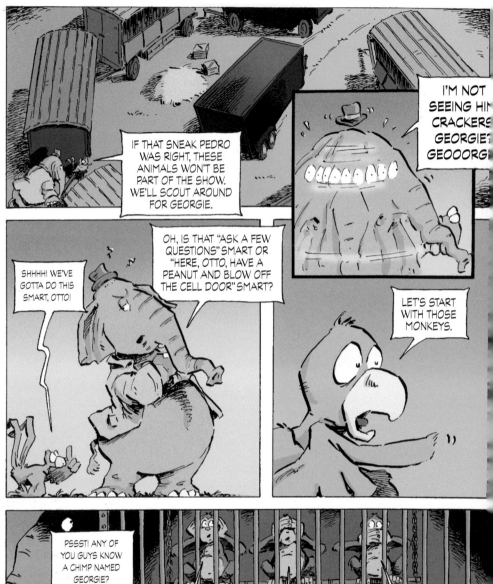

IF THAT SNEAK PEDRO WAS RIGHT, THESE ANIMALS WON'T BE PART OF THE SHOW. WE'LL SCOUT AROUND FOR GEORGIE.

I'M NOT SEEING HIM CRACKERS GEORGIE? GEOOORGI

SHHHH! WE'VE GOTTA DO THIS SMART, OTTO!

OH, IS THAT "ASK A FEW QUESTIONS" SMART OR "HERE, OTTO, HAVE A PEANUT AND BLOW OFF THE CELL DOOR" SMART?

LET'S START WITH THOSE MONKEYS.

PSSST! ANY OF YOU GUYS KNOW A CHIMP NAMED GEORGIE?

WHAT'D THE BIRD SAY?

SORRY, FEATHERS. CAN'T SAY I'VE SEEN HIM.

MGGLMBLEMMPH!

66

VERY FUNNY. YOU THREE WILL BE EVEN FUNNIER STUCK OVER BULLBLADDER'S MANTEL.

CUTE LITTLE GUY, RIGHT? INQUISITIVE?

THAT'S HIM! THAT'S GEORGIE! WHERE IS HE?!

NOT HERE, DEARIE. HE WAS, FOR A WHILE. SOLD TO THE CIRCUS BY A MAN WITH A VERY ODD NOSE.

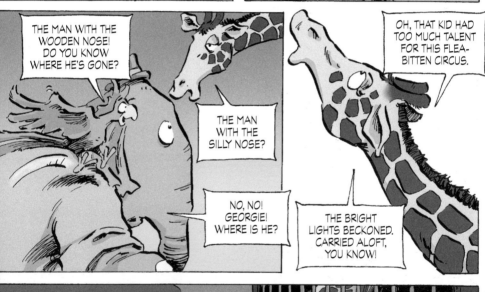

THE MAN WITH THE WOODEN NOSE! DO YOU KNOW WHERE HE'S GONE?

THE MAN WITH THE SILLY NOSE?

NO, NO! GEORGIE! WHERE IS HE?

OH, THAT KID HAD TOO MUCH TALENT FOR THIS FLEA-BITTEN CIRCUS.

THE BRIGHT LIGHTS BECKONED. CARRIED ALOFT, YOU KNOW!

NO, NO. HOLLYWOOD, THE SILVER SCREEN! HE WAS ACQUIRED BY AN ANIMAL ACTOR AGENT. SAID SHE WOULD PUT HIS NAME IN LIGHTS, MAKE HIM THE STAR OF TINSELTOWN.

GEORGIE WAS ABDUCTED BY SPACE CREATURES?!!

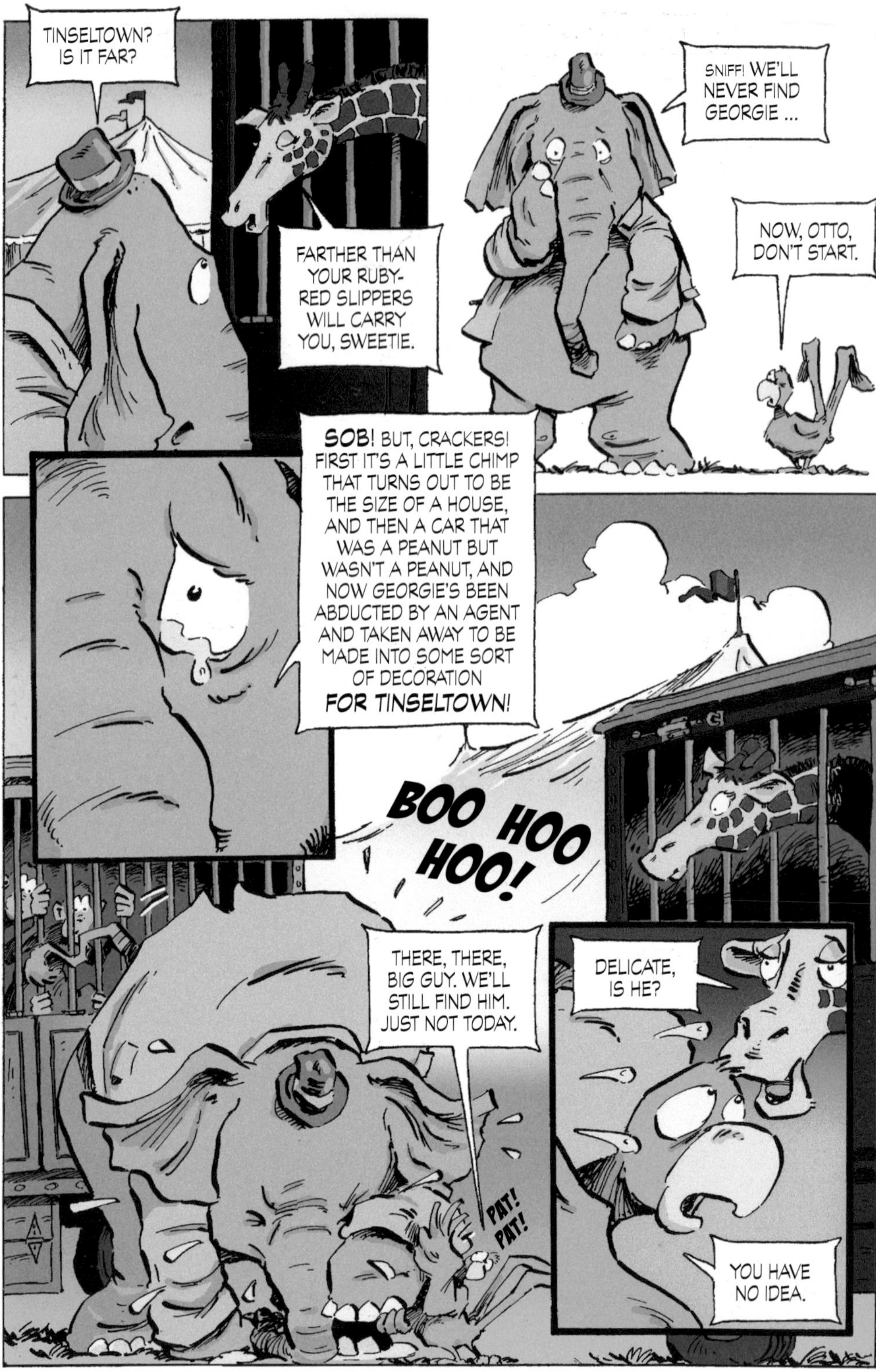

TINSELTOWN? IS IT FAR?
FARTHER THAN YOUR RUBY-RED SLIPPERS WILL CARRY YOU, SWEETIE.
SNIFF! WE'LL NEVER FIND GEORGIE ...
NOW, OTTO, DON'T START.
SOB! BUT, CRACKERS! FIRST IT'S A LITTLE CHIMP THAT TURNS OUT TO BE THE SIZE OF A HOUSE, AND THEN A CAR THAT WAS A PEANUT BUT WASN'T A PEANUT, AND NOW GEORGIE'S BEEN ABDUCTED BY AN AGENT AND TAKEN AWAY TO BE MADE INTO SOME SORT OF DECORATION FOR TINSELTOWN!
BOO HOO HOO!
THERE, THERE, BIG GUY. WE'LL STILL FIND HIM. JUST NOT TODAY.
PAT! PAT!
DELICATE, IS HE?
YOU HAVE NO IDEA.

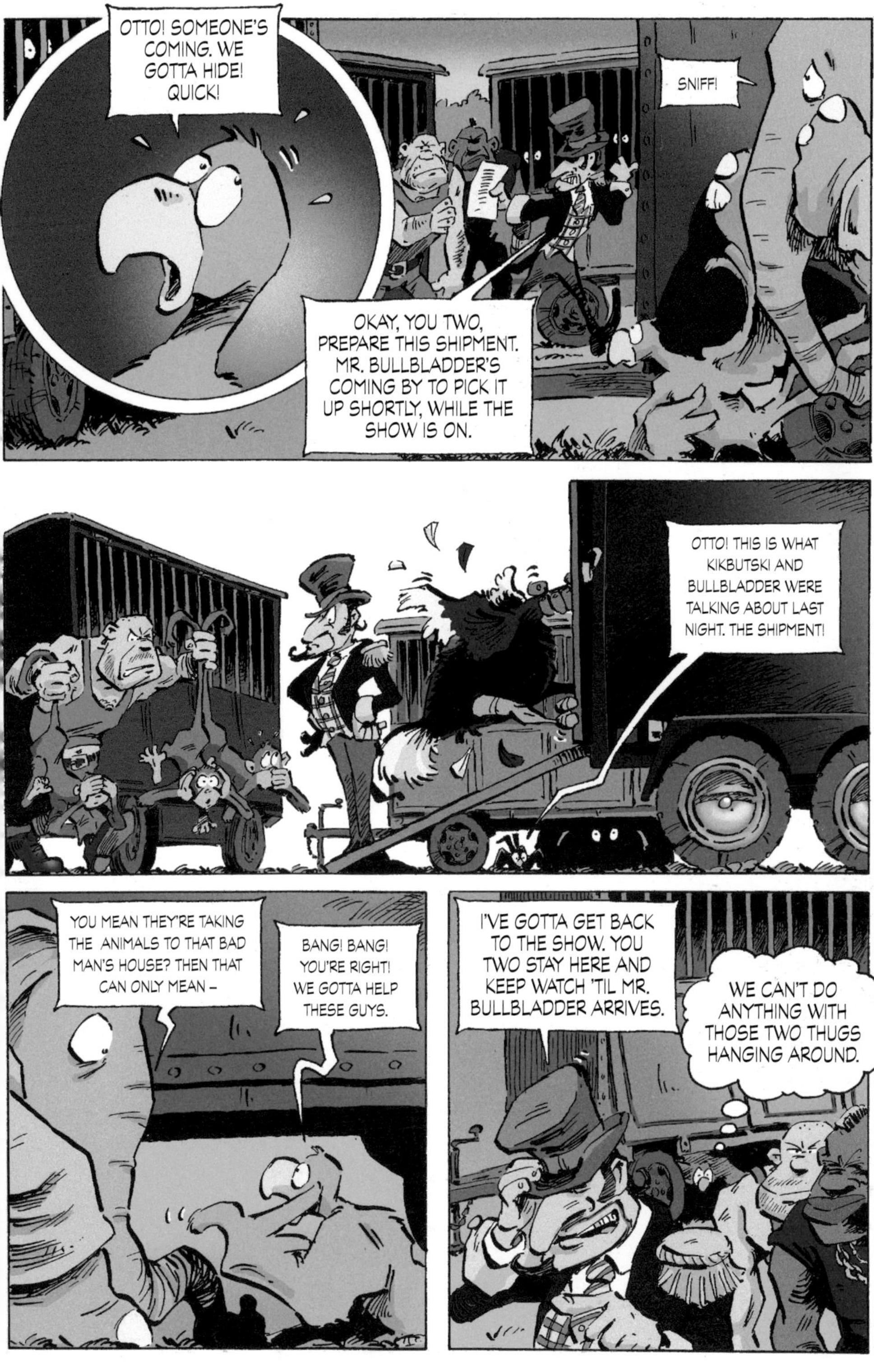
OTTO! SOMEONE'S COMING. WE GOTTA HIDE! QUICK!
SNIFF!
OKAY, YOU TWO, PREPARE THIS SHIPMENT. MR. BULLBLADDER'S COMING BY TO PICK IT UP SHORTLY, WHILE THE SHOW IS ON.
OTTO! THIS IS WHAT KIKBUTSKI AND BULLBLADDER WERE TALKING ABOUT LAST NIGHT. THE SHIPMENT!
YOU MEAN THEY'RE TAKING THE ANIMALS TO THAT BAD MAN'S HOUSE? THEN THAT CAN ONLY MEAN –
BANG! BANG! YOU'RE RIGHT! WE GOTTA HELP THESE GUYS.
I'VE GOTTA GET BACK TO THE SHOW. YOU TWO STAY HERE AND KEEP WATCH 'TIL MR. BULLBLADDER ARRIVES.
WE CAN'T DO ANYTHING WITH THOSE TWO THUGS HANGING AROUND.

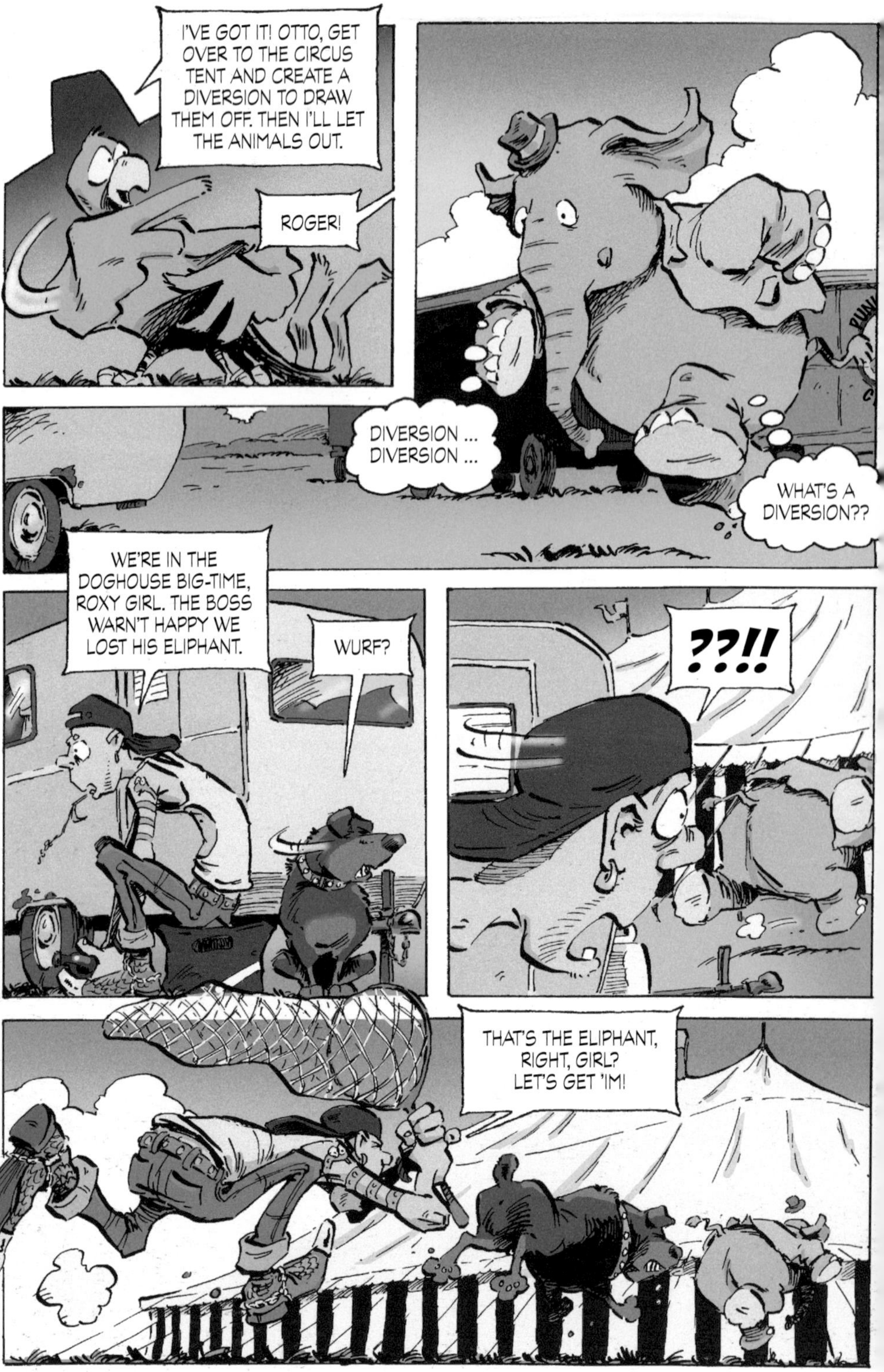

I'VE GOT IT! OTTO, GET OVER TO THE CIRCUS TENT AND CREATE A DIVERSION TO DRAW THEM OFF. THEN I'LL LET THE ANIMALS OUT.
ROGER!
DIVERSION ... DIVERSION ...
WHAT'S A DIVERSION??
WE'RE IN THE DOGHOUSE BIG-TIME, ROXY GIRL. THE BOSS WARN'T HAPPY WE LOST HIS ELIPHANT.
WURF?
??!!
THAT'S THE ELIPHANT, RIGHT, GIRL? LET'S GET 'IM!

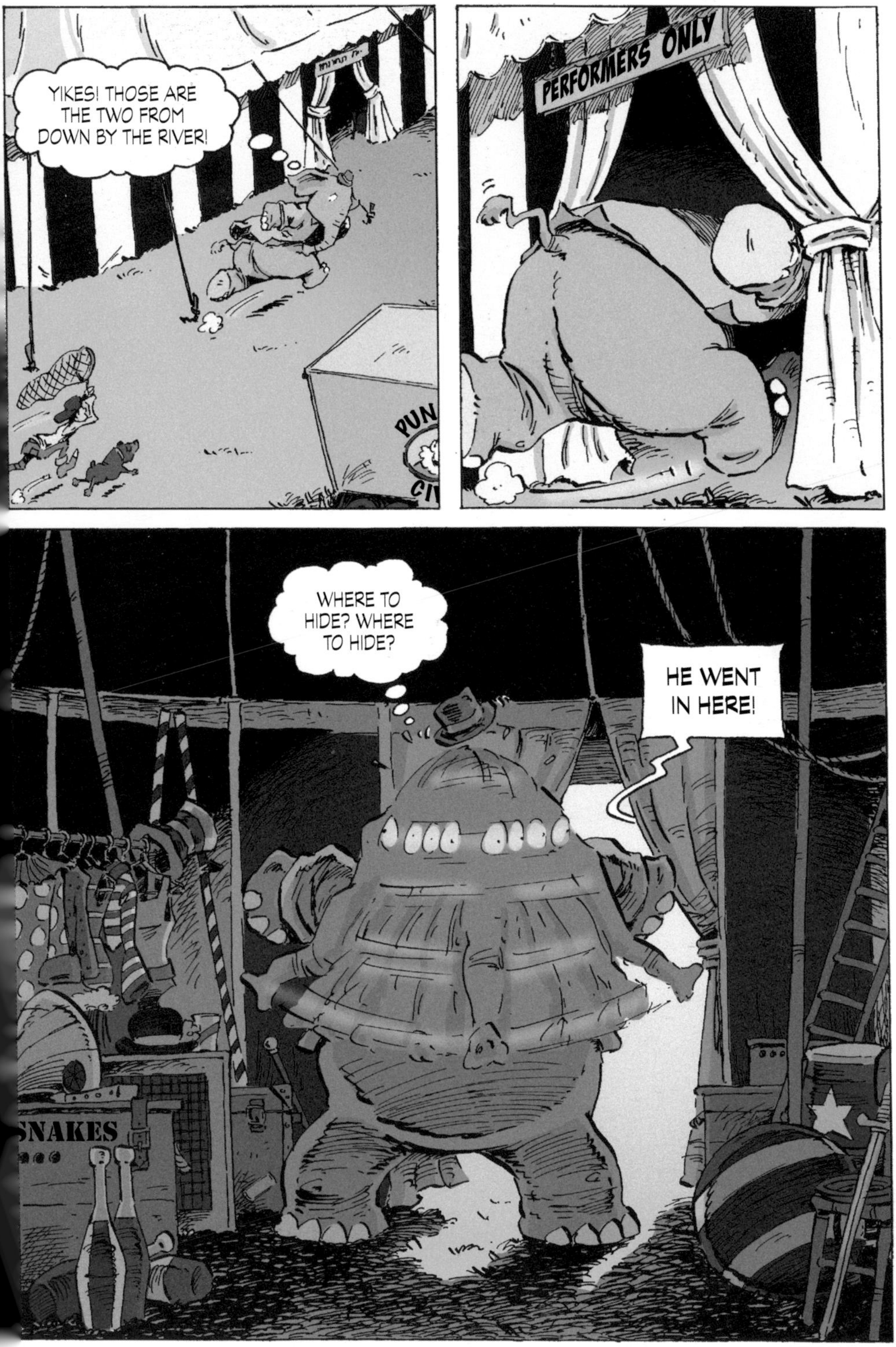
YIKES! THOSE ARE THE TWO FROM DOWN BY THE RIVER!
PERFORMERS ONLY
WHERE TO HIDE? WHERE TO HIDE?
HE WENT IN HERE!
SNAKES

HERE, BIG BOY. UNCA SNAKEY HAS SOMETHIN' FOR YA.

I'VE GOTTA GET PAST THESE GUYS CRACKERS IS COUNTING ON ME!

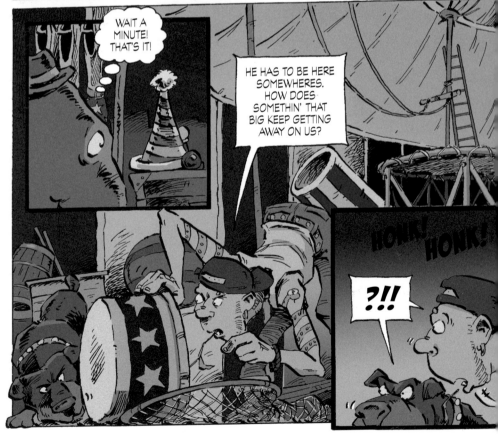

WAIT A MINUTE! THAT'S IT!

HE HAS TO BE HERE SOMEWHERES. HOW DOES SOMETHIN' THAT BIG KEEP GETTING AWAY ON US?

HONK! HONK!

?!!
•••

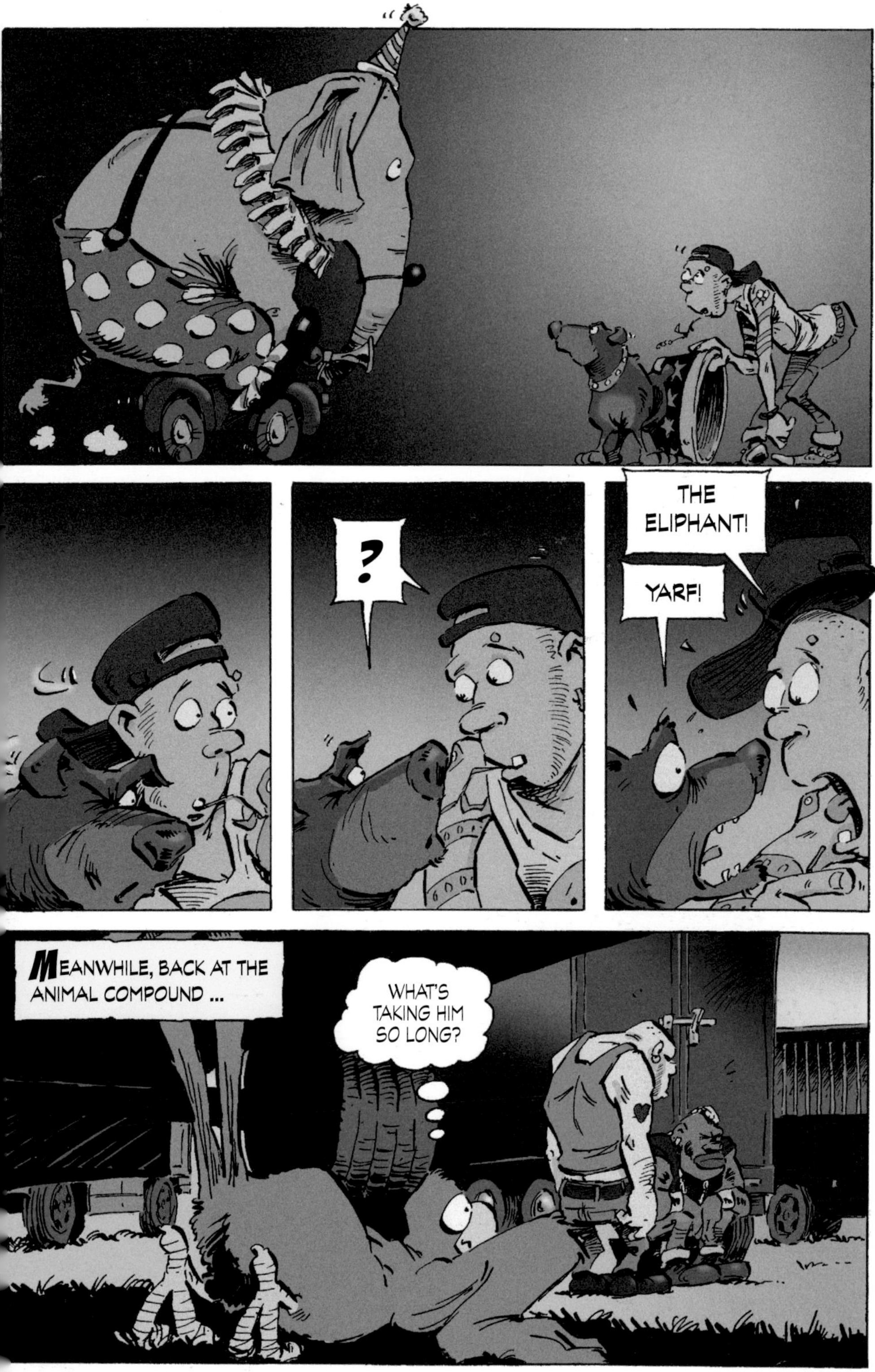
?
THE ELIPHANT!
YARF!
MEANWHILE, BACK AT THE ANIMAL COMPOUND ...
WHAT'S TAKING HIM SO LONG?

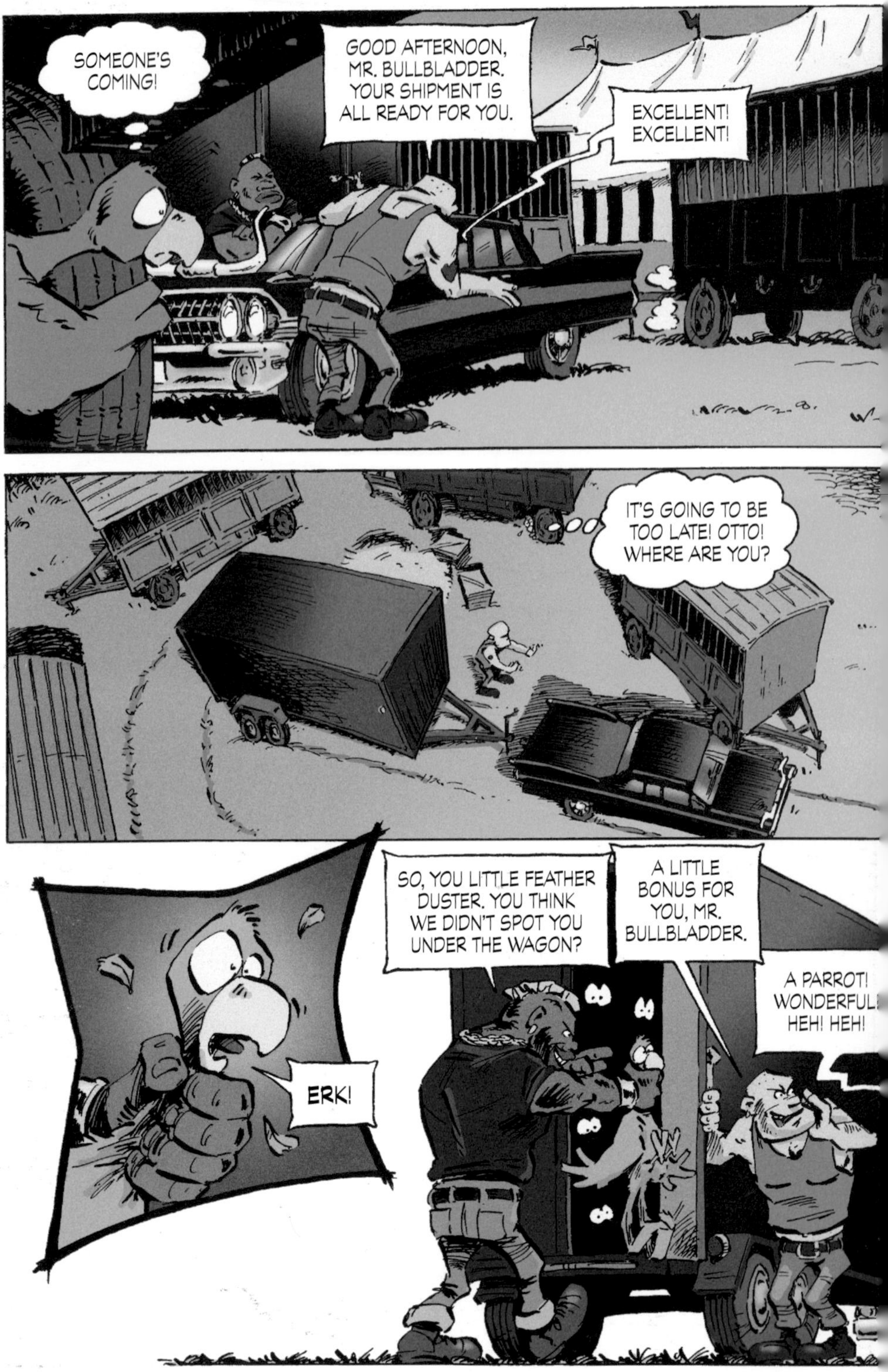
SOMEONE'S COMING!
GOOD AFTERNOON, MR. BULLBLADDER. YOUR SHIPMENT IS ALL READY FOR YOU.
EXCELLENT! EXCELLENT!
IT'S GOING TO BE TOO LATE! OTTO! WHERE ARE YOU?
ERK!
SO, YOU LITTLE FEATHER DUSTER. YOU THINK WE DIDN'T SPOT YOU UNDER THE WAGON?
A LITTLE BONUS FOR YOU, MR. BULLBLADDER.
A PARROT! WONDERFUL! HEH! HEH!

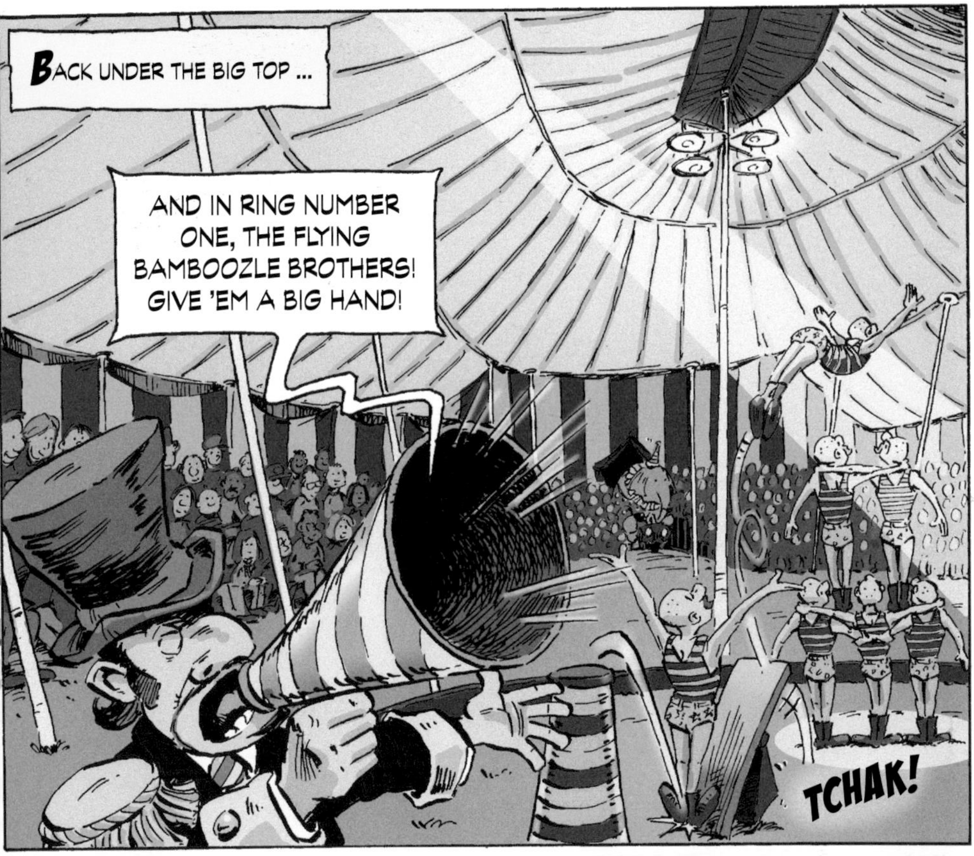
BACK UNDER THE BIG TOP ...
AND IN RING NUMBER ONE, THE FLYING BAMBOOZLE BROTHERS! GIVE 'EM A BIG HAND!
TCHAK!

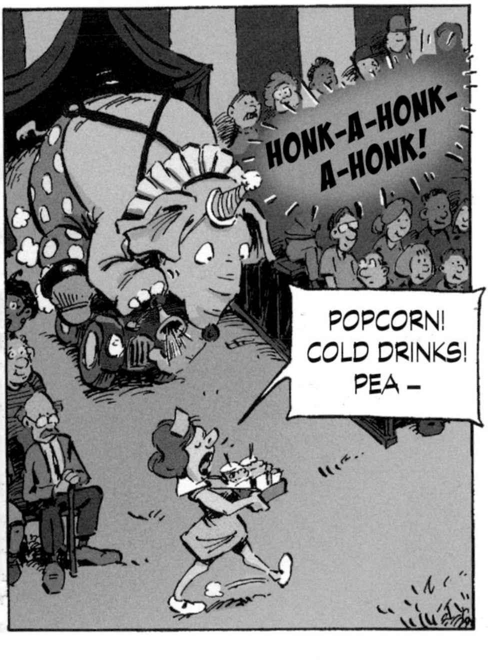
HONK-A-HONK-A-HONK!
POPCORN! COLD DRINKS! PEA –

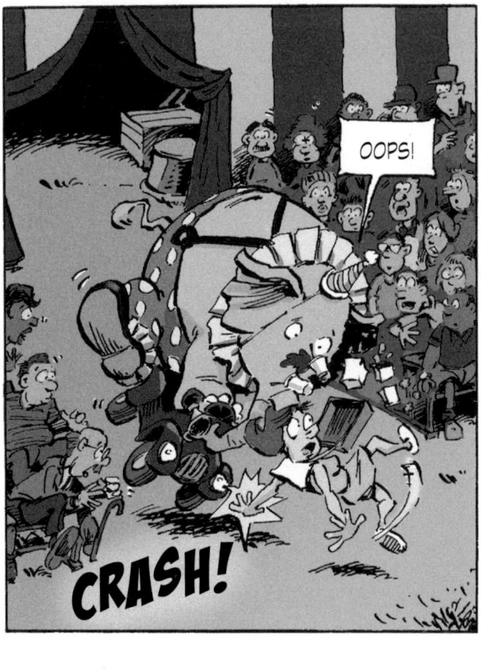
OOPS!
CRASH!

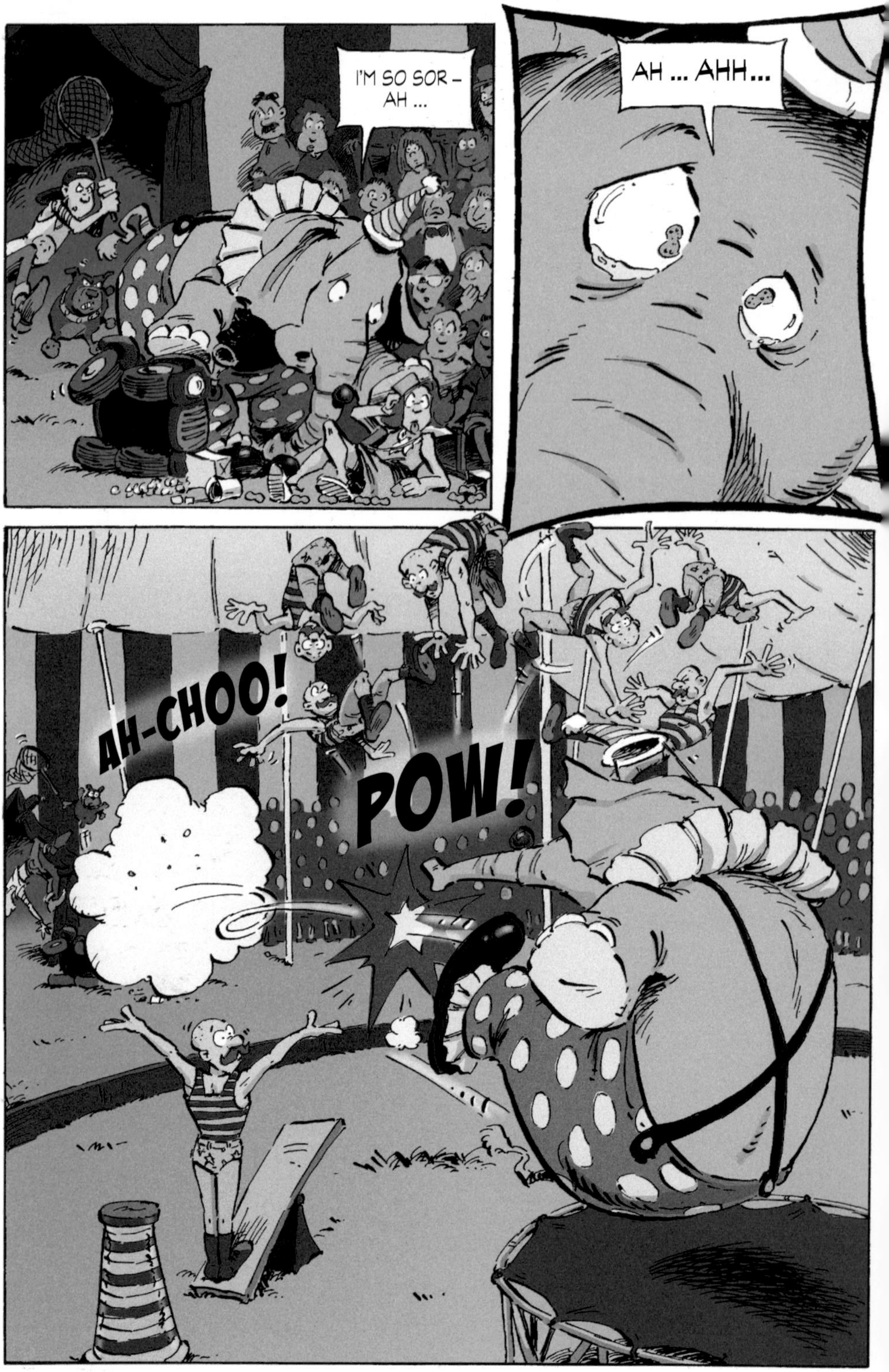
I'M SO SOR –
AH ...
AH ... AHH...
AH-CHOO!
POW!

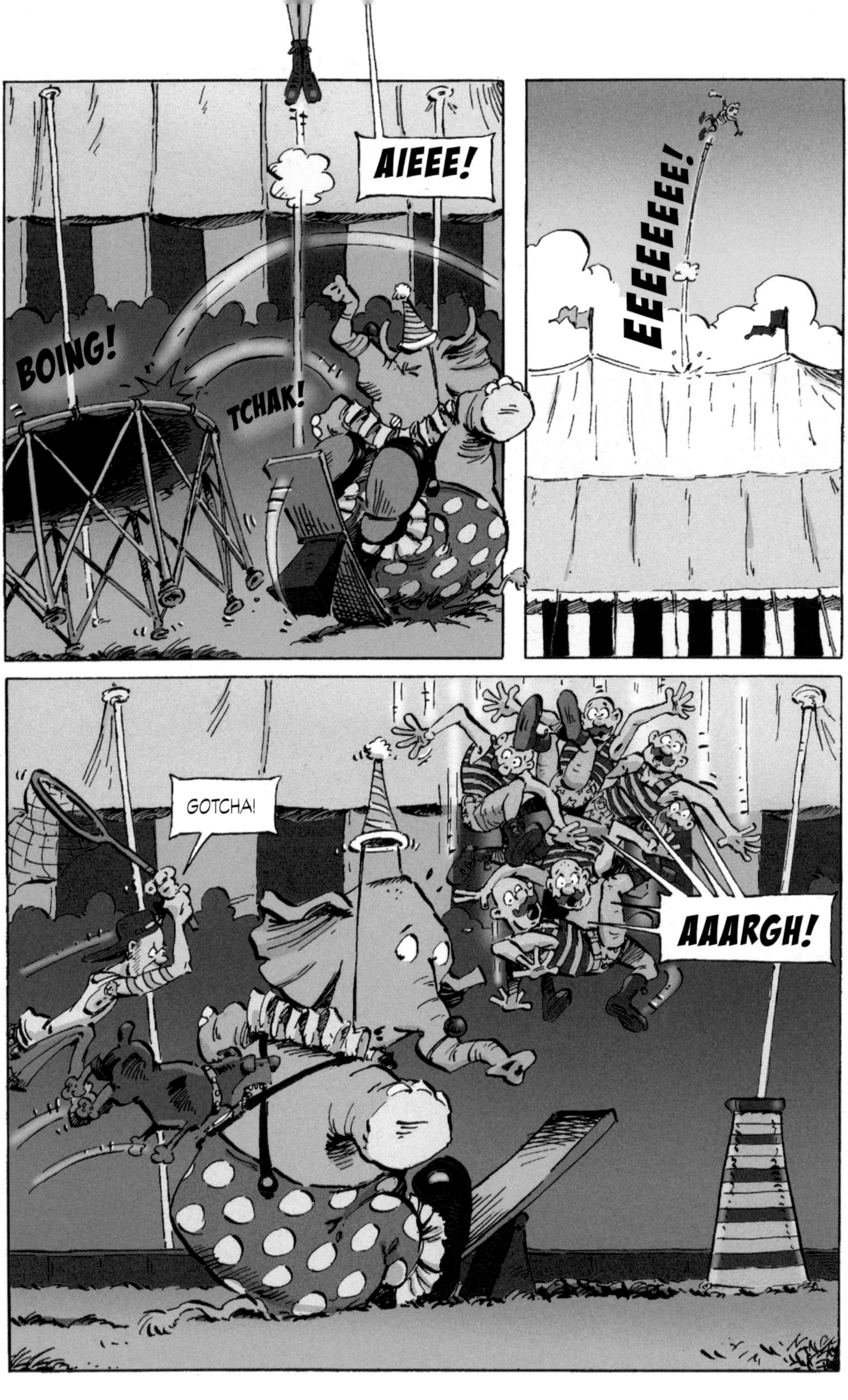
AIEEE!
BOING!
TCHAK!
EEEEEEEE!
GOTCHA!
AAARGH!

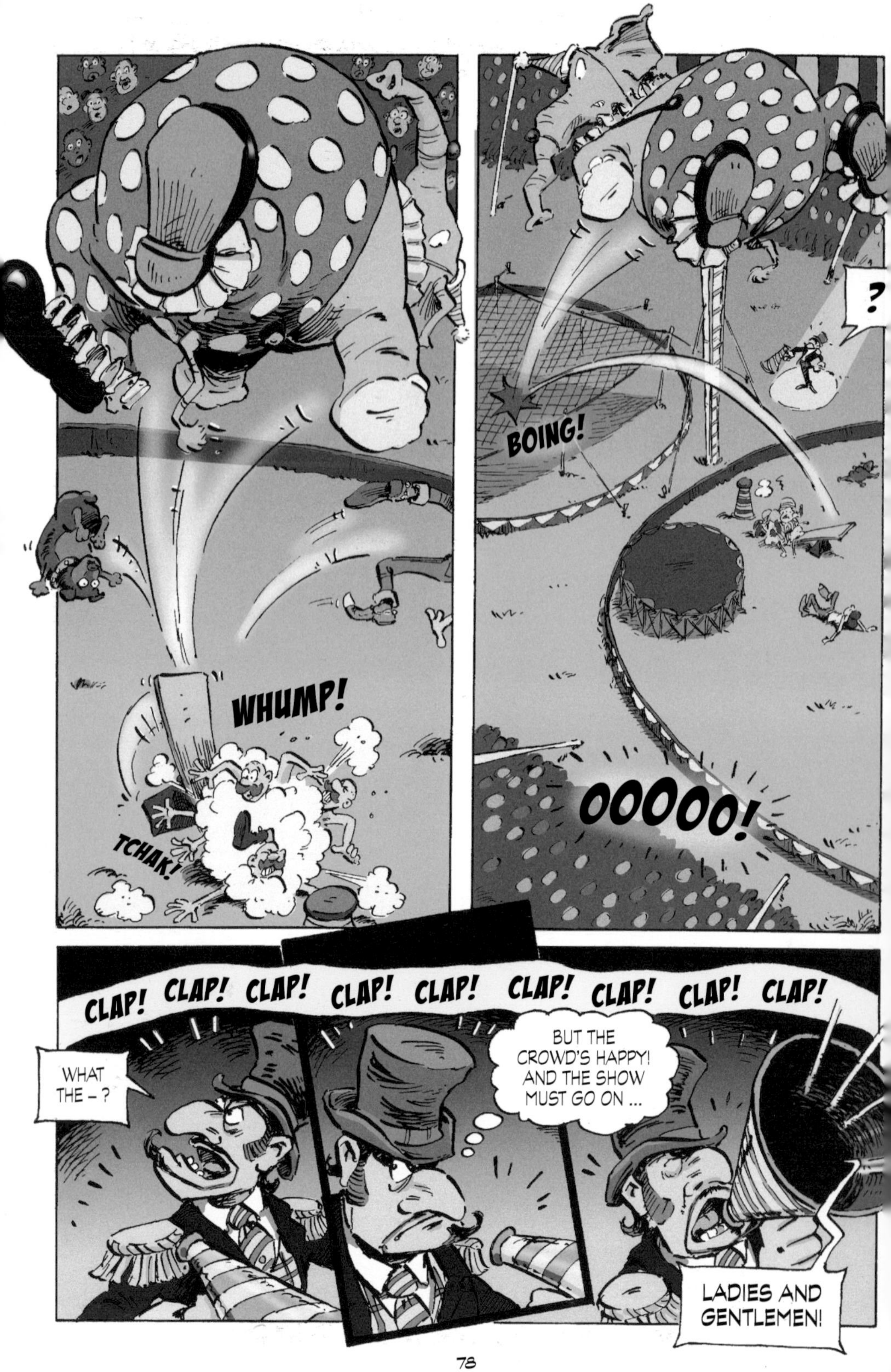
WHUMP!
TCHAK!
BOING!
?
OOOOO!
CLAP! CLAP! CLAP! CLAP! CLAP! CLAP! CLAP! CLAP! CLAP!
WHAT THE – ?
BUT THE CROWD'S HAPPY! AND THE SHOW MUST GO ON ...
LADIES AND GENTLEMEN!

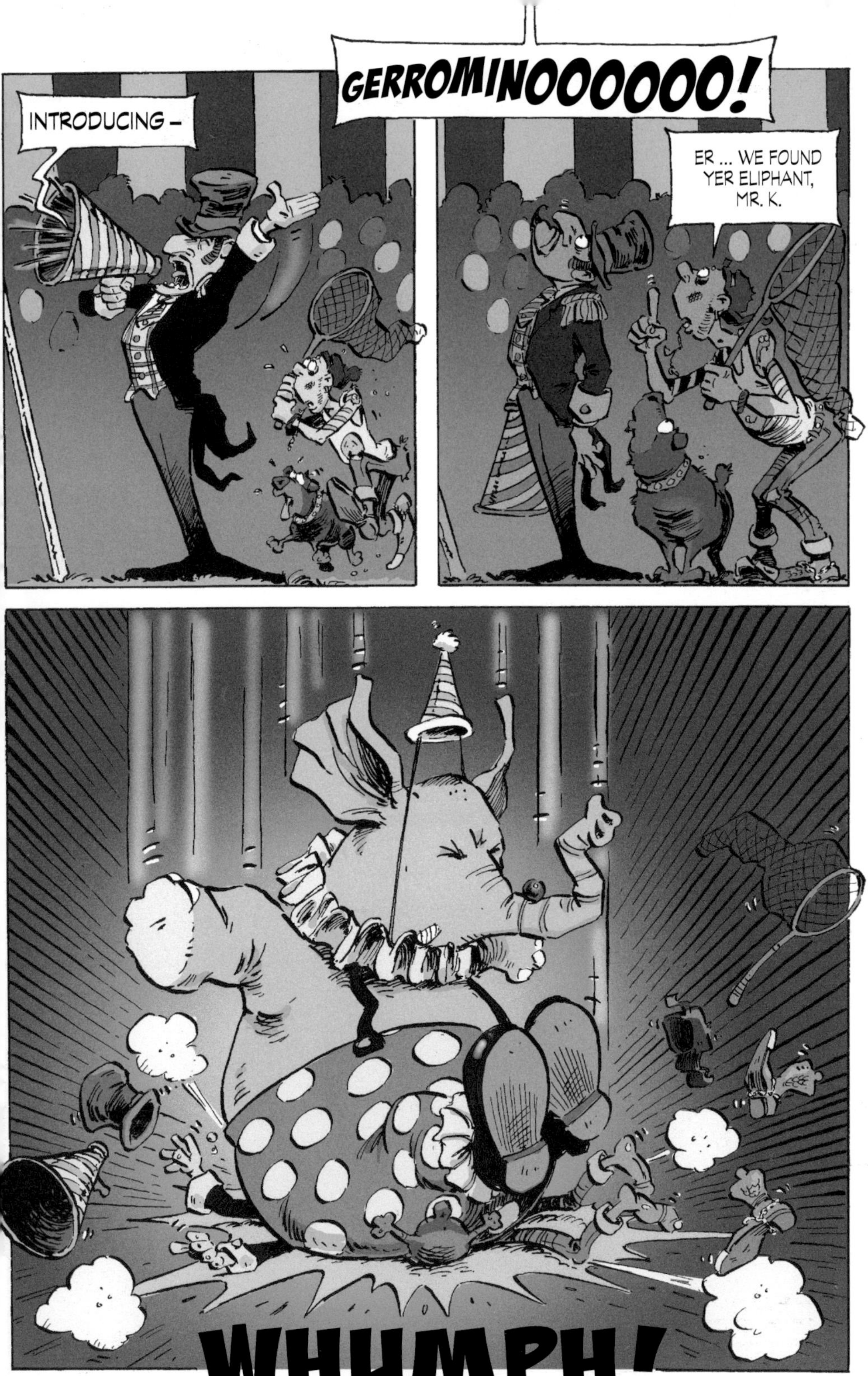
INTRODUCING –
GERROMINOOOOOO!
ER ... WE FOUND YER ELIPHANT, MR. K.
WHUMPH!

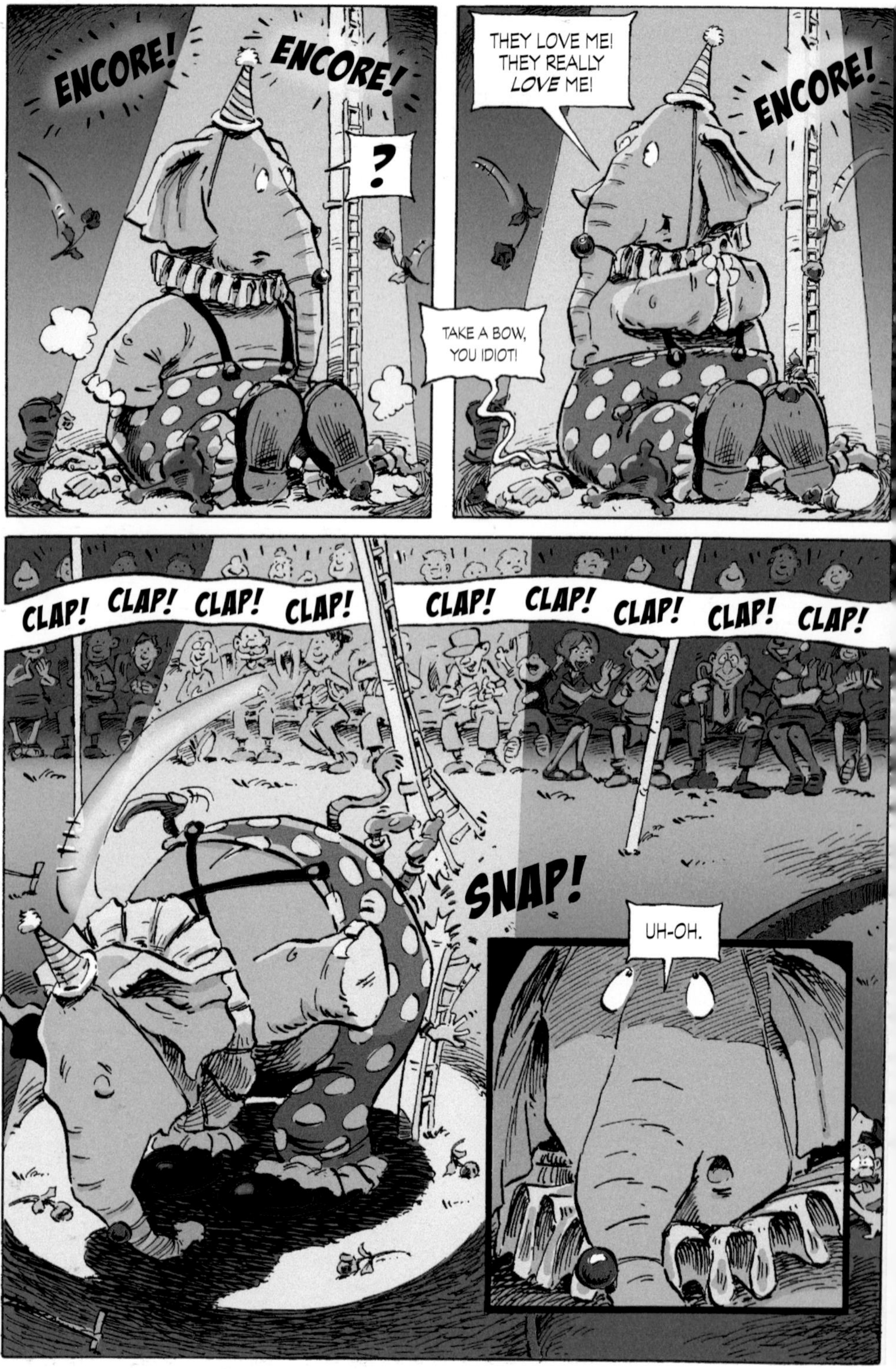
ENCORE!
ENCORE!
?
THEY LOVE ME! THEY REALLY *LOVE* ME!
ENCORE!
TAKE A BOW, YOU IDIOT!
CLAP! CLAP! CLAP! CLAP! CLAP! CLAP! CLAP! CLAP! CLAP!
SNAP!
UH-OH.

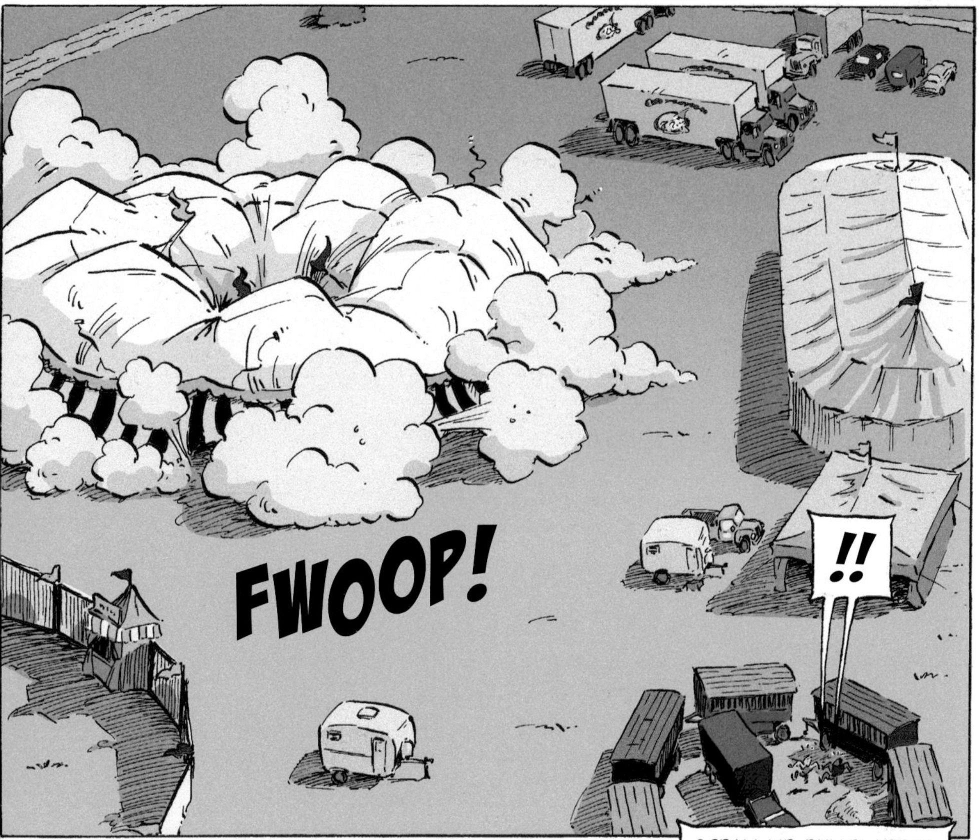
FWOOP!
!!

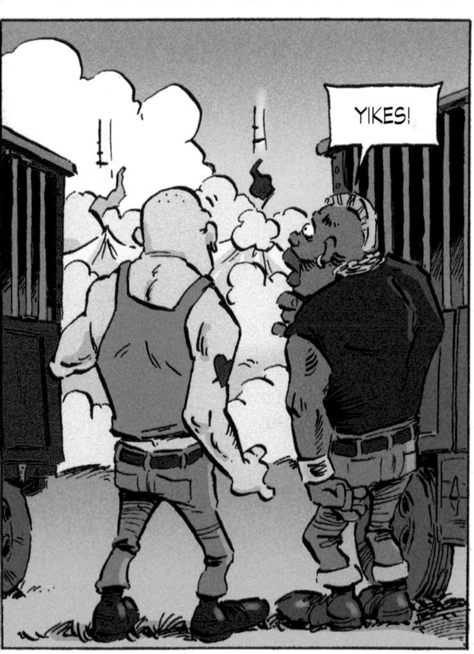
YIKES!

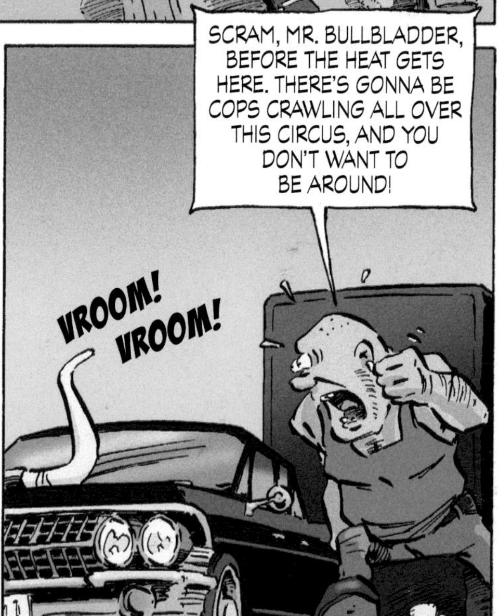
SCRAM, MR. BULLBLADDER, BEFORE THE HEAT GETS HERE. THERE'S GONNA BE COPS CRAWLING ALL OVER THIS CIRCUS, AND YOU DON'T WANT TO BE AROUND!
VROOM! VROOM!

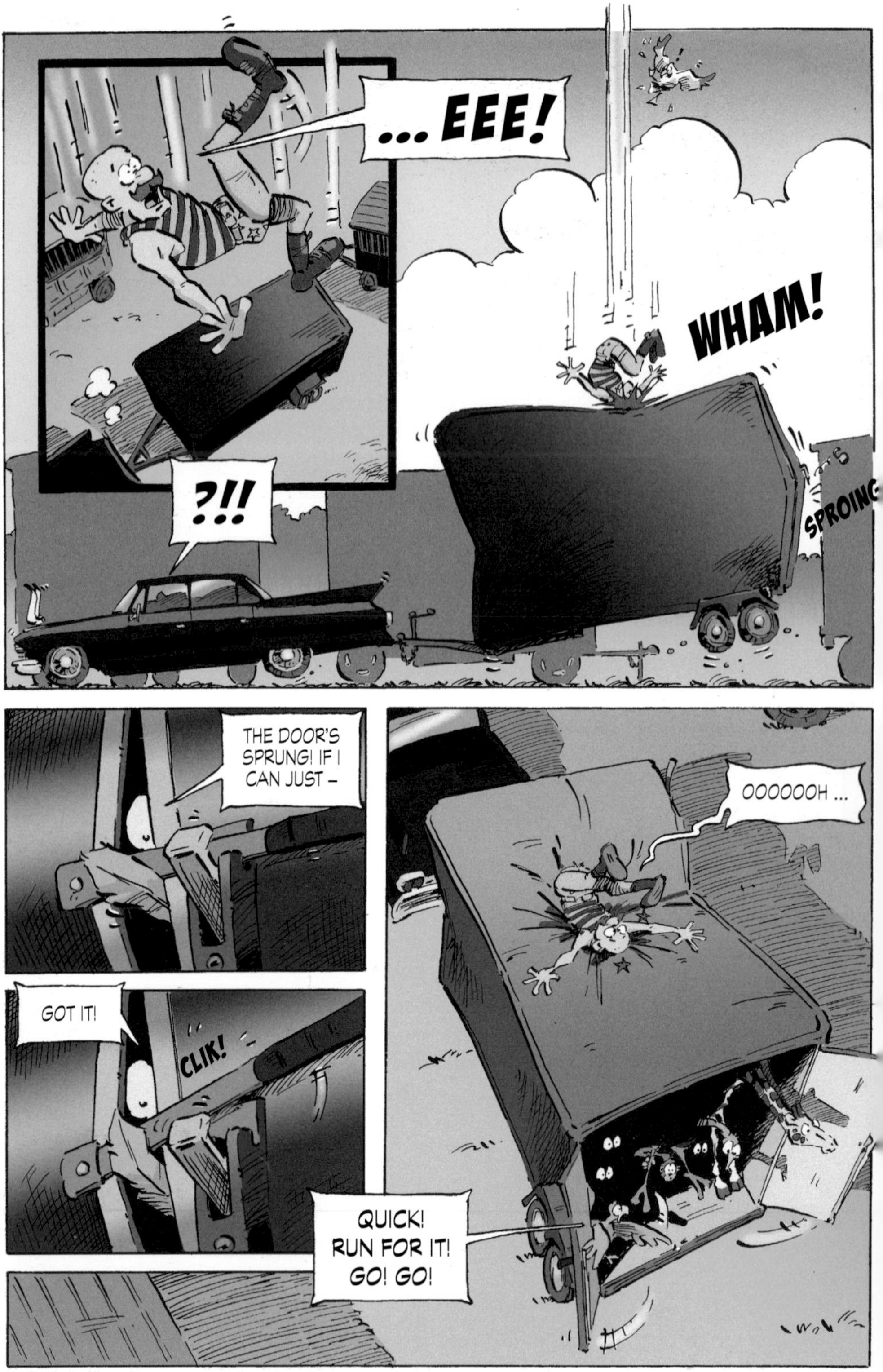
...EEE!
?!!
WHAM!
SPROING
THE DOOR'S SPRUNG! IF I CAN JUST –
OOOOOOH ...
GOT IT!
CLIK!
QUICK! RUN FOR IT! GO! GO!

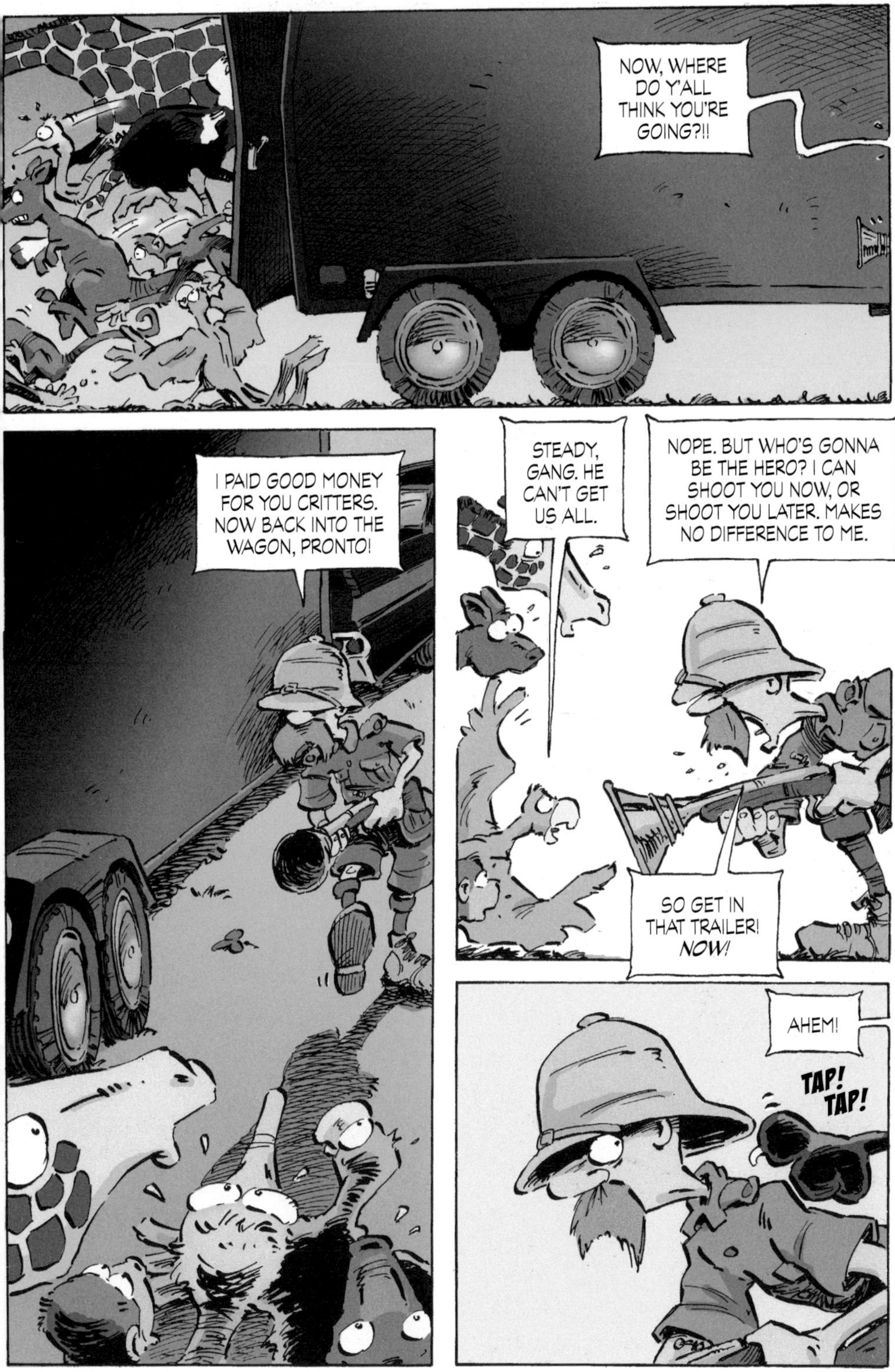
NOW, WHERE DO Y'ALL THINK YOU'RE GOING?!!
I PAID GOOD MONEY FOR YOU CRITTERS. NOW BACK INTO THE WAGON, PRONTO!
STEADY, GANG. HE CAN'T GET US ALL.
NOPE. BUT WHO'S GONNA BE THE HERO? I CAN SHOOT YOU NOW, OR SHOOT YOU LATER. MAKES NO DIFFERENCE TO ME.
SO GET IN THAT TRAILER! *NOW!*
AHEM!
TAP! TAP!

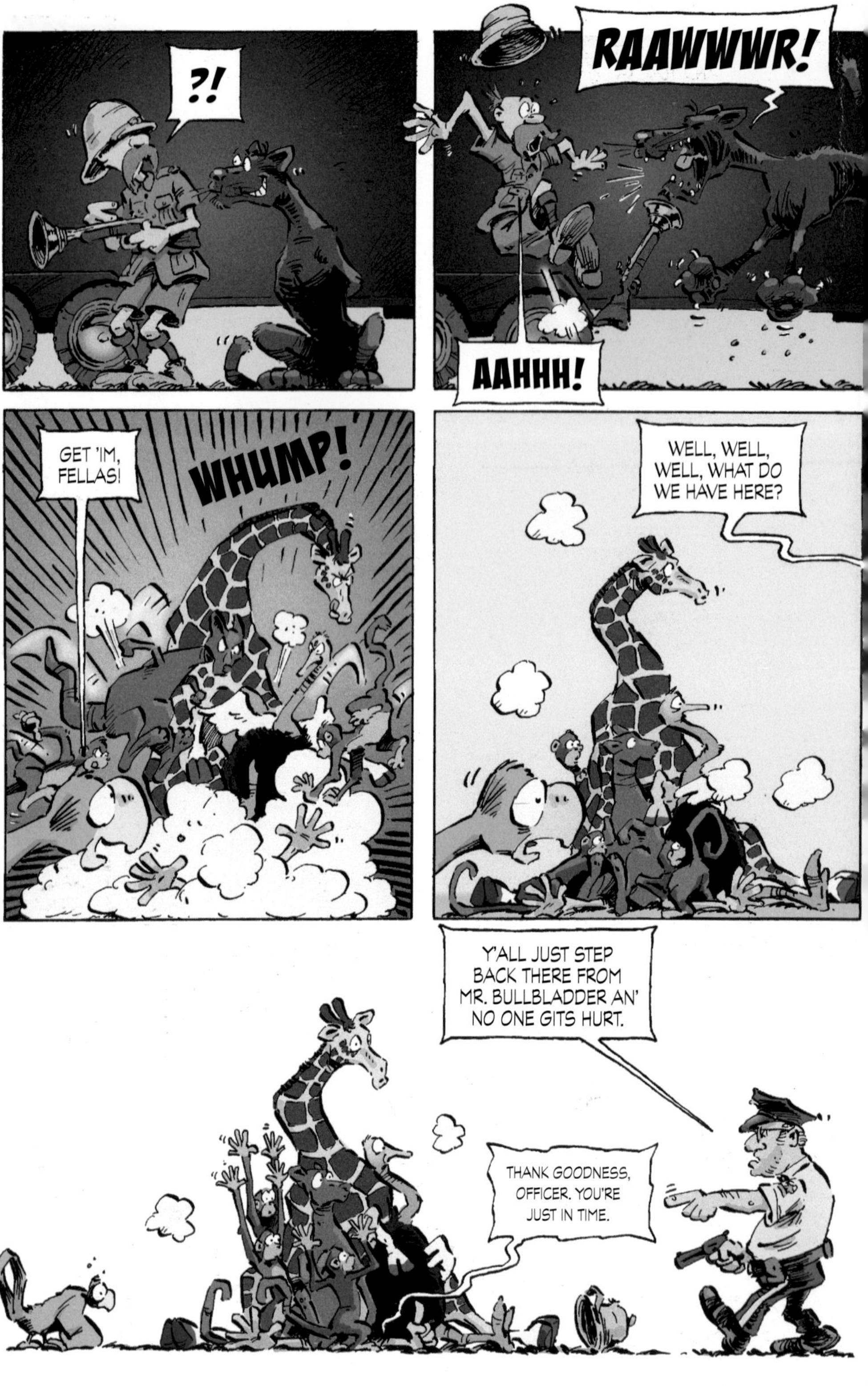
?!
RAAWWWR!
AAHHH!
GET 'IM, FELLAS!
WHUMP!
WELL, WELL, WELL, WHAT DO WE HAVE HERE?
Y'ALL JUST STEP BACK THERE FROM MR. BULLBLADDER AN' NO ONE GITS HURT.
THANK GOODNESS, OFFICER. YOU'RE JUST IN TIME.

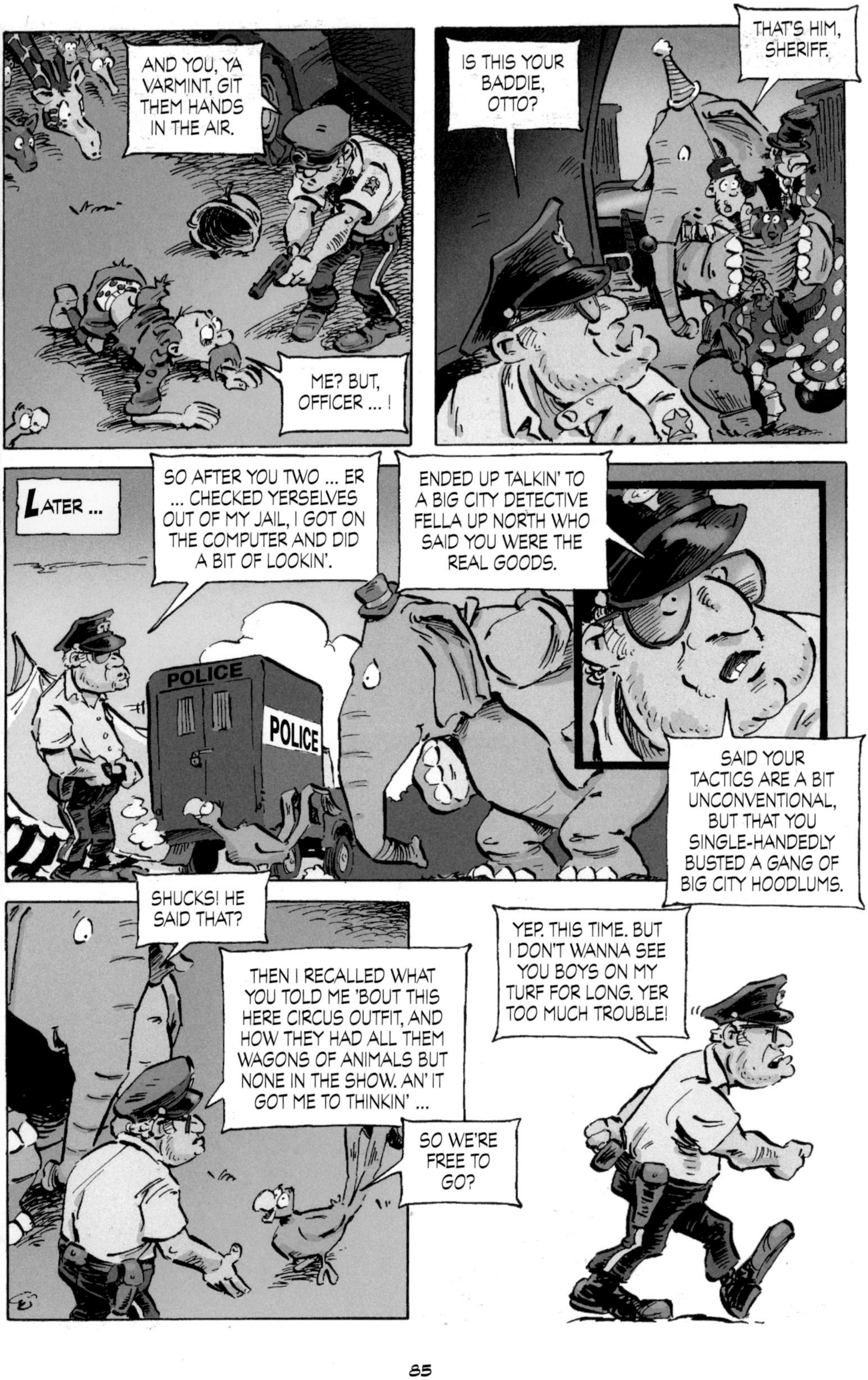
AND YOU, YA VARMINT, GIT THEM HANDS IN THE AIR.
ME? BUT, OFFICER ... !
IS THIS YOUR BADDIE, OTTO?
THAT'S HIM, SHERIFF.
LATER ...
SO AFTER YOU TWO ... ER ... CHECKED YERSELVES OUT OF MY JAIL, I GOT ON THE COMPUTER AND DID A BIT OF LOOKIN'.
ENDED UP TALKIN' TO A BIG CITY DETECTIVE FELLA UP NORTH WHO SAID YOU WERE THE REAL GOODS.
POLICE
POLICE
SAID YOUR TACTICS ARE A BIT UNCONVENTIONAL, BUT THAT YOU SINGLE-HANDEDLY BUSTED A GANG OF BIG CITY HOODLUMS.
SHUCKS! HE SAID THAT?
THEN I RECALLED WHAT YOU TOLD ME 'BOUT THIS HERE CIRCUS OUTFIT, AND HOW THEY HAD ALL THEM WAGONS OF ANIMALS BUT NONE IN THE SHOW. AN' IT GOT ME TO THINKIN' ...
SO WE'RE FREE TO GO?
YEP. THIS TIME. BUT I DON'T WANNA SEE YOU BOYS ON MY TURF FOR LONG. YER TOO MUCH TROUBLE!

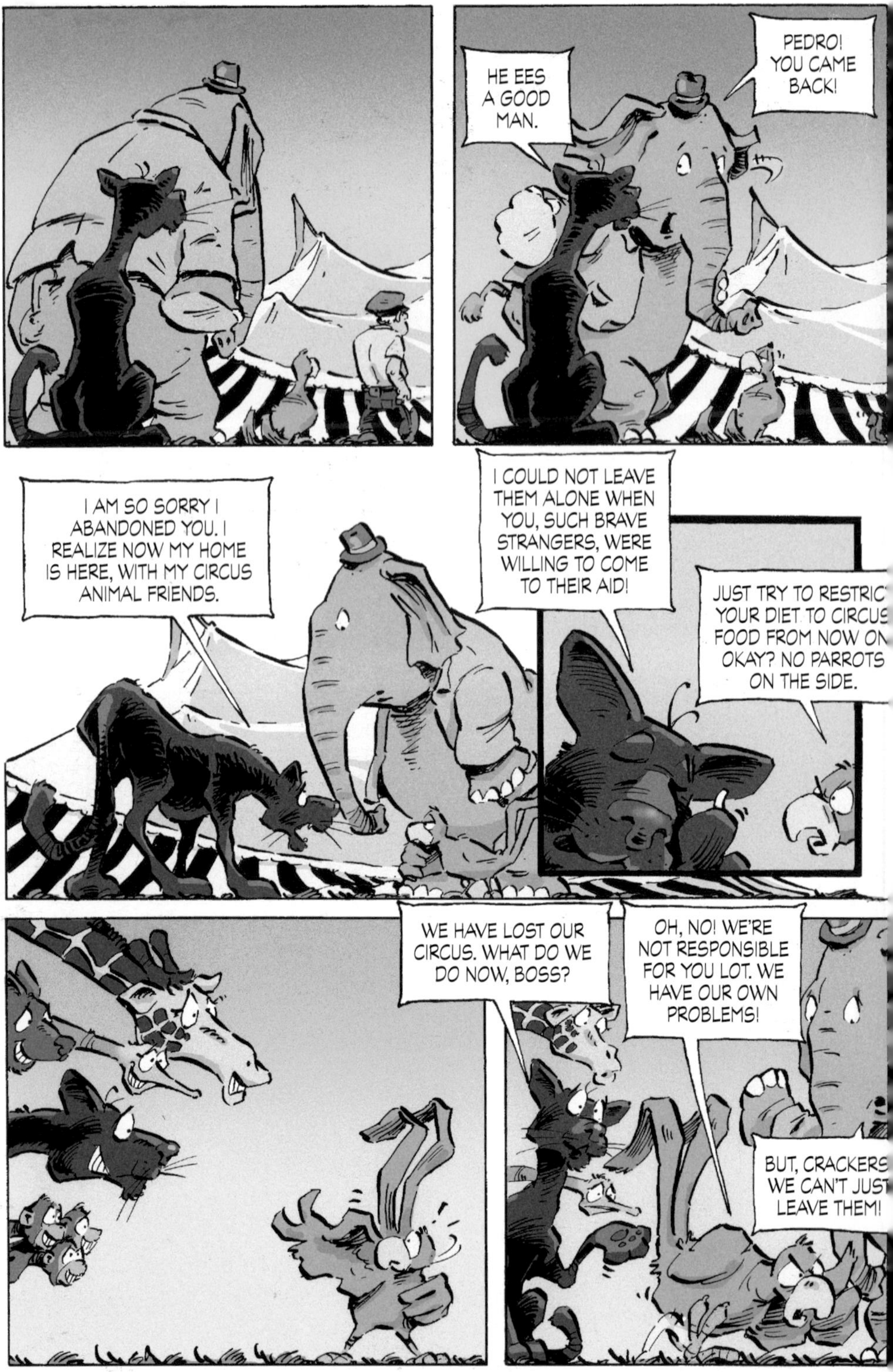
PEDRO! YOU CAME BACK!
HE EES A GOOD MAN.
I AM SO SORRY I ABANDONED YOU. I REALIZE NOW MY HOME IS HERE, WITH MY CIRCUS ANIMAL FRIENDS.
I COULD NOT LEAVE THEM ALONE WHEN YOU, SUCH BRAVE STRANGERS, WERE WILLING TO COME TO THEIR AID!
JUST TRY TO RESTRIC YOUR DIET TO CIRCUS FOOD FROM NOW ON OKAY? NO PARROTS ON THE SIDE.
WE HAVE LOST OUR CIRCUS. WHAT DO WE DO NOW, BOSS?
OH, NO! WE'RE NOT RESPONSIBLE FOR YOU LOT. WE HAVE OUR OWN PROBLEMS!
BUT, CRACKERS WE CAN'T JUST LEAVE THEM!

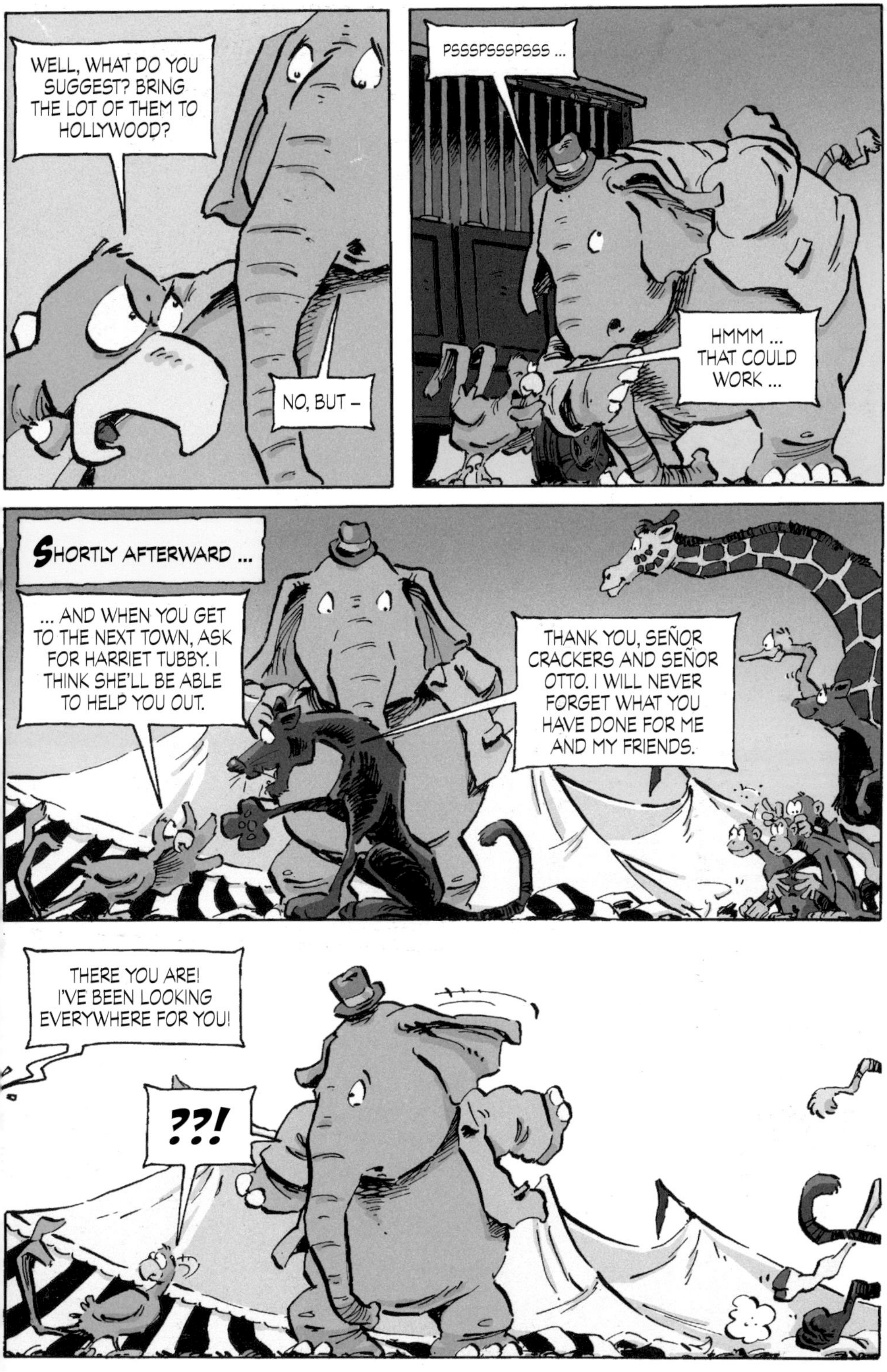
WELL, WHAT DO YOU SUGGEST? BRING THE LOT OF THEM TO HOLLYWOOD?
NO, BUT –
PSSSPSSSPSSS ...
HMMM ... THAT COULD WORK ...
SHORTLY AFTERWARD ...
... AND WHEN YOU GET TO THE NEXT TOWN, ASK FOR HARRIET TUBBY. I THINK SHE'LL BE ABLE TO HELP YOU OUT.
THANK YOU, SEÑOR CRACKERS AND SEÑOR OTTO. I WILL NEVER FORGET WHAT YOU HAVE DONE FOR ME AND MY FRIENDS.
THERE YOU ARE! I'VE BEEN LOOKING EVERYWHERE FOR YOU!
??!

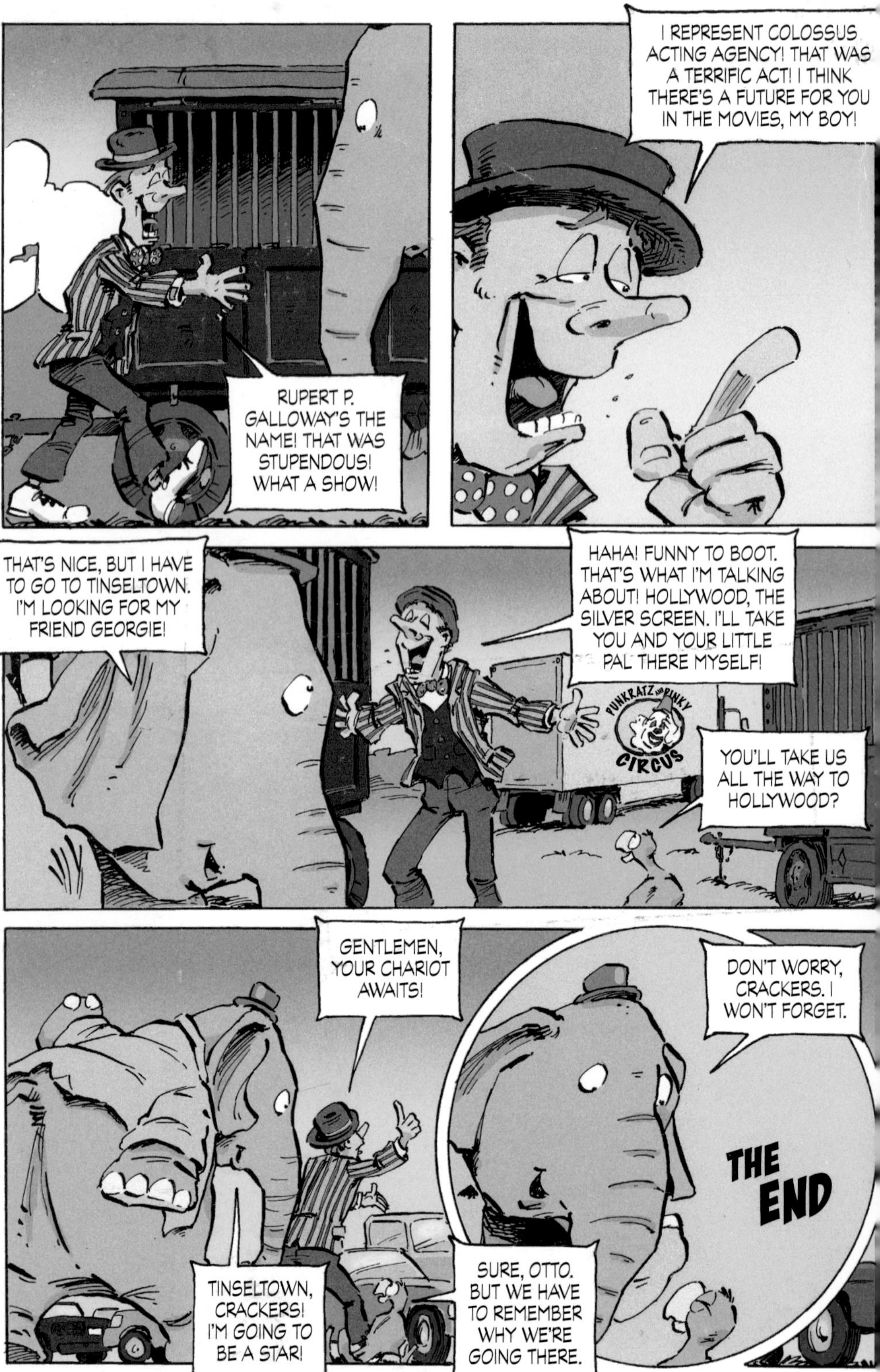
RUPERT P. GALLOWAY'S THE NAME! THAT WAS STUPENDOUS! WHAT A SHOW!
I REPRESENT COLOSSUS ACTING AGENCY! THAT WAS A TERRIFIC ACT! I THINK THERE'S A FUTURE FOR YOU IN THE MOVIES, MY BOY!
THAT'S NICE, BUT I HAVE TO GO TO TINSELTOWN. I'M LOOKING FOR MY FRIEND GEORGIE!
HAHA! FUNNY TO BOOT. THAT'S WHAT I'M TALKING ABOUT! HOLLYWOOD, THE SILVER SCREEN. I'LL TAKE YOU AND YOUR LITTLE PAL THERE MYSELF!
PUNKRATZ AND PINKY CIRCUS
YOU'LL TAKE US ALL THE WAY TO HOLLYWOOD?
GENTLEMEN, YOUR CHARIOT AWAITS!
TINSELTOWN, CRACKERS! I'M GOING TO BE A STAR!
SURE, OTTO. BUT WE HAVE TO REMEMBER WHY WE'RE GOING THERE.
DON'T WORRY, CRACKERS. I WON'T FORGET.
THE END